# THE
# CARDINAL
# CODE

# THE CARDINAL CODE

ONE KISS.
ONE CONTRACT.
BOUND BY BLOOD.

## AVERY STERLING

Sterling & Ash
LEGACIES

To the dreamers
and the beautifully broken.

## <u>Author's Note</u>

This story contains emotionally intense material and explores themes such as violence, abuse, assault, loss, psychological manipulation, questionable consent, and power imbalances. It also includes depictions of bloodletting, self-harm, moments of emotional despair, grief, and sensual encounters that may be graphic in nature.

While the heart of this book is love—tested, defiant, and enduring—it does not shy away from the darker threads woven into that journey.

Please read with care and compassion for yourself. Your wellbeing matters most.

Avery Sterling

# CODEX CARDINALIS

1. Honor the Code above all else.
2. Meddle not in the affairs of the Order, for their will is absolute.
3. Protect the sanctity of thy kin, for betrayal among Cardinales is the gravest sin.
4. Thou shall not slay man nor bring death upon thy kin.
5. Reveal thy nature to no species without necessity.
6. If a human is turned unlawfully, their fate lies with the Order.
7. Turn no human without consent from the Order.
8. Thou shalt be responsible for any human thou turnest.
9. Form no unions of procreation with humans.
10. To willfully defy the Code is to forfeit thy life by the Order's decree.

Leges istae ex Concordia Vitae dictatae sunt,
a Dominium Cardinalium custoditae.

# Prologue

P AISLEE WALKED AWAY FROM betrayal, straight into a prison she never saw coming.

But first, she had to walk in on her boyfriend screwing a blonde who clutched the sheets like they could shield her from the shame suffocating the room.

First, she had to watch Xavier scramble off the bed, panic twisting his face as if he'd been caught committing murder rather than just the worst kind of betrayal.

Then she had to lean against the doorframe, her arms crossed, swallowing the sting of tears as he fumbled with his jeans like a man who knew there was no way to explain himself.

She let out a bitter laugh.

"Go ahead," she said, with venom lacing every word. "I'm dying to hear this one."

"Pais, honey, I..."

"Oh, don't stop now." She gestured at the blonde, who was now glaring at Xavier. "Please, enlighten us both."

He sighed and threw his hands up in surrender. "I'm sorry, Paislee. I got way too drunk last night."

"Excuse me?" the blonde snapped, her voice cutting through the tension.

Xavier turned to her, stammering some half-baked apology, but Paislee had heard enough. Spinning on her heel, she stormed down the hallway, her boots striking the floor in sharp, furious beats. Xavier's footsteps pounded after her.

"Paislee, wait!"

As Paislee shoved open the front door, the crisp autumn air stung her cheeks. "Don't waste your breath."

By the time she reached her car, keys in hand, Xavier's grip on her wrist yanked her back.

"Will you just let me explain?" His voice wavered, and his eyes pleaded.

She met his gaze with ice. "There's nothing to explain." The words came out steady, but her heart pounded. "Everyone told me you were sleeping around. I just needed to see it for myself."

His face twisted, anger flickering beneath the guilt, and his grip tightened.

"What did you expect?" he snapped. "I've been waiting for you for over a year! I'm not a priest."

Paislee's breath caught. "Waiting?" Her voice rose. "From what I've heard, you've hardly been waiting."

Something in his expression faltered, but instead of defending himself, he turned on her. "I did wait," he growled. "But you...you make it impossible. How long am I supposed to wait for you to grow up? We're adults, Paislee. I know there's nothing wrong with me."

The words hit harder than she expected. She struggled to yank her wrist free, but his grip was iron.

Two guys walking toward the dorm slowed, their phones in hand.

"Bruh, let her go," one of them said, his voice firm.

Xavier sneered. "Don't play hero. She doesn't put out."

Paislee saw red. "You're a prick." She yanked her arm with all her strength, breaking free—

And stumbled straight into the street.

The impact came fast. A flash of headlights. The sickening thud of metal against flesh.

Pain—blinding, raw—ripped through her, and the world fractured into chaos. Tires screeched. Voices blurred.

"Don't move her!" someone shouted.

"Call an ambulance!"

Paislee's vision wavered. Hands gripped hers—warm, steady. A voice, urgent but reassuring.

"Hold on. Stay with me."

She tried. She really did.

But then she died.

Or at least, it felt that way.

Later, she would only remember pieces. The sirens. The flickering lights overhead. The sensation of floating while someone whispered her name.

Then a voice. Quiet. Calm. Male. "She has a medical tag. O-neg. Rare—get a proper match."

"Already requested. She's bleeding fast, Dr. Breton."

"She's stabilizing. Keep her under." Then quieter—still professional, but firm, the doctor spoke again, gently taking her hand in his. "You're in good hands, Ms. Sullivan."

The world slipped again, sound turning to static. Somewhere deep inside, something resisted—clinging to the frayed thread of breath, of pain, of memory.

She thought dying was the worst thing that could happen.

She'd survive Xavier's betrayal. She'd survive her accident.

Surviving Michael? That would be another story entirely.

# Chapter One

P AISLEE WAS IN HER bedroom, her thoughts swirling. She sighed, tying her chestnut hair back as loose strands brushed her cheekbones. Her gaze fell on the financial forms she'd signed earlier, committing to steep tuition payments for a design and development program. It was a costly but necessary investment in her future, and she was determined to move forward.

Her injury had derailed her plans two years ago, forcing her back to her family's farm in Elk County, Pennsylvania. She'd left school and worked at a local pizza place in her hometown and had been struggling to make ends meet. She couldn't pay her medical bills, let alone her school loans.

School in New York felt like a second chance—a change she so desperately needed. Her Uncle Eneko had a house on Long Island, and she was lucky enough to be staying there for the school year. When he retired, he'd moved to Florida, and his house, being so close to the Hamptons, had become passive income. When she'd told him she was looking into a school there, he'd insisted that she live at his place.

Kendra, her best friend, snapped her out of her thoughts. "Hey, girl, you ready? It's a long drive into the city."

"Yeah, give me a minute," Paislee called, grabbing a tee out of her dresser. She checked her reflection before adding eyeshadow to bring out her blue-green eyes and a swipe of gloss to her lips.

Seth Bardin's scolding voice echoed in her mind: *"We give you a hefty clothing allowance for a reason, Paislee. You're not hostessing at Applebee's."*

Paislee checked her reflection once more, willing away the sting of Seth Bardin's words. Seth, her new boss at Allusion—the Hamptons' elite nightclub—had sent her home for not meeting the dress code. He was distractingly handsome, which only made the humiliation worse. She'd thought her white tunic and black leggings were practical and stylish, but Seth didn't care about practicality.

The club's dress code was black and white, but as Paislee had learned, this meant high fashion, not simplicity. She'd left in shame, with Seth's words ringing in her ears: *"Go home. Come back tomorrow night and try again."*

"Let's go, Paislee!" Kendra called from downstairs, breaking her reverie.

Paislee grabbed her hoodie and headed out. Kendra was both her childhood friend and current roommate, though their fashion priorities couldn't have been more different. While Paislee had a practical streak, Kendra embraced city fashion with ease. Now Kendra had volunteered to help Paislee fix her "farm girl" wardrobe.

By the time they reached the boutique, Paislee was already overwhelmed. The brass doors opened to reveal the intoxicating scent of elegance—polished wood, leather, and faint florals. Clothes hung in perfect order, their price tags whispering, *"Out of your league."*

"Allusion's clothing allowance won't cover this," Paislee muttered.

With a smirk, Kendra tossed her auburn curls. "You're investing in yourself. Consider it a bonus."

Paislee sighed as she ran her fingers over a blouse's delicate fabric. "I still don't get what was wrong with my clothes."

"Paislee, seriously, you looked like you just left the farm," Kendra quipped, glancing pointedly at Paislee's worn sneakers.

"I did just leave the farm," Paislee reminded her, rolling her eyes.

"And so did I, but I don't advertise it." Kendra flashed Paislee a playful glare before asking, "Does everyone at Allusion look like they stepped off the runway?"

"I wouldn't know. I wasn't there five minutes before Seth sent me home."

"Well, he gave you one more shot," Kendra said, scanning the racks. "Don't blow it—for my sake."

Paislee arched a brow at her longtime friend. "For your sake?"

"I need you to hook me up with a job. I'm never going back to Elk County," Kendra pulled out a dress and appraised it with a critical eye.

"I'm only here for the school year. Once I'm certified, I'm leaving," Paislee said firmly, eyeing the growing pile of clothing in Kendra's arms.

"You don't even know where you're going yet," Kendra teased. "You might change your mind. Just get in tight with management and put in a good word for me."

Paislee shook her head with a small smile. "How would you afford to stay here alone? Uncle Eneko's generosity won't last forever."

"I've got time to figure it out," Kendra said, laughing as she balanced a mountain of dresses.

"All right, city fashion guru. What am I supposed to wear?"

Kendra held up a black miniskirt, and Paislee groaned. "I'm wiping down tables, Kendra."

"Get over it," Kendra said with a chuckle. "It's time to channel your steamier side."

# Chapter Two

M ICHAEL ARRIVED LATE, EXHAUSTED as he stared out the car's tinted windows. Joseph, his father's trusted chauffeur, maneuvered through the narrow, winding streets of Sagaponack with practiced ease. The charming village, framed by tall stone walls, was emblematic of quiet luxury, though it did little to lighten Michael's mood.

The pristine beaches and endless hedgerows passed unnoticed as his phone buzzed with notifications. Ignoring them, he slipped the device into his pocket just as the car came to a stop. Joseph stepped out and opened the door.

Michael swung his bag over his shoulder and climbed out. "Thanks, Joseph."

He glanced at the man who had remained loyal to the Chamberlain family for decades—and their secret. The signs of Joseph's age were obvious—graying hair, weathered skin, and eyes that had lost their once-brilliant hue. Time had taken its toll on him, a reminder of how fleeting human life was. For Michael, unchanged by time, it was sobering to witness how short human life was, especially compared to how long he, a cardinalis, lived on earth—or, as a human would say, a vampire.

Joseph's voice brought him back. "Your father's in the conservatory. He said you probably wouldn't read his messages."

Michael smirked faintly. "Thank you, Joseph. And my mother?"

"She'll join you shortly. She's wrapping up an interview with the *Times*."

Grimacing, Michael muttered a curse in his native tongue. He had no patience for reporters. As he trudged up the stone steps to the front doors, the salty breeze did little to ease his annoyance.

Inside, the massive foyer echoed with voices. A news crew was filming in the parlor, and Michael tried to slip past unnoticed. But just as he was leaving, a voice called out, "Mr. Chamberlain, you're back!"

Michael froze mid-stride, forcing himself to relax as his fangs threatened to emerge. After a moment, he turned to the reporter, plastering on a polite smile.

Then Alaitz Chamberlain, his mother, entered the hall with her usual poise, and her warmth dissolved Michael's irritation. "Ciau, Ma," he greeted, his smile softening.

"Hello, ebony eyes," she replied, kissing his cheek.

Before he could escape, Kelly McCormick—the reporter—stepped forward. He recognized her. She'd done an exposé on him nearly five years ago when he'd sold his restaurant in SoHo to one of Hollywood's leading producers. Before...everything else.

"Michael, it's been years! New York's most eligible bachelor returns at last. Where have you been?" Kelly asked.

Michael took her hand and brushed a kiss over it. "Ms. McCormick, always a pleasure. I've been...occupied."

Kelly faltered, her gaze locking on his. Michael held back a sigh. The human instinct to fear a cardinalis often surfaced in moments like these, leaving people dazed. A biological echo to an ancient threat. An inherited survival mechanism that bypassed logic or conscious awareness. He waited patiently as she blinked and recovered.

"I'm fine, of course," she stammered. "And you?"

"Thriving," he replied smoothly. "Now, if you'll excuse me, I must see my father."

He offered his mother a parting glance before heading to the conservatory. The neoclassical structure stood apart from the house, separated by sprawling gardens. Michael pushed open the French doors, bracing himself.

Saverio Chamberlain lounged on a chaise with a thin redhead draped over him. Jocelyne, his *largitor sanguinis*. She shuddered as Saverio whispered in her ear.

Michael shut the door loudly.

Saverio looked up, unbothered. "Michele, you're late."

7

Michael settled into a hammock, deliberately avoiding the scene on the chaise. "I had some errands."

"Why did you not take a flight to the landing?"

Michael turned to Saverio and gave him an odd look. Since when did he start answering to his father like a child? Michael's tone cooled. "Joseph picked me up. No problem."

Saverio smirked but pressed no further. Jocelyne stumbled as she stood, and Saverio caught her with natural precision. "To the main house, Jocelyne," he instructed softly. "Slowly."

Once she was gone, Saverio turned back. "How was Venice?"

"Magical," Michael replied dryly. "Why did you summon me?"

Saverio stretched lazily. "It's time for me to die."

Michael arched a brow. "Cancer this time, I assume?"

"Correct. Your mother's foundation will benefit."

Michael's expression hardened. "Profiting off cancer? How noble."

Saverio waved a hand dismissively. "Your mother's opening a research clinic. This will help."

Michael leaned forward, his voice cutting. "Your theatrics don't concern me. What do you want?"

"Take over Allusion. I'm done with it."

Michael's laugh was cold. "I have no interest in another business venture. Nightlife isn't what it used to be."

"It's necessary," Alaitz interjected from the doorway. "Many clubs are folding, but Allusion has remained. Because it's not just about a good party—it's about leverage. Eyes. Access. Influence. Esben can't manage it."

Michael's gaze darkened at the mention of his brother. "Let me guess, because people don't...like him?"

Alaitz sighed. "He lacks your charm."

"He's a dick." Michael stood abruptly and slung his bag over his shoulder.

Saverio cleared his throat. "Since the incident with Katya, he's become—"

Michael stilled, his jaw tightening. "The incident?" he asked quietly, though his voice carried an edge. He shook his head. "Is that what we're calling it?"

"The fallout was disastrous for everyone—especially your brother," Saverio said.

"If all this has been about Esben, you've wasted your time."

Saverio stood and stepped dangerously close to him.

Alaitz placed a hand on Michael's shoulder. "Michael," she said in her usual gentle tone. "We don't want to force you and Esben together, and your father doesn't want to put too much on you right now."

"We just want you back home, *Micu*," Saverio said. "Take over Allusion. If anyone can keep it going, it's you. And you get along with Seth much better than I do."

"I'll manage the club for the season. After that, I'm gone."

Saverio's voice followed him as he left. "Why don't you stay here, Michele? This is your home."

Michael didn't look back.

# Chapter Three

NOTHING COULD HAVE PREPARED Paislee for working at Allusion. The club was—in a word—intimidating. Its upscale, contemporary design featured sleek lines, double dance floors, and two bars that were perpetually crowded. Every night, the place pulsed with life.

Paislee feared she'd be fired, though not for the reasons she initially expected. The blaring music made it nearly impossible to hear drink orders, and she found herself momentarily frozen when celebrities performed or were escorted upstairs to the exclusive VIP room, a space strictly off-limits to her. The aura of exclusivity only added to the pressure. Her awe didn't go unnoticed by Jackie, her trainer, who promptly reminded her to stop being so hard on herself.

At least her boss made the experience bearable. Seth, likely in his thirties, had dark hair and deep blue eyes that seemed to glimmer under the club lights. She had a small crush on him. More than once, she found herself staring at him, speechless and utterly lost in his presence.

It was embarrassing, but Seth always handled it with patience, offering a reassuring smile before walking away.

Earlier that day, Paislee had gone to school, but now she stood in her bedroom, staring at her reflection in the mirror. Kendra, as usual, had taken it upon herself to dress Paislee like a human Barbie doll. Tonight was no exception. The black bodycon dress hugged Paislee's figure, with daring cutouts and a swooping back that plunged to her tailbone.

Paislee's eyes caught the thin scar running down her back, a lingering reminder of her accident. "Kendra, really? I can't show my back."

"Your scar is badass, Pais," Kendra replied from her perch on an overstuffed chair, where she sat with one foot propped against the wall. "Besides, it's not as noticeable as you think."

Paislee turned, studying the deep dip in the dress. "If I bend over, everyone's going to see my ass."

Kendra dismissed her with a wave. "You'll be fine. Think of it as letting the customers appreciate your assets."

"My assets will be on full display for the entire club," Paislee muttered.

"Don't worry, grandma," Kendra said with a sigh. "Your 'Fuck Off' vibe will keep the creeps at bay."

Paislee shot her friend a snarky glare before rummaging through her closet. She pulled out a white dress shirt and, after pulling it on, tied the front into a knot and rolled up the sleeves. She swept her hair into a bun, added silver hoop earrings, and posed for Kendra.

Kendra chuckled. "Fine, wear the shirt. You still look gorgeous." She reached for her phone just as it buzzed.

Paislee was slipping into her strappy heels when Kendra groaned. "Damn it. Tessa just texted. She's calling in."

Since Kendra had started working at the local diner, Paislee had gotten to know Tessa well. The petite strawberry blonde had a larger-than-life personality and a spontaneous streak that matched Kendra's. Her wild stories from work had often left Paislee laughing to the point of tears. Still, Tessa's unpredictability wasn't always convenient—like tonight, when Kendra was counting on her for a ride.

Kendra tossed her phone aside and sighed. "Can I borrow your car?"

"I'm off at midnight. Can you pick me up?" Paislee asked.

"Yeah, I'll finish around the same time. You might have to wait a few minutes."

"Keys are on the counter," Paislee said, grabbing her bag. "Now, let's go. I'm going to be late."

Kendra stood and snapped her fingers playfully at Paislee's composed expression. "Earn those tips tonight, mother hen."

Michael wove through the nighttime traffic on his latest acquisition—a sleek street bike—before pulling up at the curb outside Allusion. He ruffled his thick hair after freeing it from his tightly fitted helmet.

"Michael, you're back!" one of the suited bouncers called out as he approached.

Michael recognized Dante instantly. The bouncer had changed—his new hairstyle and added muscle were hard to miss—but the distinctive tattoo inked on his neck confirmed his identity. It also confirmed that he was still human.

The second bouncer, unfamiliar to Michael, grinned as he commented, "Sweet ride!"

Michael dismounted from his bike, offering a small grin and a nod as he secured his helmet and gloves. "How's it looking tonight?" he asked.

"We're packed to the brim," Dante replied.

Michael was heading towards the entrance when a voice called, "Michael Chamberlain."

He didn't stop right away, but the tone caught him. Calm, deliberate. Not aggressive. Not worshipful. Curious.

Turning slightly, he spotted the speaker just beyond the queue: a young man recording him with his phone.

"I'm Adrian Hawk from an alternative media channel, Rebel Red News. Can I ask you a couple of questions?"

"I've never heard of you," Michael said, slowing his stride towards the door but not stopping.

"I'm not surprised. I don't answer to the Order," Adrian replied. "But I have nearly five million followers, and growing by the day."

Michael stopped, slightly intrigued. "What do you want?"

The journalist looked almost surprised that Michael had stopped. "You've been off the radar for four years." He stepped closer, cautious but certain. "But we cardinales haven't forgotten." His voice lowered slightly. "The lower houses haven't forgotten."

Michael barely reacted, but the words had landed in a way he hadn't expected. Before he could ask the journalist what he meant, Adrian pressed on. "No one has heard from Katya."

The name hit like a blow.

"We suspected that the Order would bury the entire incident. But the trial—it changed everything. *You* changed everything."

Michael's gaze sharpened, but Adrian Hawk kept going, unaware that every word was an entirely new revelation to him.

"They still talk about you, you know. The way you challenged the Order in front of the entire council." Adrian watched Michael closely, frowning slightly. "The masses feel a kinship to you. Someone like you doing such a thing."

Michael's patience was wearing thin. "Someone like me?"

Adrian exhaled, clearly baffled that Michael didn't seem to understand. "A Chamberlain." His voice dipped lower. "An elite who bled in front of them. The Order wiped out all recordings of that day from the internet."

Michael didn't respond. The reporter had triggered an unwelcome memory. The cold trial chamber. Katya. Her eyes had found him once. Frightened, and already resigned.

He remembered refusing to kneel to the council. They had demanded compliance. Instead, he'd spoken. A full truth wrapped in a carefully crafted lie. His blood had hit the floor that day—whether it was symbolic or retribution, he didn't care. Until then, he'd done everything right. And still—

The journalist pulled him out of his thoughts. "Where is she, Michael? The Order silenced her. Silenced us when we reported the story." A pause. "We want to know if she's okay."

Michael remained still.

Inside, something colder stirred.

*This journalist didn't know?*

*The public didn't know about Katya?*

Before he could muster a reply, a familiar voice called out, "Michael! It's great to see you!" Seth appeared, striding through the doors to greet him with a crushing hug. "It's been too long, old friend. How've you been?"

"I've been well," Michael replied.

Seth adjusted his shirtsleeves; his usual easygoing demeanor remained intact, but there was an unmistakable edge to his humor.

The journalist turned towards Seth, and his reaction was immediate.

Recognition.

Shock.

Then something else.

Hope.

"Seth Bardin?" Adrian breathed out as if seeing something impossible. "Holy shit. You—" He actually laughed, not in mockery but in sheer disbelief. "Everything is not lost. I thought you'd vanished, too."

Seth glanced from Michael to Adrian and then just smiled, easy and unbothered. "Just keeping my head down," he said, his tone light but his eyes telling a different story.

But Michael didn't miss the way the journalist observed them standing side by side—not as outsiders or relics of the old world, but representing something Michael couldn't quite name.

Michael was grateful when Seth said, "Come on, Michael. Let's head inside."

The journalist stopped Michael once more. He raised his phone one last time. "Please, can you comment on Katya?"

Michael exhaled slowly, ignoring Seth's warning about answering any of the journalist's questions. In a low and measured voice, his gaze fixed ahead as he said, "She deserved better."

"Better?" Adrian jumped on the words, leaning forward. "Is she's still alive?"

Michael hesitated, already moving towards the door. "Better," he answered without looking back, "than what I could do for her."

Seth motioned Michael inside the buzzing club, throwing a glance back at Adrian.

The club was alive with energy, with humans and cardinales mingling seamlessly, though the humans, naturally, remained unaware of the true nature of their company.

Upstairs, Seth guided Michael into the office, a spacious and elegantly styled room that reflected his impeccable taste. Despite the club's ownership being attributed to Michael's father, it was Seth's vision that had built Allusion into what it was—his rules, his style. Michael's father, largely uninvolved, treated the club as little more than a source of income.

Seth broke the silence as they settled in. "Is Saverio coming in tonight?"

Michael nodded. "He'll be here shortly. There's some paperwork to finalize before he officially hands over the club."

The mention of Saverio noticeably stirred old tensions within Seth. Michael was aware of the friction between him and Saverio, a rivalry that had stretched over centuries. Though Seth had long shouldered the burden of running the club, frequently venting to Michael about being overworked, Michael didn't think the rivalry had anything to do with Allusion.

But Seth was Michael's lifelong friend, and Michael had often turned to him for support. Michael viewed taking over the club as a chance to finally ease Seth's load and return the favor.

Seth's usual grin faltered as he caught Michael's distant expression. "How are you holding up?" he asked gently.

Michael's jaw tightened, and his response was curt: "Fine."

The air thickened with unspoken words until Seth broke the tension. "Let me get you a drink."

# Chapter Four

T wo weeks in, Paislee was catching on quickly. She had
started managing the floor more efficiently, but tonight was
ladies' night.

Free admissions for women and half-price drinks had drawn a
monstrous crowd, leaving Paislee on the brink of collapse by the end
of her shift. No dazzling dresses or admiring glances could dull the
ache in her feet after hours in heels. Still, the growing wad of tips in
her apron was motive enough to power through.

Her shift was nearly over, and as she cashed out her sales at the
bar, her gaze snagged on a pair of dark, magnetic eyes. Their eerie
depths made her stomach twist and sent a chill crawling down her

spine. Even as the crowd swirled between them, his unwavering stare pinned her in place. When he smirked, her discomfort deepened.

The stranger came to the bar and leaned in with a casual confidence, resting his elbow on the leather inlet. "You're new here," he remarked, his voice sharp and slightly accented.

Paislee forced a tight-lipped smile. An unsettling prickle of his presence crawled along her skin, instinctive and irrational. "I am. Do you need a drink? I can have Grayson fix one for you."

He glanced at the bartender, who was lining up beers on the counter. "I'll call Gray over if I need something," he replied smoothly.

Her small smile barely masked her desire to flee. "All right, then. Goodnight."

"Esben," he interjected, extending a hand. "My name's Esben."

She hesitated. If a quick handshake could speed her escape, she'd play along. Taking his hand, she offered a brisk, "Nice to meet you, Esben," before trying to step away.

But his grip tightened, halting her. He leaned in closer, his gaze predatory. "You didn't tell me your name, *tesoru miu*."

Her brows lifted. "I know."

Maybe she should've felt flattered by his attention—he was undeniably attractive—but he was watching her too closely, and his refusal to release her hand sharpened the warning bell in her mind. As she subtly tried to pull free, Grayson called over, "You need something, Esben?"

Grayson stood watchfully behind the bar, his crisp tone breaking the tension. Paislee silently thanked her savior, who looked like he could grace a billboard with his sun-kissed skin and chiseled physique.

Esben held Grayson's gaze for a charged moment before chuckling and releasing her. "Nah, I'm good," he said with a casual wave before stepping back.

Paislee thought that was the end of it until a few minutes later, as she finished up her tasks, she felt someone behind her.

"Clock out," Esben murmured, his voice like silk over glass.

She stiffened. "Excuse me?"

He leaned close enough that his breath stirred the loose strands of her hair. "Tell whoever you planned to call for a ride not to bother. I'm driving you home."

A chill slid up her spine, slow and deliberate. "What makes you think I need a ride from you, or anyone else?"

His smile didn't reach his eyes. "I'll meet you in the breakroom," he said before turning and walking away.

Alarm blared in her head. It wasn't that he was pushy. It was the way he knew things he shouldn't.

The room felt smaller, his presence larger. Fear hit first. Anger followed close behind.

Grayson turned to her. "You okay, Country?"

She nodded, her breath uneven.

"He's an ass," she said.

Grayson's warning was quiet but firm: "Be careful with him. He's no good. But if anyone else ever asks, I never said that."

The warning stuck with her, but she didn't press. She simply promised to keep his words to herself before saying bye to Jackie and heading for the breakroom.

She faltered when she realized he hadn't been lying. Esben was leaning against the far wall, watching. Right by the breakroom door.

Paislee's gaze skittered across the bar for Grayson, but he was busy with a knot of customers. Seth was nowhere in sight.

"Shit," she muttered. Gathering her resolve, she prepared for a confrontation, but as she approached, her nerve waned. Esben pushed off the wall, closing the distance between them.

Her unease deepened, and Grayson's warning replayed in her mind. Her heart thudding, she looked for an escape—and fast. That's when she spotted him: a man descending the stairs from the VIP room.

Before she could second-guess it, she moved. Straight towards him. Before she could lose her nerve, she slid her arms around his neck and kissed him. The stranger froze and then recovered, kissing her back. He didn't hesitate. Just met her there.

Her hands trembled as she pulled back. His features were stunning—sculpted cheekbones, a strong jawline, and eyes so piercing they made her knees weaken. His lips curved into a slow, knowing smile as he slid his hand to the back of her neck, drawing her in for another kiss. Paislee momentarily forgot everything: Esben, the crowd, even where she was.

When she managed to catch her breath, her voice lowered. "C-Can you help me?"

The stranger's smile widened. "Anything."

She swallowed hard. "Pretend to be my boyfriend?"

That sounded ridiculous the second they left her mouth. But she didn't take them back. "F-For like five minutes. I know it sounds—"

"It does," he interrupted with a slight chuckle, his tone almost amused. But just as quickly, his expression softened. "Someone's bothering you?"

She nodded, unable to form a coherent reply as his gaze swept over her like an intimate touch. There was something about him—weight, presence—like everything around him bent just slightly in his direction. Everyone in the Hamptons looked like they were sculpted by celestial beings, but this man took the crown. He looked like he had been plucked from the dreams of ancient sculptors and brought to life for mere mortals to marvel at.

"I'm sorry," she whispered, unsteadily. "There's something about him I can't shake. The fear is paralyzing—I can't explain it. But do you understand what I'm saying?"

For a moment, something unreadable crossed his gaze. The corner of his mouth twitched into a slow, knowing smile. "More than you'd think," he replied.

"Maybe if he thinks I'm with you, I can slip away. If you don't want to—"

"I'll handle it," he interrupted, his hand firm on the small of her back. "What's your name?"

"Paislee," she managed. "And if we're doing this, I guess I should know yours."

"Michael."

She wanted to say something witty or flirty—anything—but his name alone sent a fresh wave of heat through her.

He guided her downstairs, his touch steady.

# Chapter Five

MICHAEL WRAPPED UP HIS meeting with Seth and his father, eager to leave. The reunion with his family, especially his brother, had dredged up memories he'd spent years trying to forget. Now those memories had torn their way back to the surface, leaving him restless.

To make matters worse, he needed blood—soon. Finding a largitor wasn't easy with the Order's strict rules. He hadn't renewed Ariel's contract before leaving Venice. A foolish oversight.

He prided himself on restraint, but tonight, even his willpower was faltering.

When the server kissed him, it was as if every dormant instinct roared to life. Her scent, the warmth of her blood, the wild rhythm of her heartbeat—it called to him. Kissing her back, he was consumed by a surge of hunger and desire he could barely hold back.

Her skin glowed under the dim lights, and her bright blue-green eyes pierced through him like sunlight on water. Something about her woke a part of him he didn't recognize. He hadn't allowed himself to truly look at her before, but now, as she descended the stairs, she was all he could see. The softness of her features, the delicate strength of her frame—she was striking in a way that made his hunger sharpen and his self-control teeter.

Then he saw Esben.

And he realized that the man she feared was his brother.

"I just want to get to the breakroom so I can leave," Paislee whispered.

"I understand," Michael said, his voice calm, and as steadying as the hand on the small of her back.

Paislee hesitated as Esben smirked at Michael. The tension between the two men was palpable, and she suspected that they already knew each other. Whatever history they shared, her plan to escape had only made it worse.

"Out of the frying pan, sweetheart," Esben remarked, his dark gaze darting between them.

Michael's arm slid around Paislee's shoulders, and he pulled her close. His cool smile was sharp as he guided her past Esben. They headed into the breakroom, but Michael didn't let go. His hold was a calculated move meant to provoke. And judging by the murderous glint in Esben's eyes, it had worked.

"Do you need a ride home, ducizza?" Michael asked.

"Hmm, what?" Paislee had gotten lost somewhere in his gaze, and it was difficult to snap out of it. She shook her head and removed her sneakers from her locker. Fumbling with her laces, she sat down. "I have a ride, thanks."

"Esben doesn't strike me as the type to give up easily," he said. "I'll wait with you."

"I didn't tell you his name," she said, glancing up at him as she removed her heels. "You clearly know him. And you enjoyed using my situation to get under his skin."

Michael chuckled, and the sound was rich and low. "You're right. I don't care for him. But, in my defense, I agreed to be your boyfriend before I knew who I was rescuing you from."

Paislee flushed, and her heartbeat stuttering as his gaze dropped to her lips. She stood abruptly, clutching her bag. "Thanks for the help. I think he got the message."

Michael took her hand and pressed a kiss to her knuckles. The old-fashioned gesture left her stunned. "My job isn't done," he murmured. "I insist on staying with you until your ride arrives."

Paislee was ready to argue, but her phone buzzed with a message from Kendra, who was running late. Her chest tightened as she weighed her options.

Michael, noticing her hesitation, gently guided her out of the club, where a sleek street bike was parked out front.

"I was leaving anyway," he said smoothly. "Let me take you home."

She hesitated. "I...I can't."

Michael's brow arched, and his smirk was disarming. "Why not?"

Paislee's cheeks burned. "There's no way I can climb on that bike in this dress."

He laughed softly. "Then we wait together."

As they lingered in silence, Esben appeared. His presence struck like static, again sparking unease in her chest. *What was his problem?* She pulled out her phone and messaged Kendra, telling her not to bother. She slipped the phone back in her bag and turned to Michael.

"I'll make it work," she said, quietly. "Let's go."

Michael's grin widened with a flicker of satisfaction. "Yes, ma'am." He handed her his helmet and jacket.

Despite the absurdity, her doubts faded. She felt safer with him than she expected to. Even with her heart pounding as she climbed on, even with the way he felt beneath her arms, she felt something strange. Something like trust.

Then headlights swept over the curb.

Kendra's car pulled up.

Paislee let out a breathy groan. Of course.

She slid off the bike reluctantly, avoiding Michael's eyes as she handed him back the helmet and jacket. "Goodnight, Michael," she said softly.

His disappointment was hard to miss.

"Goodbye for now," he said with a lopsided smile. "I'll see you again."

She turned away before her resolve crumbled.

Once in the car, Kendra wasted no time. "Oh, my God, who was that?"

Michael, Paislee nearly said aloud, but she kept it to a mutter, staring out the window. "Nobody."

"Nobody?" Kendra arched a brow. "He looked like he was going to devour you. Why didn't you let him?"

Paislee laughed, despite herself. "Nice, Kendra. You make me sound like a snack."

# Chapter Six

F RUSTRATION SIMMERED IN MICHAEL as Paislee climbed
into the car and disappeared into the distance. Her presence
lingered, with her heartbeat still echoing faintly in his ears and the
taste of her lips clinging in his memory. The overwhelming need to
claim her was almost too much to bear.

He'd found his next *largitor sanguinis*. Better yet, she'd found
him. The question was whether he could restrain himself long
enough to secure her signature on the contract. Something told him
she wouldn't be easy prey. The thought brought a smirk to his lips.
A challenge was always more fun...but time wasn't on his side.

"You really are an asshole, Michael."

He leaned back slightly as Esben stormed over, his expression as perpetually thunderous as ever.

Michael raised an eyebrow. "And you're as charming as ever," he said dryly. "Scared off another target, did you, brother?"

Esben straightened to his full height and glared down at Michael, who remained unmoved by his ire.

Sliding on his helmet, Michael ended the conversation the way he preferred—by riding away.

The following night, Paislee slipped on a black miniskirt that hugged her hips; its silver D-rings and removable straps lent it an edgy flair. She paused, studying it—bold in a way she wasn't used to.

"Yes, Pais, you're wearing that," Kendra said, amused, tossing her a white cropped halter top with a single-loop closure at the neck. "You know that guy's coming back tonight."

Paislee tugged the halter into place, then dropped onto the chair as Kendra began braiding her hair.

"Someone like him doesn't want someone like me, Kendra," Paislee muttered.

Her best friend secured one braid and started another on the other side, unfazed. "That's the spirit, Pais. Talk yourself out of it before it even begins."

Through the mirror, Paislee shot her friend a snarky look. "Come on, Kendra. You saw him. He can have anyone he wants. Why would he wait around for someone like me? The outcome is predictable."

"He scared you."

"No," Paislee retorted quickly. "Esben scared me. Michael was...friendly."

"Nobody has a name, after all." Kendra pinned Paislee's braids into a loose bun and then tugged out random tresses, letting loose strands fall around her face. "You've waited long enough, Pais. You deserve to be with someone who looks at you like you matter. *Really* matter."

Paislee scoffed, shifting uncomfortably. "I don't think he's that kind of guy."

Kendra's laugh was equal parts amused and triumphant. "I've never seen someone's eyes say so much in the few seconds he watched you walk away. Admit it—every guy you've dated has been a tool."

Paislee opened her mouth but then closed it again, her cheeks heating.

"He got to you."

"How do you know he's not a tool?" Paislee snapped.

"Call it intuition." Kendra dug through Paislee's jewelry box and then held up a pair of earrings for inspection. "Every guy before thought waiting was some kind of game. When it stopped being fun, they moved on."

"I don't need forever," Paislee said softer. "I just want it to mean something when it happens. I want if to feel right."

"And whoever you choose is going to feel damn lucky." Kendra squeezed Paislee's hand then smirked, handing over a pair of simple diamond studs. "Wow, I get to play mother hen. This is fun. Can I borrow your car again? I'm meeting up with Tessa after work."

33

"I'm closing tonight."

"I'll be there on time. I promise."

By the time Paislee arrived at the club, the place was already packed. Music hit her the second she stepped inside, low and heavy in her chest.

"We're swamped, Pais. Hurry up and get on the floor," Jackie called, peeking into the breakroom.

Paislee nodded, clocked in, and grabbed a tray. By the time she reached the floor, chaos had already taken over—servers weaving through bodies, trays tipping under the weight of too many orders. She maneuvered through the throng, barely avoiding collisions as customers spilled from the dance floor to the carpeted seating area. She nearly collided with another server, twisting at the last second to keep the tray steady.

The front bar was nearly inaccessible, so she shifted to the smaller junior bar in the back, where Seth was holding his own against the flood of drink orders. Even there, space soon disappeared as patrons swarmed the area.

Paislee gave up trying to memorize orders and started writing everything down. Eventually, she braved the main bar again, threading her way through the crowd until her eyes landed on a familiar face: Michael.

He was behind the bar.

She stilled.

Bottles turned in his hands like it was nothing—clean, controlled, practiced in a way that drew eyes whether he meant it or not.

Her grip slipped on the notepad.

Michael worked here?

His gaze caught on hers and he paused.

Then the corner of his mouth tipped—quick, deliberate—before he turned back the bar.

Something in her chest tightened, sharp and unexpected. She wasn't ready for this—not yet. Grayson's station opened up, and she made a beeline for him. She quickly recited her order.

"Got it," Grayson said, setting up shot glasses with rapid efficiency. "Here you go, Country. Anything else?"

Paislee loaded her tray and slipped back into the crowd, avoiding the main bar for as long as possible. Until Seth became too busy, and she was forced to return.

This time, the crowd pressed in around Michael, tighter, louder, drawn to him without even realizing it.

"Paislee—what do you need? I'm swamped," Michael called out, his brows raised in her direction.

Her first instinct was to confront him—why he hadn't said a word about working here, last night?

But with all the chaos, this wasn't the time or place. Swallowing her irritation, she called out her drink order. Michael's hands moved with theatrical precision, bottles spinning, catching light—performing without ever looking like he was trying. She caught herself staring when he snapped his fingers in front of her.

"Wake up, Country!" he teased, his voice cutting over the music.

Heat climbed up her neck as she grabbed the drinks and slipped back into the crowd.

For the rest of the night, Paislee avoided Michael. He was swarmed by customers—some even took selfies and begged for his attention. A bachelorette party descended on the bar at one point—loud, relentless. The bride grabbed Michael by the shirt and pulled him in, laughing as she kissed him. Phones flashed. The room ate it up.

Paislee didn't stay to watch.

She stuck to Grayson for orders. When he got too busy, she slipped behind the bar herself—until even that stopped working. Frustrated, she had no choice but to call out to Michael again.

At first, he ignored her; his attention was on a group of customers taking shots with him. Irritation pressed tight under her kin. She signaled him for a second time, but he didn't so much as glance her way.

"What the hell?" she muttered under her breath. She forced her way through the crowd and shouted her order straight at him.

Michael cupped his hand to his ear. "Speak up!" he said, leaning in—just enough to make it worse. "I can't hear you over the music!"

Gritting her teeth, Paislee ripped a sheet from her notepad, scrawled her order, and slid it across the bar. Michael glanced at it before pushing it back.

"I can't read chicken scratch."

Her temper flared. "Are you serious?"

"Then write so I can read it—or say it louder."

Jackie arrived at the bar, and Michael immediately started mixing her drinks. Paislee stared in disbelief. Was he deliberately being difficult?

Her customers had been waiting for far too long. Before she could think better of it, she planted a hand on the counter, hoisted herself up, and swung her legs over the bar. She landed hard—too close—Michael stumbled back a step, caught off guard.

"What the hell are you doing?"

Ignoring him, she grabbed her drinks, loaded them onto her tray, and swung herself back over the bar just as quickly.

She tore a page from her notepad, wrote one word in large, bold letters—*ASSHOLE*—and shoved it towards him.

He stared at it, then a grin pulled at the corner of his mouth.

"That clear enough?"

Paislee avoided him the rest of the night. She focused on her customers, and kept her distance from the main bar. The club was relentless, with people flagging her down at every turn. She didn't have time to dwell on her frustration, though the memory of Michael's smug grin lingered in the back of her mind.

When DJ finally announced last call, relief washed over her. She hurried to serve her final orders and then began cashing out her tables as the crowds slowly thinned. The chaos ebbed, and the music dimmed, signaling the end of a grueling night.

As she rounded the bar, a commotion erupted. Shouts echoed over the fading music as two men smashed their beer bottles and lunged at each other. A full-blown fight broke out within seconds, dragging nearby patrons into the fray.

Before Paislee could react, Michael vaulted over the bar with a speed that didn't quite make sense. Seth appeared moments later, and the two of them worked in tandem to subdue the brawlers. They moved fast—controlled and precise—forcing the fight apart. The fight dissipated as quickly as it had started, leaving a tense but calming silence in its wake.

The bouncers led them out as Paislee turned to leave—and collided hard. Cold liquid soaked through her shirt as she went down, her ankle twisting under her before she could catch herself. A jolt of pain shot through her leg before she hit the floor.

"Oh, my God, I'm so sorry," the man slurred, reaching out a hand to help her. But he was barely steady on his feet, and Paislee waved him off, gritting her teeth as she struggled to sit up. The pain hit fast and didn't let up.

Jackie appeared moments later. She slipped an arm around Paislee's shoulders and helped her to the breakroom. "Let's get you off your feet."

Paislee winced as Jackie eased her onto the couch. "I'm fine," she muttered, though her voice betrayed her pain.

A few minutes later, Seth poked his head in. "Hey, Country, go ahead and call it a night."

"Thanks, Seth," she replied, leaning back against the couch with a sigh. Her shirt was still damp, and her ankle throbbed, but at least the night was over.

Paislee hobbled to her locker, grabbed her sneakers, and began the slow process of putting them on. The muffled hum of the club still buzzed in her ears, and she welcomed the relative silence of the breakroom.

That was when she sensed someone behind her.

Turning slowly, she found Michael standing there, his expression unreadable. The noise of the club had faded enough for her to clearly hear his voice when he asked, "Are you all right?"

# Chapter Seven

P AISLEE STRAIGHTENED, HER FINGERS pausing mid-lace as she glanced at him. "I'm fine," she said curtly, though the ache in her ankle and the damp fabric clinging to her skin suggested otherwise.

Michael tilted his head, and his sharp eyes scanned her. "Doesn't look like it. You're limping, and you look like someone dumped a drink on you."

She scowled, pulling the laces tighter in her sneakers. "Thanks for pointing that out. Oh, so helpful."

He crossed his arms and leaned casually against the doorframe, a faint smirk playing on his lips. "It's part of my charm."

Paislee shot him a glare and then rose carefully to her feet. A pain shot through her leg, and she bit back a wince. "If you're here to gloat, don't bother. I've had enough of you for one night."

"Gloat?" Michael echoed, his tone feigning innocence. "Now, why should I do that?"

"Because you've been an absolute pain in the ass since the second I walked in tonight."

Michael's smirk widened, though his gaze softened. "I've been busy, Country. It's not personal."

"Not personal?" she snapped, brushing past him with her bag slung over her shoulder. "You ignored me, made my job harder, and then acted like it was a joke."

He followed her into the hallway, his pace matching her limping steps. "If I ignored you, it's because I was working. And you? You were the one writing love notes." He pulled out the crumpled note from his pocket and held it up. "Eloquent, by the way."

Paislee stopped abruptly and turned to face him. "You deserved that, and you know it."

Michael's grin faltered for the briefest moment before it returned, softer this time. "Maybe I did." He stepped closer. "But you didn't have to climb over the bar like that," he said in a low voice. "Impressive though it was."

She stared at him, caught off guard by his tone. "I did what I had to do. Unlike some people, I take my job seriously."

Michael's grin faded completely. "We both do."

"Could've fooled me," she muttered, pulling out her phone.

His hand shot out and gently caught her elbow. The contact sent a spark down her arm, and she froze. "Paislee," he said softly, his voice no longer teasing, "I wasn't trying to make things harder for you. If I did, I'm sorry."

She looked at him, surprised by the sincerity in his tone. His dark eyes searched hers, and for a moment, the noise of the club, the ache in her ankle, and the frustration of the night all melted away.

"I'll let it slide," she said finally, her voice quieter. "This time."

Michael released her elbow, and a faint smile tugged at his lips. "I'll take it."

Leaning against the wall, he watched her open an app and begin ordering a ride. "Let me take you home. It's the least I can do after being an ass."

"I don't want you getting in trouble with Seth," she said, hesitating.

"I won't get in trouble with Seth." He reached out and gently took her bag off her shoulder. "Let me carry that."

She faltered, not entirely sure why she let him. "I hurt my ankle and don't really feel like climbing on a bike tonight." It was a terrible excuse, and she knew it, but his steady gaze was making it hard to think straight.

His smile widened as he took a step closer, his presence commanding without being overbearing. "It's a good thing I have my car, then," he said softly.

She released a breath and thought she heard herself sigh. *Just let it go, Paislee.* "All right."

They exited through the back door into a small, dim parking lot. Two cars were parked under a flickering streetlamp: a sleek roadster with white stripes and a flat-black Mercedes with carbon fiber accents.

The Mercedes's headlights blinked.

"You've got to be kidding me."

"What did I do now?"

She gestured toward the car, her tone incredulous. "There's no way you bought this on a bartender's tips."

Michael cocked a brow, his expression teasing. "I'm not just a bartender, Paislee."

"Then what are you?" she asked, folding her arms. "Seriously, who are you?"

Bracing one arm on the car door, he leaned closer, and his voice dripped into something almost intimate as he said, "You'll figure me out soon enough."

She blinked, taken aback. "That...sounded creepy."

His deep laugh echoed through the lot, and her stomach did a somersault. "I guess it did," he admitted, stepping back and motioning toward the passenger side. "Get in."

Her lips twitched in reluctant amusement. "Hm." She slid into the car and melted into the soft leather seat, momentarily distracted by the red ambient lighting that bathed the interior.

"My brother races cars back home," she said, laughing as Michael started the car. "He'd give his left nut just to *sit* in this thing."

Michael chuckled and shook his head. "The most country thing I've heard you say yet. Are you ready to go from zero to sixty in two-point-seven seconds?"

"What? Wait—"

As they pulled into her uncle's driveway, the house was shrouded in darkness.

Michael killed the engine and was out of the car in an instant. She fumbled for her keys and was surprised when he opened her door.

"Thanks," she murmured, taking his outstretched hand as she stepped onto the driveway.

"How's your ankle?"

She tested it. "Actually, it's not that bad. Thanks for the ride."

"Let me walk you in," he offered.

Her heart thudded in her chest. "That's...really not necessary."

His lips quirked. "You have to let me finish redeeming myself, Paislee."

With a dramatic sigh, she dangled her keys in front of him. "Very well, Sir Knightly. Here."

Michael unlocked the front door, and they stepped into the house. His gaze swept over the modest furnishings as she turned on the lights.

"How long have you been working at Allusion?" he asked, pausing in the living room.

"A couple of weeks." She slid her bag off her shoulder and set it on a nearby chair. "I came here for school. Allusion helps pay the bills."

He stepped further into the room.

"What about you?" She glanced at him. "Where are you from? You're obviously not from Long Island."

"Sicily."

"You're Italian." Her brows lifted.

"Sicilian," he corrected.

"Aren't they the same thing?" The look on his face answered her question. "Well, Michael Chamberlain doesn't sound all that Sicilian—or Italian."

He chuckled but didn't elaborate. She busied herself with slipping off her sneakers, but the silence stretched long enough that she turned around.

He was inches away, his eyes dark and unreadable.

Her breath quickened as the weight of his gaze stirred something both thrilling and terrifying inside her. His eyes swept over her, stopping at the straps on her skirt.

"I...uh...Seth wasn't a fan of my wardrobe," she stammered, nervously toying with the dangling hoops. "I've been my roommate's project ever since."

"She's got good taste," he said with a teasing glint in his eyes.

Her cheeks flushed, and she quickly changed the subject. "So, am I safe? No danger lurking in the shadows of my house?"

Michael reached for the strap on her skirt, and his fingers traced it slowly before he hooked it and tugged her forward. She gasped, and her hands instinctively splayed against his chest.

"Why do you look so frightened?" he murmured, his brow furrowing.

"I'm not frightened," she shot back, though her trembling hands betrayed her.

He arched a brow. "You're shaking."

Her cheeks burned. "Because I know you're going to kiss me," she admitted.

His lips curved into a slow, wicked smile. "Last night, you didn't seem so afraid."

Her resolve ebbed as his face inched closer. "That was impulsive," she whispered. "Now I'm just...questioning what I've gotten myself into."

He laughed softly, and the sound was rich and unguarded. "You have no idea what you've gotten yourself into, ducizza," he breathed.

Then he closed the space between them.

His lips moved over hers with a tenderness that made her heart stutter, and her initial hesitation melted away as she leaned into him. His grip on her waist tightened, and his kiss deepened, turning into something more consuming. Her fingers tangled in his hair as his lips moved over hers, and she felt herself drowning in the heat of it.

A strange, almost electric sensation pulsed through her, starting where his lips met hers and spreading outward. It was warmth and sweetness, like honeyed sunlight, but there was something else—something sharper, more intense—that made her senses reel. Her body responded instinctively, and she leaned closer.

He tasted sweet but...otherworldly. She really couldn't understand why that term cemented in her mind. But her senses heightened as she indulged the delicate fusion of honeyed warmth and an inexplicable, almost celestial essence. She couldn't get enough of it.

Beholding her hungry response, he inhaled sharply and slid one hand down the length of her spine. He stopped at the lower curve of her bottom and used his other hand to slide up her skirt. She released an uneven breath and heard a throaty sound as he braced her against the wall, making a trail of kisses along her jaw and down her neck. His lips captured the curve of her shoulder and lingered, becoming more demanding on her flesh. She tipped her head back slightly, giving him better access as his teeth grazed the sensitive hollow at the base of her throat. Her body responded instinctively, leaning in closer, even as her mind screamed that something was wrong.

With a gasp, she pulled back slightly. "What...what are you doing?" she whispered, shaky.

He was breathing heavily against her flesh, sending shivers down her body. "You're safe, ducizza," he murmured, his voice like velvet.

But she didn't feel safe. Her head was spinning, and her pulse was racing in a way that wasn't normal. She tried to step away, but he straightened and followed. Michael's eyes darkened, and his expression shifted into something almost predatory.

"Michael," she said, her words slurring as a warmth spread through her limbs. "I feel...strange."

For a moment, his expression faltered as a flicker of something—guilt, hesitation—crossed his face. But then it was gone, replaced by that same heated intensity. "You're fine. It's just...me."

"What does that even mean?" she demanded, her voice rising as a mix of fear and confusion welled up inside her.

Michael's grip on her tightened. "You're feeling what I feel."

Her lips parted, but no words came out. Instead, she became acutely aware of the way her body was reacting—her pulse thrumming in time with his, the overwhelming heat coursing through her veins, the way every touch from him seemed to set her skin on fire. She was dizzy, overwhelmed. "I can't," she managed to say, barely audible. "I don't know you."

"Of course you can," he said gently against her mouth, and then he clasped her lower lip between his teeth and slowly released it, fixing his eyes on hers. She was trapped between his body and the wall, scorching under his gaze. "This is the perfect way to get to know me," he said with a mischievous glint in his eyes.

She nodded and heard herself say, "You're right."

*What?*

She melded with him, and he swiftly lifted her and headed for the stairs.

All the while, she was being drugged by his kisses, and she basked in the sweetness unfurling on her tongue like liquid starlight.

She was vaguely aware of him carrying her up the stairs and then asking her where her room was.

Michael carefully set her feet on the floor and unzipped her skirt. Then he tore off her halter and unclasped her bra so quickly that she didn't even realize it until she was lying naked on the bed and he was gently kissing her as his other hand slid down her side. She could barely speak, and her breath caught in her throat as she tried to comprehend the whirlwind sweeping her into another world.

She had crazed feelings, and her body ached to release the tension building inside. She began pulling at his shirt, and he eagerly helped her remove it before he climbed back over her and his mouth crushed hers.

"Michael," she breathed, her voice trembling as his lips trailed along her jaw. "I've never..."

He pulled back slightly, his gaze dark and searching. "Never what?"

She forced herself to meet his gaze, even as her cheeks burned with embarrassment. "I don't really...know what I'm doing."

"Like, in this moment?"

She lost her voice, and her body cried out with longing. She shook her head, her frustration so intense that tears welled in her eyes.

"Paislee." His expression shifted, and the fire in his eyes dimmed as something softer and more protective took its place. "Are you telling me you've never had sex?"

Paislee wrapped her arms around herself as if trying to hold herself together.

Michael froze and then quickly got off the bed, his eyes wide. The shift was sudden, and the loss of his touch made her feel strangely bereft, even as she struggled to regain her composure.

"I don't even know what's happening." She pulled the blanket over her and watched him, looking just as shaken as she felt. "You should go," she said, her voice firmer now.

For a moment, he didn't move. Then he slowly drove his hand through his hair and grabbed his shirt. "You're right," he said quietly, his gaze softening. "I'll go."

He stepped towards the door, but before he left her room, his eyes lingered on her. "I'm sorry if I scared you. Goodnight, Paislee."

She covered her eyes briefly before she said, "Goodnight, Michael."

Then he was gone, leaving Paislee alone in silence, with her heart pounding and her thoughts spinning.

# Chapter Eight

MICHAEL STALKED OUT OF Paislee's house, a growl rumbling low in his throat. "What a cruel, fucking joke."

Frustration gripped him, twisting like a vice. He turned up the stereo as he drove back to Allusion, but the music did little to silence the thoughts gnawing at him.

Of all the women he could have, he wanted the virgin. Really? Her innocence wasn't just inconvenient—it was a complication he hadn't accounted for. And now the thought of approaching her with a contract felt...shameful.

As he pulled into Allusion's private lot, he cut the engine and stepped out, slamming the car door harder than necessary. His fingers habitually twirled his keys as he strode inside, his mind still tangled with unwanted thoughts.

The moment he entered, he spotted Saverio standing on the staircase.

If Saverio had been human, he might have passed for someone in his early fifties—distinguished, sharp, effortlessly commanding attention. Even now, the younger women on the cleaning crew cast lingering glances at him, their dreamy expressions betraying their fascination. Saverio ignored them. His focus remained on Michael as he crossed the dance floor and ascended the stairs.

"How long have you been here?" Michael asked, sidestepping his father and heading into the office.

"Long enough for Seth to tell me you took one of the servers home," Saverio replied evenly. He followed Michael into the office, stopping by the windows overlooking the dance floor. "I was late, but I guess you found a way to pass the time."

Michael didn't dignify that with an answer, though he shot a glare at Seth.

Seth cleared his throat and poured three tumblers of scotch, setting one in front of each of them.

Saverio's gaze briefly flicking to the dance floor below. "Are you looking for a largitor?"

Michael took his drink, and he swirled the amber liquid before taking a slow sip. "Maybe."

"I'll have Bishop draft a contract. You can use Jocelyne in the meantime."

"I'll draw up my own paperwork," Michael said tersely.

Saverio shrugged, unbothered. "Suit yourself. What happened to...what was her name? Gianna?"

"Her contract ended years ago. She'd grown...pale."

Saverio gave a perfunctory nod, already disinterested. Seth, meanwhile, flipped through ledgers, feigning focus.

"You're a Regnanti," Saverio mused. "Our thirst is demanding. It's a wonder I've kept Jocelyne as long as I have."

Michael set down his glass with a soft thud. "I'm a Chamberlain," he corrected, his voice like steel.

Yet, even as he said it, he questioned his own restraint—especially where Paislee was concerned.

Exhaling sharply, he tilted his head back and finished his drink. "You're here for a reason. Let's get on with it."

Seth handed Saverio a folder. "Here's the list of donations for July's Liberty Benefit. This year, we're raising money for Mrs. Chamberlain's research center. I've outlined expenses and event ideas."

Michael extended a hand. "If I'm going to be running this place, I should be reading that."

Saverio handed over the folder without argument. Michael scanned it, unimpressed.

"Your age is showing in this proposal, Seth." Michael smirked. "This club will be filled with young cardinales and human elites."

Seth frowned. "These plans make a good party for the youth."

Michael shook his head. "This isn't just a party—it's theater. And elites don't pay to be entertained. They pay to be seen."

Seth exchanged a glance with Saverio. "What do you suggest?"

"I'll rewrite the plan tomorrow," Michael said, suppressing a yawn. "I'm tired. Let's just handle the legal paperwork tonight."

"So be it," Saverio said, settling into business mode.

Michael forced himself to focus, though fatigue dragged at him. When they were finished, Saverio stood and extended his hand.

"Allusion is yours," he declared. "Find a blood donor soon, Michele, before your lethargy consumes you."

Michael said nothing, only watched as Saverio exited the office.

Silence stretched between him and Seth as they sat nursing another round of scotch.

Seth finally broke it. "So...you met Paislee."

Michael's grip tightened around his glass. The memory of their encounter flared in his mind, sharp and vivid.

"I did." His voice was unreadable. "I can see why you hired her."

Seth smirked. "She's something, isn't she?"

Michael grunted and finished his drink in one sharp swig. No amount of liquor could dull the ache coursing through him.

Her scent. Her touch.

They lingered.

And damn it all—how the hell was he supposed to stay away?

# Chapter Nine

I T HAD BEEN NEARLY a week since Michael had driven Paislee home. She'd seen him every night at the club, and their encounters remained civil—civil as if they hadn't almost had sex.

Her memory of that night was hazy, but one thing was clear: it hadn't gone well—for either of them. The haunting thought of Michael kissing her with such passion, as if he were taking the life right from her, lingered. It felt raw and unsettling. He was in a league far beyond her experience, and now he was keeping his distance.

A part of her didn't blame him. Why would he want to entangle himself with someone who couldn't match his passion? She'd been too stunned to process anything after he'd left, but at least he hadn't taken advantage of her vulnerability. Yet, his eyes—those enigmatic eyes—still pulled her in, coaxing her to abandon reason and surrender to her primal instincts.

Since meeting Michael, she'd been questioning everything that had shaped her—her values, her desires, her very identity.

At the club, she watched other women practically throw themselves at him, some nearly dragging him over the bar for a kiss. He handled it all with ease, laughing it off. Paislee couldn't forget that she'd been one of those women. But unlike her, these women were polished, poised, and undoubtedly his type. They wore heels worth thousands, were dripping in diamonds, and exuded an effortless elegance that matched his taste for the finer things in life: luxury cars, tailored suits, and champagne-soaked nights with celebrities.

Michael took all their attention in stride, but there was more to him than his playboy exterior. He had a way of stripping people down to their most primal selves, igniting desires they didn't even know they had. He was impossible to resist—and equally impossible to understand.

As the night dragged on, Paislee sighed with relief when the DJ announced last call. Exhausting and feeling less than her best, she focused on cashing out. Her next two days off couldn't come soon enough.

While she organized her tips, a voice called out to her. Esben. She hadn't seen him since the night she'd met Michael. She'd assumed that he'd moved on.

She turned away, hoping he'd lose interest, but he blocked her path. His smirk made her skin crawl.

"Look, I'm sorry about last week. Do you want to join me in the VIP room?" Esben asked, his tone slick.

"I don't work in the VIP room, and we're closing soon," she said curtly.

"That doesn't matter. Come as my guest. Have you ever been up there?"

"No. Seth made it clear I'm not supposed to go in there."

"Leave her alone, Esben."

Michael's voice cut through the tension as he strode toward them with a towel slung over his shoulder.

Paislee used the distraction to step away, but Esben grabbed her arm and slid his hand down her back and along the curve of her bottom. Furious, she spun and slammed her tray into his chest. Drinks splashed over his face and tailored shirt, and the glasses shattered on the floor.

The entire club seemed to freeze. A few patrons nearby recoiled as if burned, dragging their drinks back as they shared in rapt silence.

For a breathless moment, nobody spoke.

Esben stood rigid, lips pulled back in a feral snarl that was part fury, part disbelief. Every face that that turned towards him fed the mounting heat under his skin. Humiliation burned up his neck like wildfire.

He grabbed Paislee, his fingers digging into her arm.

Michael stepped between them, forcing Esben to release her.

"Shake it off," Michael said, tossing a towel at Esben.

Paislee stormed off, ignoring Esben's glare. She'd had enough—enough of Michael's indifference and Esben's aggression.

In the break room, she switched her heels for sneakers and then went to the sink. As she washed the drinks off her hands, she smiled, recalling the look of shock on Esben's face.

The door flew open, and Michael stood there, glowering. "What the hell were you doing?"

She crossed her arms and leaned against the sink. "Me? I was defending myself," she shot back. "He grabbed my ass."

"I was handling it," Michael said sharply. "He's a customer. If there's a problem, you get management or the security staff. You don't throw a tray of drinks in their face."

Her mouth dropped open. "You were there. You saw what he did, and you're giving me grief? Tell Seth if you want," she added bitterly. "If I was wrong, he'll handle it—he's the boss. I don't need a lecture from the bartender."

Michael's eyes hardened, and with a single, deliberate motion, he slammed the door shut behind him. His jaw tightened as he stepped closer and the space between them shrank.

"I'm not the bartender, Paislee. *I'm* the boss."

Her world tilted, and she was stunned into silence as his words ricocheted in her mind.

"What?" she whispered.

"That's right," he said, his tone firm but not unkind. "I bought this club from my father. And if you assault another customer, you're fired."

"But, we almost..." Her stomach twisted, and a rush of heat crept up her neck. Her boss? The man she'd kissed. The man she'd almost had sex with? Her ears burned as the implications pounded into her one at a time.

"You've been here over a week. You should've told me," she said. "I deserved to know."

He tilted his head, his gaze steady. "Would it have changed anything?"

Yes. No. She didn't know. All she could think about was the way his hands had roamed her body, how her own hands pulled him closer, and how closely they'd come to crossing a line she couldn't uncross.

Her chest tightened as anger and embarrassment warred inside her. "I can't believe this. You let me make a fool of myself. You took off my clothes. You kissed me—"

"After you kissed me," he interrupted, his voice hardening again. "And you didn't seem to care who I was then."

Her face flushed crimson. "Because I didn't know!"

"Exactly," he said, stepping closer. His voice softened but lost none of its intensity. "And now you do. So, tell me—does it change anything?"

Her breath caught. She hated the way his words struck something raw and vulnerable inside her. She hated even more how the answer wasn't as clear as she wanted it to be.

She swallowed hard, breaking eye contact. "You should've told me," she repeated, her voice quieter now. "Before I almost had sex with you."

"You're right," he admitted, catching her off guard. "But now that you know, you need to understand something. What happens on this floor—what happens between you and any customer—is my responsibility. You can't go rogue, no matter how justified you feel."

His words should've stung, but all she could focus on was what had happened that night and how tangled it had just become. She nodded reluctantly, her pride swallowing her retort.

She couldn't resist one last jab. "I was justified. Esben is a douche."

To her surprise, Michael's sternness cracked, and his mouth twitched into a faint smile. "I agree."

His sudden shift only added to her disorientation. Without another word, she turned on her heel and snatched up her bag. Her thoughts were a whirlwind of confusion, anger, and something she wasn't ready to name.

"Don't worry about your customers," he said, stopping her just as she reached the door. "I made sure they got their drinks."

She turned to him and glared. If he was expecting a thank you, he was mistaken.

"They didn't tip you, being that they had to wait so long," he added.

"Fuck their tip. It was worth it."

Michael felt like shit. His muscles ached, his head was pounding, and his patience was nonexistent. Images of Paislee kept flashing in his mind, and his thirst was growing unbearable. He needed to find a largitor, yet his body and mind refused to let go of her.

He sat in Seth's office, staring at the bracelet on his desk. Paislee's bracelet. After their heated conversation, she'd angrily thrown open the door, and she hadn't realized that it had fallen off her wrist on the way out. The room was silent save for the faint hum of the building's air system, but his mind was anything but quiet. The slim, silver band seemed harmless at first glance, innocuous, even, yet the engraving made it heavier than any object he'd ever had.

*PAISLEE SULLIVAN – O NEGATIVE – MEDICAL ALERT*

Seth entered the office, pulling Michael from his miserably confusing thoughts. Seth didn't say a word, just went to his collection of fine crystal decanters and poured two tumblers full of whisky. After handing Michael one, he sat opposite at the desk. They remained in silence for a long while, counting the cash and looking over the inventory.

Michael tried to focus, but images of Paislee kept flashing in his mind. He'd planned to keep his distance, but the thirst tore at his restraint, eroding his control and amplifying the pull toward her. He needed to find another prospective donor because Paislee was an innocent. She was off-limits despite the strange effect she had on him. After indulging in her charms, and now discovering that she had the caviar of blood types, no one else could come close to satisfying his desires.

Even now, his body betrayed him, with tension coiling tightly beneath his skin as every nerve screamed for more of her. His hands itched to touch her. Each time she came to the bar for drinks, he had a mind to scale the counter and take her to the office. He convinced himself that his insatiable need for her was only because he'd been deprived of blood for too long.

It was true that she had the purest of blood types, and her body could tempt a saint, but his willpower was usually unshakable. His resolve was faltering only because he'd gone so long without feeding, and the effects were beginning to show. Truthfully, he wanted her. Badly. The very idea that she'd remained untouched all this time was another matter.

"I'm going to make it an early night, Michael." Seth gathered his paperwork into a loose pile.

"No problem. Get out of here, Seth. I'll lock up," Michael replied, trying again to focus on counting and separating the money.

Seth didn't leave right away, though. Instead, he poured another drink. "I heard your brother was here again."

Michael chuckled. "Paislee threw a tray in his face."

Seth raised a brow. "I'm sure he deserved it."

Michael tossed aside a stack of money. He'd sorted through it three times and still didn't have a final count. He rubbed his eyes and then pinched the bridge of his nose, fighting a horrible ache in his head. "He did," he admitted. "But I had to scold her, nonetheless. She didn't like that too much."

Seth sat back in his chair. "I wouldn't let Esben anywhere near her."

Michael sighed. "I didn't realize he'd come down from the VIP room. Soon enough, he won't be able to touch her."

"You plan to make her your contracted blood source," Seth observed.

"I just decided this moment. But I shouldn't," Michael said, his eyes fixed on the ceiling as he rested his head back on his chair. "There are a lot of complications that come with Paislee Sullivan."

"You're obviously conflicted about it." Seth cocked a brow. "There are plenty of humans willing to give their blood with a lot less drama."

Michael grimaced as another searing pain shot from his temple to the center of his forehead. "I've met some prospects, but...I want Paislee."

Seth was silent for a moment as he sipped his drink. "I've never seen you so determined when it came to a particular human."

Michael scoffed as he took a drink. "I have to say, for the first time, I'm not certain I'll succeed in this."

"Paislee Sullivan is something special," Seth laughed softly as he drank the dark contents of his tumbler. "You may have to really work for it this time, Michael."

It was the admiration in Seth's voice that triggered Michael's attention, and he looked at his old friend. Seth's voice, always so sharp and fast, had softened slightly when he'd said her name. Not in an obvious way, not enough for anyone else to catch, but Michael had.

It wasn't the words but the weight behind them.

Seth rarely involved himself in the hiring process, yet he'd hired Paislee personally. He handed off resumés, skimmed credentials, but he didn't personally bring people on. That wasn't part of his job. Saverio hadn't expected it of him, nor was it something Michael expected.

"Seth? Were you planning on making Paislee yours?" Michael asked.

Seth finished his drink and set it on the desk with a clunk. "I'd considered it," he admitted.

"Why didn't you tell me?"

"I knew she wasn't going to be mine when I saw her kiss you," Seth said. "I'm not a fool. I couldn't miss your response to her that night—or that daft look on your face every time you look at her."

Michael looked defensively at him. Dropping his arms from the desk, he sat back in the chair.

"I wish you would've said something," he said. "I can back off."

Seth raised a brow. "*Can* you? Your venom emanated from her last week. That doesn't happen from one simple kiss. So, having gotten that close, could you let her go now?"

When he didn't answer, Seth chuckled.

"It's all right, Michael. Take her with a clear conscience; I have several largitores. You need one soon. I can see the signs. You've been without blood for a while."

Michael knew he was right. He felt it. He was weaker—and tired.

"Esben is still sniffing around," Seth said. "He was watching Paislee from the VIP windows, so you might want to hurry up and seal the deal."

Michael let out a disgusted grunt. "My brother can't force her to be his largitor—and legally, he can't touch her if she's under my contract."

"But she's not under your contract, is she? And now he'll want to make her pay for insulting him."

There was enough bad history between the two of them that one would have thought that Esben would leave him well enough alone and stay out of his club. But Esben couldn't do that.

Michael stood and walked to the window. He scanned the empty floor below. The club was silent now, its patrons long gone, and Paislee with them.

Seth's words echoed in his mind like the crack of thunder before a storm. Michael's fists clenched, and his nails bit into his palms as his body barely contained his rage. Esben was watching her tonight. He'd targeted her again. The thought ignited a fire in Michael's chest, and fury rushed through him like a dam breaking under pressure.

The bastard couldn't help himself. Esben never could resist playing games, never could leave well enough alone. Michael should've known better than to think his brother would stay out of his business—or away from Paislee.

*She's not under contract, is she?*

Seth's question replayed in his mind, dragging Michael's teeth into a tight clench. His jaw ached from the strain, but the physical pain was nothing compared to the inferno burning inside him.

He'd jumped to Paislee's defense when she'd thrown the tray in Esben's face. Seth was right. Esben had wanted Paislee, and not only had she rejected him, but she had also humiliated him. He'd want to make her pay.

Michael's fury was matched only by his concern. Paislee had no idea of the danger she was in, walking through the night like she was untouchable. She didn't know the monsters watching from the shadows.

The memory of Paislee's defiance, her fire, flashed through his mind. She was bold and brave, but she was also human. Mortal. Fragile. And Esben would break her just to make a point.

A violent hiss escaped him as his fangs emerged, a physical manifestation of the rage and hunger swirling inside.

"I have to go." Michael grabbed his keys, his movements fast and deliberate. He was already halfway to the door when Seth's voice stopped him.

"Michael—don't let him bait you."

Michael stopped. His shoulders were tense, his body as taut as a bowstring. He turned his head slightly, just enough to respond without looking back.

"It's not about him," Michael said. "It's about her."

And with that, he was gone, slamming the door shut behind him.

# Chapter Ten

P AISLEE ARRIVED HOME JUST as Kendra pulled up with her
coworker, Tessa. They'd spent the early hours of the morning
chatting and unwinding, and at some point, Kendra had floated the
idea of letting Tessa stay in the third bedroom. Paislee had promised
to bring it up with her uncle.

As dawn approached, Tessa said her goodbyes and drove off,
leaving Paislee and Kendra alone in the house.

Kendra sat cross-legged on the blue denim couch, brushing her
hair as Paislee paced the room, ranting about Esben grabbing her,
and Michael's scolding reaction.

"Maybe Michael was just in a bad mood," Kendra suggested, her
fingers deftly braiding her long curls.

Paislee shrugged, relieved that it was finally Sunday. She had the next two days off, a break from Michael, Esben, and the chaos they brought. She opened the fridge, and her face scrunched at its pitiful contents: an open bottle of Yoo-hoo, questionable lunchmeat, and a bag of apples. She grabbed an apple and bit into it with more force than necessary as her mind wandered back to her conversation with Michael earlier.

Paislee groaned, leaning against the counter. "Maybe," she muttered, though the memory of his cutting tone still stung, "but I can't believe he's Allusion's owner."

Kendra snorted. "That's awesome, Pais. I never thought you were the type to screw the boss."

"I'm not screwing anyone, Kendra," Paislee shot back, taking another angry bite of her apple.

"Give it time."

Paislee rolled her eyes and muttered under her breath as she stormed upstairs. "Me and my apple are going to bed."

Her room was a sanctuary of dim light and quiet. She kicked off her slippers, grabbed her comfiest pajama pants and halter, slipped into them, sighing at the familiar softness despite the faded frog print. Her hair fell loose as she tugged out the clips, and she stretched, feeling the exhaustion that had finally settled into her muscles.

"That was quite a show," a voice drawled from the shadows.

Paislee gasped and spun around, nearly choking on the bite of apple in her mouth. A figure stepped into the faint light cast by her bedside lamp.

"Esben," she whispered, and the name caught in her throat.

He leaned against the wall, his posture casual but his presence suffocating. His eyes gleamed with menace, and a smirk curled at the corner of his mouth, a cruel mockery of the fear tightening in her chest.

"Oh, shit," she breathed. Her voice trembled despite her efforts to sound firm when she demanded, "Get the hell out of my room before I call the cops."

Esben glanced at her phone set next to him on the dresser.

*Fuck.*

He tilted his head, and his silence was louder than any words. Her pulse thundered in her ears as she edged toward the door, her mind racing with ways to escape.

She didn't make it far. Before she could reach the knob, he was there, moving faster than she thought possible. His hand forced the door closed while the other wrapped around her waist, pulling her flush against him. She thrashed against him, her screams muffled by his palm.

"I saw you first," he hissed, his breath hot against her ear. "And imagine my fury when I learned that Michael is trying to claim you for himself."

Her struggles intensified, but his grip was solid. Iron. His words didn't make sense—*claiming* her? What did that even mean? She tried to twist away, and her nails dug into his arm, but he didn't flinch.

"You humans," he continued, his tone almost mocking. "So fragile. So predictable."

His grip shifted, and one hand tugged at the drawstring of her pajama pants. Panic flared, white-hot in her chest. With a surge of adrenaline, she jammed her knee upward and connected with his groin. He stumbled back, growling, and she didn't hesitate. She swung the apple in her fist, smashing it against his face before darting for the door.

She'd barely unlocked it when his hand clamped around her waist and hauled her back. A scream tore up her throat, but it broke into a panicked gasp as he dragged her toward the bed. She clawed at his hands, kicked blindly—anything to break his grip. But his strength was unyielding.

And then glass shattered.

Michael.

He was there in an instant, a dark streak in her periphery before he crashed into Esben with a brutal impact that rocked the floorboards. Paislee stumbled backward, landing against the wall as she fought to catch her breath. Paislee scrambled to the far corner, where she watched in stunned horror. The fight exploded around her, too fast for her eyes to track. Snarls, hisses, the sickening scrape of shoe against wood. They moved like beasts, shadows locked together, fists and teeth and something wilder. Michael's hands closed around Esben's collar and he drove him into the wall so hard a picture frame fell and splintered.

But Esben recovered with feral speed, producing a glint of steel. Paislee flinched as the knife sliced the air, and Michael twisted away just in time. He seized Esben and heaved him across the room, sending him tumbling into the chair.

That was her chance. Paislee surged to her feet and sprinted for the door. Her hands fumbled at the knob. Almost. Almost.

And then something yanked her back again. Her scream broke free with pure terror, stifled by a hand over her mouth. But this time, the grip was gentler.

"Paislee, it's me. Stop it," Michael said, his voice low and urgent. "He's gone."

The sound of footsteps pounded up the stairs. "Paislee! Are you okay? What's going on?" Kendra called out, her voice muffled by the closed door.

"Listen to me," Michael whispered. "It's important that you don't say anything—" Paislee pushed at his chest, but he only tightened his hold on her. "If you tell her anything, you risk her life. Understand?"

Paislee's heart thundered. No, she didn't understand! What the hell was going on? She was frantic. Esben had invaded her room and tried to assault her! After watching how violently the two men had fought, even Michael frightened her. Now he was threatening Kendra's safety?

Kendra banged on the door and jiggled the knob. "Hey, Pais, what's all that noise? Answer me!"

Paislee and Michael peered at each other.

"Don't. You'll endanger her," he whispered again, giving her one last, loaded look before removing his hand from her mouth.

The weight of his words hit like a stone. After what she'd just witnessed, Kendra had no idea the monster she'd be facing if she crossed that threshold. Paislee's thoughts scattered, she imagined

Kendra frozen in terror, dialing 911 too late—or worse. Paislee realized she couldn't let that happen. She dragged in a shaky breath and gave a tiny nod. Shaking out the trembling in her hands as Michael soundlessly stepped back, she opened the door.

"What happened?" Kendra demanded, her phone clutched tightly in one hand.

"It's...it's nothing," Paislee stammered, forcing a weak laugh. "I...I tripped. Sorry for the noise."

"Jesus, I was ready to call the cops, Pais." Kendra frowned, her eyes wide as she tried to peek past Paislee and into the room.

Behind her, Michael appeared, his expression composed despite everything that had happened moments before. "Apologies for startling you, Kendra," he said smoothly. "We haven't been introduced. I'm Michael."

Kendra's eyes narrowed as she took Michael's outstretched hand. "Hi, boss-man. Come to apologize for being a dick?"

"Something like that." Michael chuckled, scratching the back of his neck. "Apparently, climbing up the window isn't romantic like in the movies—"

"What? No, it's terrifying—and fucking weird," Kendra interrupted. "Knock on the front door like a normal person."

Michael drove his hand through his hair. "I've learned my lesson after stumbling. I knocked over some shit. Not to mention that I startled Paislee."

"You think?" Kendra asked, her tone dripping with sarcasm.

Michael let out a soft laugh, and he dropped his gaze as if he were truly embarrassed. Paislee couldn't believe it. She glanced at Kendra, who was buying all his charm, eating it up.

"I'll do that next time. Paislee and I were just going to get some breakfast. Talk it out."

Kendra leaned to the side, trying to peer around him. "Everything's good, then, Pais?" she asked.

Paislee's thoughts were sluggish, as if she were moving through molasses. She opened her mouth, but no words came out. She stared blankly at the apple still in her hand, the bruised fruit a bizarre reminder of the chaos moments earlier. Michael stepped beside her and gently took the apple from her hand. The movement jolted her back to reality. With his warning echoing in her head, she pasted on a smile and nodded. "I...yeah," she croaked, her voice barely audible. "He just jumped me, and I threw...something at him."

Kendra's gaze flickered between them before she finally sighed. "Fine. You're lucky I didn't call the cops." She shook her head and started back downstairs.

Michael waited until she was out of earshot before he shut the door and locked it, his movements quick and precise. When he turned back to Paislee, his expression was a blend of urgency and determination. "You're leaving with me," he said, his tone brooking no argument. Finding her bookbag in the closet, he handed it to her. "Pack your things."

Paislee froze, staring at him as if he'd just spoken another language. "Excuse me?" she said slowly, her voice thick with disbelief. Her brows drew together as the initial shock gave way to a spark of anger. "What the hell are you talking about?"

Michael stepped close and held her gaze. "Esben will come back for you, and if your friends are here, they'll be caught in the crossfire."

The mention of her friends sent a chill through her, but she refused to let it show. And the mention of Esben's name chilled her blood. She clenched her fists as the fire in her rose to meet the fear. "Not if he's arrested for assault!"

"Keep your voice down." Michael's jaw tightened as he shook his head. "Calling the cops on Esben isn't going to stop him."

"I don't care who he is; he's not above the law. How do you know—"

"Because he's my brother," Michael interjected, and his words sliced through the space between them. He sighed, his frustration evident, but there was a flicker of something softer in his tone that matched his eyes. "The cops wouldn't stop me, and they're not going to stop him. Now, pack, Paislee."

Her heart thudded against her ribs, and her body was still trembling from everything that had just happened, but the fire inside her burned brighter now. "Your brother?" she repeated, her voice barely above a whisper.

"Yes." Michael's expression darkened. "But don't confuse me with him. We're nothing alike."

"Oh, really?" she snapped. "Because, from where I'm standing, you're both storming into my life and tearing everything apart. I'm supposed to go with you now? Why? For how long? You act like I'm just supposed to go along with it!"

"I didn't ask for this, either!" Michael shot back, his voice rising before he quickly reined it in. "Pack, or I'll pack for you," he said bluntly as he opened one of her drawers.

"Get out of my underwear drawer," she snapped, closing the drawer so quickly that she nearly caught his fingers in it.

He smirked faintly and raised his hands. "Then start packing."

"Fine," she spat, her voice cutting like a whip.

"And I'll pick up this mess."

"But I'm not doing this because you told me to," she snapped. "I'm doing it so Esben doesn't return and harm my friends."

"If that suits you." Michael's lips pressed into a thin line. "Now, hurry."

Still grumbling under her breath, Paislee began tossing clothes into her bag. "I swear, this is the worst night of my life."

She zipped the bag shut with a tug and then, her glare burning into him, headed for the door.

He glanced at her bare feet. "Shoes?"

Her glare never faltered as she marched to her closet and put on her bunny slippers, with their soft fabric thrusting against her skin. "These better survive this mess," she muttered as she exited her room.

# Chapter Eleven

**M**ICHAEL PULLED HIS BIKE to a stop and killed the engine. The sudden silence was broken only by the distant crashing of waves against the shore. The air was heavy with salt, cool and damp against Paislee's skin. Her arms were still around him, trembling with an adrenaline she couldn't suppress. He climbed off first, turning to help her. Her legs felt too shaky to move on their own.

"You okay?" he asked, his tone even, almost calm—a stark contrast to the turmoil still swirling inside her.

She didn't answer, not trusting herself to speak. Her legs felt unsteady as she let him guide her, and his hands were firm but strangely gentle on her arms. The warmth of his touch unsettled her, clashing with the memory of him throwing Esben across the room with monstrous strength. It wasn't natural. None of it was.

"This way," he said, taking her bag and leading her up the stone path to the front door.

"Where am I?"

"My place," he replied.

Her breath caught as she looked up and his house came into view in the dim, shifting light of dawn. It loomed over the dunes like a monolith of glass and stone, like something out of a luxury magazine—a modern beach house with a touch of cottage charm. It was striking, all sleek angles and expansive windows, with soft exterior lighting illuminating an imposing yet elegant structure. Beyond, the ocean stretched into infinity, dark and restless, reflecting the horizon's pink hues.

It was stunning, but in the stillness of the hour, it felt like another world entirely—isolating and unyielding—the kind of place where time seemed to stand still...and no one could hear you scream.

Inside was equally mesmerizing. The entryway opened into an expansive living area where floor-to-ceiling windows framed the Atlantic Ocean, now bathed in the pale colors of early morning. The soft, golden glow of ambient lighting made the polished floors gleam, casting long shadows. Everything was immaculate and sleek, from the modern furniture to the abstract art adorning the walls. It felt cold and impersonal, like no one truly lived there.

"Sit," Michael said, gesturing toward the kitchen. His tone made it clear that he expected obedience, and her legs carried her forward on autopilot.

She sank into one of the high-backed chairs at the kitchen's island, her hands trembling uncontrollably. Michael poured her a glass of water and placed it in front of her, but her fingers shook so violently that the glass rattled against the marble countertop, sending water splashing over the rim.

He took it from her before she could drop it. "All right, you need to calm down," he said, his voice firm but low. He crouched in front of her and cupped her face in his hands.

She jerked back.

Michael released her immediately, and his expression softened as he straightened. "Paislee," he said gently, "you're safe now. If I wanted to hurt you, I could've done it already. Trust me."

The calm in his tone felt like a command, one her body obeyed even as her mind screamed not to. She swallowed hard, unable to meet his eyes.

"Please trust me," he repeated, his fingers brushing a strand of hair behind her ear.

She felt herself leaning into him despite the turmoil inside her. Her instincts were warring with logic. His voice—his touch—it was like something had reached into her chest and quieted the storm there.

When he lowered his head and pressed his lips to hers, a strange warmth washed over her, calming the tremors in her hands and slowing the frantic rhythm of her heart. She hated that it felt good, hated how her body seemed to welcome it.

He pulled back. "Your shaking has stopped. Your heart's steady now," he said softly. "Do you think we can talk?"

Her voice was barely above a whisper. "How did you do that?"

"I'll explain as best I can."

"Esben is your brother. Why didn't you tell me sooner?"

Michael let out a short laugh, though it didn't reach his eyes. "I didn't think it was relevant."

"How about now?"

His expression grew serious, and he lowered his gaze. "I'm sorry about my brother. I didn't want you to find out like this."

"Find out what?" she asked, narrowing her eyes.

He rested his hands on the counter to steady himself, as if the question were a heavier weight than he wanted to admit. "Would you stay here with me?"

The absurdity of his words jolted her back to reality. She stood and backed away from him. "What are you talking about?"

He hesitated, his frustrations crackling under the careful mask he wore. "I need you, Paislee. I'll pay you—substantially."

Her stomach dropped. "I'm not a prostitute, Michael."

"I'm not asking for sex," he replied as a faint smirk tugged at his lips. "Not that I'd turn it down, but...that's not what I need."

She stared at him, her pulse pounding in her ears. "What do you need from me, then?"

His jaw tensed, and he turned away, shrugging off his jacket. It landed on the counter with a soft thud, but she barely noticed. Her attention was drawn to the blood soaking through his shirt.

"Michael," she breathed, stepping toward him. "You're bleeding."

He looked down as if noticing it for the first time. "It's nothing."

"Nothing?" The word slipped out sharper than she'd meant it. He'd rescued her from Esben, throwing himself between them without hesitation. And now, he was hurt. She grabbed the stained hem of his shirt to inspect the wound. "You need a doctor."

His hand shot out and caught her wrist. "Don't." His voice cracked through the air like a whip. "Don't touch my blood."

She froze, stunned by the sudden change in him. The sharpness. The panic.

"Why?" she whispered.

Michael's grip loosened. He didn't answer—just pulled her toward the sink with a desperate kind of urgency and shoved her hand under the faucet. The water ran cold as he scrubbed her hand with frantic determination, washing away any trace of blood. "Never touch my blood, Paislee. Promise me."

"You're not making any sense," she said, yanking her hand back. She stared at him, her pulse pounding in her ears. "You save me from your brother, then freak out when I try to help you. What's going on? What do you want from me?"

He let her go. Slowly, he turned. His body stayed rigid, his shoulders drawn tight, as his hands braced against the counter. "Your blood," he said quietly.

Her heart stuttered. She blinked at him, confused and suddenly aware of how quiet the room had gone. "What about it?"

"I need it. I need...you."

Michael's words hung in the air. She backed up a step.

She gawked at him, struggling to piece his words together. "That sounds really creepy," she whispered. "I think you're injured and saying crazy things—"

He moved slowly, like he was trying not to spook her. "You've heard the stories, Paislee," he said, his voice softer now, more careful. "They've called us creatures of the dark, feeding off the living."

Her heart stumbled in her chest. "No, you're not saying—"

Michael growled, dragging his hand through his thick hair. "Vampire. That's the word your kind uses."

She stared at him and for a moment, she didn't breathe. She couldn't.

Then she shook her head. "No. No, you're not—vampires aren't real."

He winced at the word. "We don't like that term," he said, his tone clipped. "That word was never ours. It was made up. By humans who didn't understand us. We were never undead. Never crawling out of graves. I'm not a corpse. And I'm not cursed. That's theater. That's folklore."

She stiffened. Her whole body felt locked in place. "Then, what do you call yourself?"

"A cardinalis," he said. "And we're real."

She clenched her jaw, forcing her tone steady. "You're bleeding. A lot. We need to get you to the hospital."

Michael exhaled.

"You already know the truth."

He stepped closer—she stepped back.

"You've felt it. The pull."

His dark eyes drew her in.

She stared at him, her mouth dry, as his words continued to sink in. "Stop," she said, the word shaken.

"Paislee," he said, his tone low and almost pleading. His gaze was unwavering as he leaned against the counter. "I was trying to explain it without scaring you."

*Too late for that*, she thought.

"Okay," she said slowly, stepping back again. "Let's say I believe you. Why me? Can't you just go to a blood bank?"

Michael's shoulders relaxed, and his lips curved into a faint, almost relieved smile. His tension appeared to ease, slightly.

"It doesn't work like that."

He shook his head as his expression softened. "It has to be fresh. Alive."

"So what—you just... drink it?"

She suppressed a shudder and tilted her head, forcing her tone to remain light. "Do you have a deficiency or something?"

Subtle amusement passed over his face. "In a way. Our bodies need something from human blood to survive—a protein we can't produce naturally. Without it, we grow sick. Weak."

Her brow furrowed as she feigned interest while taking another small step back. "But you don't kill people, right? You don't like...suck us dry?"

His gaze locked with hers, and there was a strange intensity in his eyes. "It's not necessary."

"Comforting," she muttered under her breath.

Michael's jaw tightened, but he didn't respond. Instead, he began pacing. "Your blood is valuable. Rare. I'm willing to pay more for yours."

"Lucky me," she said dryly, glancing toward the hallway leading to the front door. She needed to keep him focused on her words, not her movements. "What's your plan—keep me in a cage and drain me like a keg at a frat party?"

His eyes snapped to hers, darkening. "It's not like that."

"Then what is it like?" she shot back, her voice rising. She couldn't help it.

She caught herself, forcing her tone to soften.

Nothing was adding up.

He believed what he was saying.

Every word.

She nodded slowly, and softened her expression.

For a moment, he didn't speak. Frustration and something deeper crossed his face. Regret, maybe?

Every instinct in her body said the same thing—she wasn't safe.

Silence ticked by until he sighed and turned away. He was opening the fridge—for what, she didn't care.

Paislee bolted for the door, slipping slightly on the polished floor as adrenaline surged through her.

But she didn't make it far.

He caught her before she reached the door, fingers locking around her wrist. She was spun back—hard—her back hitting the wall. His eyes blazed with anger—and something darker beneath it.

"How far did you think you'd get in bunny slippers?"

Paislee squirmed against his grip, but he didn't budge. Her pulse spiked as his gaze locked on hers—dark and unreadable.

"You're fucking crazy, Michael."

"I've been patient, Paislee—"

"Let me go, you fu—"

"More patient than I've been with anyone. But you're testing my reasonable nature," he said, his tone dangerously soft.

She snapped. "Claiming you're a vampire and wanting to drink my blood doesn't sound reasonable! You sound fucking insane!"

His jaw tightened, and he closed his eyes briefly, taking a deep breath, as if gathering his restraint. "I didn't want it to be like this."

Before she could react, he lifted her off the ground—over his shoulder. He ignored her cries of protest and carried her up the wide, curved staircase with infuriating ease.

He kicked open the door at the end of the hallway and stepped into a massive bedroom.

She kicked and pounded at him. When none of it mattered. She twisted, biting down hard enough to draw a reaction—any reaction.

He didn't so much as stumble or flinch. He dropped her onto the bed—not hard but not gently, either.

"Don't do that again," he warned, voice flat with quiet menace. His expression darkened. "I bite way harder than you."

She scrambled to her knees, her eyes darting between him and the door.

"You're out of your mind," she said, her voice shaking. "Do you even hear yourself right now?"

Michael's expression looked pained. "I knew you wouldn't believe me," he said at last, his tone grim. "That's why I need to show you."

Her stomach flipped as he reached for the hem of his shirt. The fabric clinging to his chest was stained with blood from his knife wound. But when he pulled it off, the wound was...gone.

She froze, and her jaw slackened. The gash from Esben's blade had been deep and bleeding, and now it was little more than a faint line. She stared at his side—at the skin that should've been cut and wasn't.

Michael used his shirt to wipe away any remaining blood from his skin, then tossed it aside. He held up his hand and slowly kneeled on the bed. He moved closer. Her pulse kicked harder. Too loud. Too fast.

He inched closer.

"Michael, please," she whispered. "Just let me go."

He stopped, merely a breath away. "I can't," he said, his voice breaking slightly.

Before she could react, he tilted her head gently. His lips brushed her neck.

Her body locked, every instinct screaming at her to pull away.

"I'm not going to hurt you."

His words reached her, but they didn't land the way they should have. Her mind was so clouded, her body so heightened, that her sense of reason had shut down. His kisses on her ear and down the column of her neck sent goosebumps across her skin.

He kissed the curve of her shoulder. His mouth found her pulse.

A soft sound left him. Low. Sharp. Almost a hiss. It was barely audible, and too close to her ear.

The sound stopped her cold.

It wasn't imagined.

Not in her head.

Real.

Her breath hitched. Then again—too fast.

Her chest tightened as panic surged. Everything was trying to fall into place at once.

If he wasn't lying—he was going to bite her.

She felt paralyzed. Fear sank in fast, cold, and absolute as the room blurred.

"Paislee, are you all right?" Michael asked.

The ringing in her ears swallowed her voice.

He drew away from her neck and clasped her face. "Paislee, look at me. Are you okay?"

She looked at him, and something in her chest dropped.

Michael wasn't crazy.

His parted lips revealed sharp fangs.

Her breathing broke, uneven, out of control.

Her fingers lifted and brushed his mouth.

His eyes had changed completely. They weren't human. They couldn't be.

Vampires were real.

It hit her all at once. Too much. Too fast...

The room tilted.

Then everything went black.

Michael caught her as her body went limp, and her head rolled against his shoulder. His arms instinctively cradled her, holding her carefully.

"Paislee," he whispered, his voice tight. He lowered her to the bed, brushing her hair back.

Her breathing slowed into a shallow, even rhythm. Her expression was soft now, no longer twisted with fear.

Fear. He'd seen it before, countless times. On prey. On enemies.

It should've meant nothing.

Instead, it tore at him.

"Fuck."

He let out a shaky breath as he stepped back from the bed. The echoes of her pulse still echoed in his ears. Relentless.

"What have I done?"

# Chapter Twelve

T HE SUNLIGHT STREAMED THROUGH the windows, stabbing into Paislee's eyes like needles. She groaned and rolled onto her side, the pounding in her head forcing her to stay still. Hangover? No, this was different.

Slowly, she opened her eyes again. The bright light illuminated an unfamiliar room. Tall windows lined an entire wall, framing a breathtaking view of the ocean. The grandeur of it all screamed wealth. Her chest tightened with unease. She didn't belong here.

And then it hit her.

Michael.

Her gaze darted to the man lying beside her. He was peaceful, almost serene, his chest rising and falling steadily as he slept.

Memories of last night surged back—his eyes, his fangs, the unearthly strength.

She touched her neck instinctively. Nothing. No bite marks. What the hell was he? Her rational mind searched for explanations: mental illness, some rare blood disease, or maybe just a man with a twisted obsession. Yet the vivid images of his supernatural abilities refused to fade. She shook her head. It couldn't be real.

Her pulse hammered as she glanced back at him, his skin bathing in the sunlight. Wasn't he supposed to cook or sparkle—something? It didn't make sense. None of it did.

Escape. The word whispered urgently in her mind. She wasn't going to stick around to figure out if her suspicions were correct. Quietly, she slipped from the bed and crept toward the door, her bare feet barely making a sound on the hardwood floor. Freedom was so close—until an arm snaked around her waist and yanked her off the ground.

"Damn it!" She thrashed in his grip. "Let go of me, Michael!"

"Stop." His voice was calm and commanding as he kicked the door shut and set her down. She backed away as he leaned against the door, maddeningly composed, dressed only in black boxer briefs. His toned body glistened faintly in the sunlight, and he had the audacity to smirk.

"If you keep staring at me like that, you're going to make me self-conscious," he teased.

"Doubtful," she spat. Her voice rose as anger drowned out her fear. "I'm trying to figure out how to get the hell out of here!"

"That would be unwise."

Paislee's gaze darted around the room, searching for another escape route. She spotted a partially open door leading to what she assumed was a bathroom. Before she could take another step, Michael was there, slamming the door shut with a speed that made her stomach flip.

"I don't have the patience for this, Paislee," he growled, lifting her effortlessly. He carried her back to the bed, ignoring her kicks and curses, and deposited her like a misbehaving child. "Sit. Stay. Listen."

She crossed her arms and glared at him.

A muscle in Michael's jaw was working as he slowly exhaled. "I owe you an apology," he began, his tone softer now. "I didn't handle things well before. After finding my brother in your room, I...lost my temper. Everything seemed to spiral from there."

She frowned. "Esben. Your brother." Her voice wavered as the memory of his grin sent a chill down her spine.

"He's dangerous, Paislee. More than you realize."

"Dangerous? Like you?" she shot back. "Neither of you is... normal."

Michael's silence felt dark, and for a moment, she thought he wouldn't answer. "You know what I am. Whether you want to believe it or not."

His words hung between them, heavy and absurd. She stared at him, waiting for the punchline. When none came, she laughed—a swift, nervous sound. "This is wild."

"Is it?" He stepped closer, his eyes gleaming with an intensity that stopped the breath in her lungs. "You saw what I can do. You saw what I am." His eyes bored into her, unflinching. "And if you're smart, you'll accept what I'm offering. Protection. Security."

Her laugh was hollow. "You call this security? You've turned my life into a nightmare—literally!"

Michael's eyes lightened, as did the hard lines of his face, but his voice remained firm. "I need an answer from you, Paislee."

Paislee rubbed her temples, her thoughts spiraling in endless circles.

Michael broke the silence as he sighed. "Stop trying to run away long enough for us to talk. Come downstairs." Without waiting for a reply, he grabbed his jeans and shirt and walked out, leaving her alone in the cavernous bedroom.

She exhaled shakily and glanced around, searching for something—anything—that could ground her. Her eyes landed on the ocean view and the waves crashing onto the shore. She focused on the sound, letting it drown out her jumbled thoughts.

When she finally mustered the strength to move, she followed the faint sounds of clinking dishes down the hallway. The house was enormous, its every detail meticulously designed. It represented the kind of wealth that was overwhelming, almost alien.

She found Michael in the kitchen, moving easily through his task of pouring steaming coffee into delicate cups. He glanced at her briefly, his expression unreadable, before sliding a cup toward the counter's edge.

"Macchiato," he said simply, his tone neutral. "Not the kind you bring to work in venti cups, iced with caramel, whipped cream, and...all that other stuff you put in it. This is the real thing."

Paislee hesitated before walking to the kitchen's marble-topped island and sitting on one of the high-backed stools. Her fingers curled around the cup. "You were paying attention to my coffee?" she asked, her voice cautious.

"It was a painful observation," he replied, sipping from his own cup.

"So, my macchiato wasn't 'real,' then?"

"Eh," he said with a charming wrinkling of his nose before sliding a red leather folder in front of her. The cover was embossed with a gold crest—a bird with its wings outstretched.

Her fingers brushed the smooth leather. "What's this?"

"The contract," he said simply. "I told you I'd compensate you if you remained with me. It outlines everything you need to know. Your obligations and rights, your compensation, all the terms of our arrangement."

Paislee opened the folder and read the heading: *Cardinalis et Largitor Sanguinis Pactum*. She scanned the text, which was thick with legal jargon, a lot of it in Latin.

"This is for three years," she said, creasing her brow.

"Yes," he replied as he placed a small plate with a pastry on it in front of her. "I don't know what you eat. I have *cornetto cu l'albicocca. Teni...è friscu. Mancia.*"

She stared at him while he puttered around the kitchen, drinking his coffee. When he turned back to her, she quickly diverted her gaze and picked up the fruit-filled pastry. She had no idea what he'd called it. It looked like a croissant. "Do you eat...food?"

"Yes, I eat food," he said as he sipped his macchiato. "I require various means of nourishment, just as you do."

"I guess I don't understand why you consider yourself a vampire. I didn't see a coffin, and you're walking in daylight. I've even seen your reflection in the mirrors behind the bar."

A soft laugh passed his lips as he set down his cup. He crossed his arms and relaxed against the counter, looking as though he were bracing himself for a conversation he'd had many times already. "I've heard it all. I've watched movies and read the books, too. That's not reality."

She closed the folder and rested her chin on her fist. "What's reality, then?"

"Reality is that I respectfully carry my mother's name, but embrace my Sicilian raising. I have a soft spot for pasta—and I'm partial to garlic."

"You barely have an accent."

"*Grazzii*. I've had many years to perfect my English. Let's see. I don't burst into flames if I walk into a church. I find the crucifix and religious architecture rather stunning. I'm indifferent to bats and rather enjoy my own reflection. Blessed water is as cold as any other. Did I cover all the bases?"

"You don't have supernatural abilities?"

"My abilities could be considered supernatural, compared to a human's."

"Like what?"

"I'll outlive you by centuries," he replied. "My body is like armor, nearly impenetrable and heals quickly—as you witnessed last night."

"But you still need human blood."

"Yes," Michael said before taking another sip of his coffee.

Paislee let her pastry roll around a little longer in her mouth to give herself another moment to respond.

"I'll get back to you if I think of anything else," she said after she swallowed her food.

She returned to the contract in front of her. Her breakfast almost fell out of her mouth when she turned the page and saw her pay. Her gaze shot to him. "Are you serious?" she asked, her voice incredulous.

"Completely," he replied. "All expenses are covered. Anything you need, I provide."

She stared at all the zeros and imagined all that she could do with so much. She could pay off her medical bills, her student loans... She could help her family. Her perspective shifted as she continued reading through the contract. "You're offering me health and dental?"

"We have our own doctors," he replied.

"Can you throw in Wi-Fi and bundle it?"

Michael's expression darkened. He finished his macchiato, brusquely set his cup in the sink, and then left the kitchen.

She snapped the folder shut, but the substantial sum he was offering stuck with her. She shook her head, muttering, "The cost of my freedom."

Life as she'd known it had just changed before her eyes. When she imagined what it would be like being Michael's donor, it terrified her. But then she considered how that kind of money could improve her life and her family's. It was all like some cruel joke.

Paislee read the header on the contract, *Cardo & Aegis LLP*, and searched the main floor for her bag. She found it on the sectional. After digging out her phone, she looked up the firm. Dread washed over her when she discovered that it was legit, a major New York firm with several international branches.

She was beginning to think this was no joke. If it were real, then there were vampires in the world, and there was even a system in place for them. They had their own doctors and lawyers, and judging from Michael's lifestyle, they weren't paupers. They had influence and power.

Her stomach churned. She was unable to eat the rest of her pastry and shoved away the plate. It was all too much, really. Her phone vibrated, and several messages from Kendra popped up.

Paislee sent her a quick message letting her know that everything was fine. But it wasn't.

Michael was offering her security. Comfort. A solution. All she had to do was allow him to take her blood.

Should it have been an easy yes? Maybe. But something in her gut twisted. Sharp and cold.

In the contract, she was addressed as little more than property. According to an authority she didn't recognize, she'd *belong* to Michael. It wasn't a job offer. It was a cage.

She couldn't calm her shaking hands as she slid her bag onto her shoulder and headed for the door. It hurt to think she was walking away from something that could've fixed so much.

But it wasn't a gift. It was a transaction. And she wasn't for sale.

She swore when she left that she'd bury all thoughts of what she'd experienced since meeting Michael and Esben. That gave her a sense of peace and calm. The further away she got from Michael's beach house, the easier it would be to forget everything she'd learned.

She was close to the exit—and freedom—when Michael stopped her.

"Where are you going?" he asked, walking up behind her.

His shadow stretched across her, swallowing her presence beneath his. It loomed over her, pressing down on her like an unseen weight. She didn't turn around; instead, she kept her gaze fixed on the door. "I'm going home," she said.

"You're rejecting my offer?"

He sounded shocked, and she shook her head. Was he truly surprised? She squared her shoulders and spun around.

"You have contracts for blood donors," she said, creasing her brow. "I'll donate to the Red Cross. They don't almost give me an orgasm every time they take my blood."

"It's my venom, Paislee." He crossed his arms over his chest and planted his feet apart, looking at her incredulously. "And it's necessary so you don't feel pain. It's also why your signed consent is required."

"Because it makes me powerless against you," she said.

"I can't help what I am. I do the best I can to make you feel comfortable."

"But, while you're getting what you need from me, I'm building an emotional bond built on nothing real. It's not personal at all for you? Everything about you seduces me! It sounds like torture."

"It's never been reported by any donor as torturous, Paislee," he quickly defended. "Quite the opposite. It can be incredibly enjoyable."

His eyes were darkening again, but she stood her ground. "No human has ever mistaken your transactional relationship for something more?"

The muscles in his jaw tightened, and his eyes glimmered at her. His silent struggle was clear...and telling.

"To mistake such intimacy sounds awful," she said as she adjusted her bag over her shoulder. She spotted her slippers by the front door and slid them onto her feet. "I can't do it. It may be in your nature, but it's against mine. I can't be so detached. Do you even have emotions?"

Michael was silent for a long moment, his gaze gave nothing away. "I understand it's difficult for humans, and that's one of the reasons why you're so handsomely compensated. We try to be considerate of the human heart. I assure you this contract is standard and all my *largitores* have left my employment sane and sound."

"I respectfully *decline*," she said, and then she went for the door again. But again, he halted her. "What?" she asked once more, her voice rising with anger and frustration.

"Your situation is precarious. I don't understand your hesitation. This solves both of our problems."

Paislee shook her head, laughing bitterly. "If you were a human, you'd know exactly what the problem is."

Her phone went off, and she opened another message from Kendra.

His eyes narrowed with a dangerous gleam. "Paislee."

Her name on his lips was terse, but she ignored the warning in his tone.

She turned back to the door. "I'm heading out, and I'll have Kendra pick me up."

As far as she was concerned, the conversation was over. Michael was incredibly screwed up, and maybe his whole species was, too. It was best to leave it be. She needed to go home. If she left now, Kendra could meet her along the way.

"Paislee, stop."

She was about to send her message when he spun her around once more.

Paislee straightened and stepped up to him, glaring. "Michael, back off!" She was no match for his height or dominating presence, but she'd make her best attempt. "You made me an offer, and I declined. Thanks but no thanks. I'm not a human juice box."

One second, her phone was in her hand; the next, it was in his. Before she could even send her message. He stared down at the device, his eyes cold and unreadable.

"The fuck, Michael. Give it back!"

Michael didn't reply. Instead, he tightened his grip, and the unmistakable sound of glass and plastic shattering filled the room. He dropped the broken pieces at her slippered feet, and the shards clinked onto the floor.

Paislee stared at the remains of her phone, her jaw slack. "Are you serious?" she finally managed. "That phone was under a contract I *did* agree to! What the hell is wrong with you?"

Despite his actions, his voice was low and controlled. "I can't protect you if you don't listen and continue to ignore the reality or your situation."

"No, I see how it is," she said, her anger boiling over. "You give humans the *choice*, but no one's ever turned you down. I bet a lot of people jump at the chance to let you suck on them while you fill their bank accounts. So, I get this is uncharted territory, but let me give you a heads-up," She pointed her finger at his angry expression. "You need to work on all this because you don't handle rejection very well."

Michael took another step toward her, swallowing the distance between them. Paislee's instinct was to back away, but her pride held her in place. She'd thought he was charming and warm, but now she suspected that was an act. Underneath his fun-loving nature, he seemed cold and arrogant. Her fists clenched at her sides as her fear warred with the simmering anger beneath it.

"Do you think this is a game?" He was seething now and nearly nose to nose with her.

"No, I get it. I know exactly what you can do to me," she said. "I know exactly how you make me feel. And I can't be your donor, Michael. It will destroy me."

He stared at her for a long moment, his expression shifting unpredictably, revealing glimpses of something she couldn't quite name. Her certainty wavered, and she began to question her initial assumption that he lacked emotions altogether. She didn't fully understand what he was or how his feelings worked, but in that moment, she suspected he had them—however alien they might seem.

"I'm sorry, Michael," she said more gently. "I think you're more than reasonable in your offer. It's flattering; that's *a lot* of money. But I just can't."

He shook his head and sighed heavily. "You're impossible."

They stared at one another for a long moment as the tension crackled between them like static. Finally, Michael stepped back, giving her space. "But you're forgetting one key factor in all this. My brother."

Paislee's heart sank, and her stomach twisted. She swallowed hard, her resolve wavering. The fear she'd been trying to bury seeped to the surface, but she pushed it down, clinging to her defiance.

"Esben won't ask for your consent. He'll take what he wants. Since he knows my interest in you, he's going to look for you. Without a contract, the law can't defend you."

At the sincerity in Michael's eyes, Paislee swallowed the lump forming in her throat.

She remained quiet for a moment. "Legal contracts and laws, where does all this come from?"

For a long moment, he said nothing, his gaze locked on hers. Then, finally, he spoke. "There's a system, a hierarchy, that governs us. Dominium Cardinalium. We call it the Cardinal Order."

She frowned. "You have your own government?"

"It's complicated, but yes. The Dominium Cardinalium is our governing authority," he replied. "We have our own laws and enforcers to keep our kind in line. Feeding is strictly regulated. Contracts are part of that system. They ensure that humans are willing participants."

"And Esben?" she asked. "He doesn't follow the rules?"

Michael's jaw clenched. "Esben does whatever benefits him, no matter the cost. His status holds privilege. And if he finds a loophole, he'll use it."

Her stomach churned. "And I'm just another pawn in whatever game he's playing."

Michael leaned his shoulder against the wall and tucked his hands in his pockets. "You're more than that. To him, you're leverage. To me, you're...important."

The way he said the word made her chest tighten. She looked away, unsure how to respond. "I don't want to be important," she muttered. "I want to go back to my normal life."

His expression didn't change right away. He studied her in silence for a beat too long. And when he spoke, his voice was calm, but it carried weight. "I know," he said, his voice low. "But you were pulled into my world and you can't go back."

She let out a shaky breath, her shoulders slumping. She could feel tears welling behind her eyes.

He shook his head. "You weren't just exposed to me, Paislee. You were exposed to *them*. To the shadow of what truly governs this world. Whether by choice or by force, it can't be undone."

Her chest tightened, breath sticking at the base of her throat. She wanted to scream. Argue. Deny it all.

But he wasn't wrong.

"I'll respect your decision," he finally said, though he didn't meet her gaze. "But if you're not going to accept my protection, please leave the Hamptons. Go back to Pennsylvania; it'll be safer."

"Do you think he'd follow me?"

"If he thinks he's going to get one over on me, he'll look for you. I can't guarantee your safety."

"Is your brother really that sadistic?"

"He's done far worse for less. I'm sorry you were brought into this. Though I suspected you might deny me, your rejection has still been...humbling."

Silence hovered for a long time. Paislee's gaze drifted to the house he occupied alone. The sweeping arches, the tall windows that caught the light just right, the quiet hush of opulence wrapped around every inch..

She imagined herself there, trailing barefoot across cool marble floors, waking up in a massive bed. Space. Safety. Silence.

She glanced at Michael and wondered if he ever got lonely in such a place. It was perfect and glamorous—as everything in his world seemed to be. Even him.

What would it feel like to be him? To live with the power he seemed to possess. The knowledge that couldn't be unlearned. She imagined the weight of it, and it pressed against her chest.

The way he looked at her, not just with hunger or intensity, but with something quieter, an ache she didn't understand. Could she keep herself from falling for him? Would it be real, or just the pull of something ancient and unnatural? The allure of him?

Was that why he had offered to pay her so much money? Because he knew what it would truly cost her?

Then her thoughts shifted. Esben. Last night, was real. He would've hurt her and enjoyed it. And Michael...Michael had saved her.

Safety came with a price, didn't it? And this world—his world—wasn't offering her a life. It was offering her the choice to stay and become someone else, or walk away and pretend none of it had happened.

Her heart pounded as she reached for the door. "I-I can't give you an answer right now," she whispered.

"If I never see you again, Paislee," he said, taking slow steps towards her, "don't speak about this to anyone. Ever. I don't care if it's been two days or twenty years. Every human is tracked. Their conversations, their correspondences, everything. The Order will find out if you say anything."

She glanced over her shoulder at him and raised her brows. "What will they do? I have the freedom to speak."

The seriousness she witnessed in him just then was dire, and the severity was injected straight into her soul. "Your freedom is an illusion. You're a slave to our system like the rest of the world. If you speak, they'll find you and anyone you told. And everyone will be eliminated without prejudice."

# Chapter Thirteen

P AISLEE HAD BARELY MADE it half a mile before Seth's sports car pulled up beside her. He rolled down the window and flashed her a smile. "Need a ride, Country? It's a long walk to your uncle's."

She climbed in, relieved and grateful for the break. Her phone was a shattered casualty of Michael's temper, and a dangerous vampire was hunting her. Holding her breath, she braced herself as Seth took off, his speed almost reckless. "Perfect timing," she said, trying to sound casual. "Glad you happened to see me."

"It wasn't a coincidence," he replied matter-of-factly. "Michael called me. Said he owes you a phone. And an apology."

Her stomach knotted at the mention of Michael. She kept silent, even as Seth chuckled at her reaction. Studying his profile, she noted how perfect he looked—sculpted features, flawless skin. The sunglasses hid his eyes, but she remembered all too well the times he'd left her tongue-tied.

"You're one of them, aren't you?" she said with a resigned sighed. "Of course you are."

He didn't even pause as he wove effortlessly through morning traffic. "*Oui, mam'selle.*"

"So, not all of them are Italian. You're French?"

"Not anymore."

Her brow furrowed. "Can you just decide not to be French anymore? Is that even a thing?"

"Yes," he said, his tone final. "When you've lived as we have, you can be whoever you choose."

Paislee let out a dry laugh. "Michael says my freedom is an illusion. Sounds like vampires have it all."

Seth tsked and waved a finger at her. "Don't call us that. Surely, Michael warned you. And we have our limitations."

She remembered Michael's reaction when she'd used the term *vampire*, all too well. She shook her head. "I don't want to know any more about your world."

"Fair," he said. "It's not for everyone. But you're in a different situation, Paislee. If you're going to refuse Michael's offer, I can help you disappear. Esben won't be able to find you—at least not until he loses interest."

Hope flickered, and Paislee straightened in her seat. "You can help me?"

"You'd have to give up your identity, but yes."

Her hope was shattered. "Give up who I am? That's ridiculous! Esben is just some stranger, and he's ruined my life!"

"Could you tone it down?" Seth winced and gestured for her to lower her voice. "That hysterical squeak is like nails down a chalkboard."

Her jaw dropped. "Are you serious?"

"Mm-hmm," he hummed, unbothered.

The rest of the ride was steeped in strained silence. When Seth finally pulled into her uncle's driveway, she was more than ready to get out. She prayed that this would be her last interaction with a vampire.

As he parked, Seth removed his sunglasses and handed her a thick envelope. "Michael feels responsible for your predicament. There's cash inside. He asked me to remind you—again—that you should return to Pennsylvania as quickly and quietly as possible. Oh, and I've erased your employment records. You never worked at Allusion."

"You already fired me."

"It's for your own good." Seth sighed. "Your circumstances suck, but it is what it is. You're caught in a feud between Michael and Esben. If you're not going to take Michael's protection, stay far away from the Hamptons."

"I can't imagine Esben will waste his time hunting me. It all seems so exaggerated. I'm not special, Seth."

"If there's one thing we have, Country, it's time." Seth's tone turned grim. "Esben values you because of Michael's reaction. That alone tells Esben you're worth exploiting."

Paislee froze, the envelope trembling in her hand. She didn't want to consider what Esben or Michael intended. She didn't want to be part of their war.

Feeling defeated, she accepted the envelope and trudged into the house. The stillness inside seemed amplified by her spiraling thoughts. Seth's words lodged deep.

Silence wrapped around her like a noose, and the weight of everything clawed its way to the surface. Her knees buckled, and she slumped onto the living room floor. Tears spilled freely as her composure crumbled under the strain of fear, anger, and exhaustion. Her grief rushed out, released in raw cries. How had her life unraveled so quickly?

Moving to New York for school had felt like a chance to reclaim a dream she'd lost years ago. But now, that dream needed to be abandoned—again. Because staying without Michael's protection didn't just put her at risk. It put her friends in danger. Michael had offered to keep her safe. Part of her wanted to accept. Deep down, she knew she wasn't safe on her own. But she couldn't accept his help. The price was too high. There was something about him, something that pulled at her in ways she didn't understand. It wasn't just the danger he carried. It was the way he saw her, the way she responded. She'd confronted Esben. She'd been around Seth. They had presence and power. But neither of them held that kind sway over her. Only Michael.

And it was terrifying.

Her uncle had confirmed that Tessa could stay. Kendra wouldn't leave New York, but at least she wouldn't be alone. It wasn't ideal, but it was the one piece of comfort Paislee could hold onto in a world that no longer felt safe.

Michael's offer lingered in her mind as she hurried past her bedroom door. She didn't glance inside. She couldn't. Not yet. The memory of what happened there was still too raw to face. Esben's assault, Michael's fury, the moment her reality shattered.

She almost said yes to Michael. Almost let herself believe she'd be protected in his care. But the gravity of that choice—the power he held over her already—brought her back to her uncle's home. Letting distance be her only solution.

In the bathroom, she stripped off her clothes and stepped under the scalding water. She relived Esben grabbing her. His cold voice made her body freeze. She scrubbed until her skin burned, until her knees trembled beneath her.

By the time she dried off, there was nothing left to weigh. Slowly, almost numbly, she packed her things and loaded them into her car. It was mind-boggling how one vampire's frivolous whim could dismantle her entire life.

She drove away on the north road, seeking clarity and distance, and the rural route offered the quiet escape she craved. Driving past small towns and villages, she drifted into reflection, her thoughts tangled in the chaos of recent events.

The open road stretched ahead, flanked by endless trees. So wrapped up in her internal world as she left another small town, gazing at a long stretch of open road lined with trees, she barely noticed a silver car appeared in her rearview until it was speeding up behind her. She switched to the slow lane to let it pass, but the car veered into her lane, tailing her dangerously.

Her chest tightened, and she pressed the accelerator, but the car mirrored her movements, staying inches from her bumper. When she moved back into the passing lane, it followed. She strained to see through the tinted windshield, but the driver remained hidden. She almost reached for her phone—then cursed Michael for smashing it.

Without warning, the car sped around her and disappeared. She exhaled a shaky breath. Relief washed over. She didn't need to add a road-raging stranger to her list of traumatic events.

But Paislee's relief was short-lived. The silver car reappeared, swerving into her lane and charging straight towards her. "Oh, my God," she whispered, yanking the wheel and slamming on the brakes. Her car screeched off the road and slid into the grass.

A jarring mixture of honking blared behind her as the silver car executed a sharp turn and barreled back in her direction. Her adrenaline surged. She steered her car back onto the road, but it sputtered.

"Fucker!" she yelled, realizing that she had blown a tire. *No, no, no!*

The car screeched to a halt in front of her, and her stomach dropped when Esben stepped out.

Then a black Mercedes shot past them and rammed into his car, forcing him to leap onto the roof. Then the Mercedes screeched to a stop, sending nearby vehicles swerving into the emergency lane to avoid collisions.

Michael.

Paislee snapped out of her paralyzed state, and dread overtook instinct. She flung her door open and bolted toward oncoming traffic, waving her arms desperately. Horns blared again, louder, closer.

Esben grabbed her flailing arms and yanked her away from traffic. She frantically shoved at him, pulling herself free but losing her balance at the same time.

Time slowed as Paislee stumbled back into the road and the roar of approaching traffic grew louder.

She'd been here before—trapped in the unforgiving path of a speeding car, the inevitability of pain rushing toward her like a tidal wave.

Memories flashed: the screeching of tires, the searing pain, the helplessness as her body crumpled under the force of impact. She braced for it—the familiar agony, the moment of impact. Shutting her eyes, she prepared for the anguish she knew too well.

But the impact never came—at least not the way she expected. Instead of pain, there was warmth. A protective force surrounded her, cocooning her against the crushing blow. The sound of the car hitting rang out in a deafening clap. But it wasn't her body that absorbed it. Someone had thrown themselves between her and the car, an unbreakable barrier taking the impact. There was a deafening crack, the sound of metal on metal. She barely registered it. The force spun her across the pavement, but the pain she expected never came.

When she opened her eyes, she wasn't alone. A crowd had gathered, their concerned voices a distant hum.

Michael cradled her in his arms, dirt and blood streaking his face, his breathing ragged. His gaze, dazed and desperate, locked onto hers.

"Are you okay?" she asked, her voice catching. "You're bleeding."

"No, I'm not," he murmured, brushing off her concern. His hand rose to her cheek—gentle, grounding. "You are."

A bystander's voice broke through the chaos. "We have an ambulance on the way!"

Phones recorded the scene, capturing every moment. Paislee's gaze shifted to the distance. Esben gave a mocking wave before flicking off Michael. He vanished into the traffic, leaving behind only the echo of sirens and the scent of scorched rubber.

"Come on," Michael urged, standing and pulling her to her feet. His grip was firm, but she could see he was straining. Someone called after them, warning them to wait for the authorities, but Michael ignored them. He guided her to his car. "Get in."

# Chapter Fourteen

P AISLEE HAD BARELY SHUT the car door before Michael sped away. The drive was tense, heavy with unspoken words. She stole glances at him, noting his pale complexion and the sheen of sweat on his brow. The bruises from the accident were still evident on his arms.

"Do you need me to drive?" she asked, finally breaking the silence.

"No," he said.

"Do bruises take longer to heal than cuts?"

He cocked a brow at her. "What?"

"I don't know," she replied, a little exasperated by his condition. Honestly, he didn't look good. "When Esben cut you, it healed in minutes."

"Hm." He returned his gaze to the road, and his grip on the wheel tightened. "This is different."

"How?"

Michael didn't answer, keeping his focus locked on the road as he accelerated and wove through traffic. By the time they returned to his beach house, his condition had worsened. His steps were sluggish, and his breathing was labored.

He unlocked his house and held open the door for her. "Michael, you're not okay," she said, her voice edged with worry.

He tossed aside his keys and weakly brushed his hair out of his eyes, mumbling something undecipherable, something in his native tongue.

"I didn't understand you," she said.

He continued speaking in Italian.

"Michael, is there someone I can call? Do you need some help? I-I don't know what's wrong with you."

He straightened, and his hazy expression seemed to clear slightly as he glanced at his surroundings, like he'd just noticed where he was. "Nothing is wrong. I just need to rest."

"Why didn't you wait for the ambulance? You need medical attention."

He laughed softly. "No, ducizza, I don't need medical attention."

"What do you need?"

He slowly climbed the stairs. "A shower."

Soon after, she heard the shower turn on. Sitting on the steps, chewing her lip, Paislee wrestled with an uneasy truth—the truth of what was wrong with him...and what he needed.

Her stomach twisted. Helping him crossed a line she wasn't sure she could come back from. Her instinct told her to run, to shut the door on this, and never look back. But leaving wasn't easy. Not when she could feel him falling apart.

She stayed on the step. Listening. Breathing. Waiting.

Minutes later, a crash shattered the quiet.

"Michael!"

She raced up the stairs and found him collapsed on the bathroom floor, completely bare, in a wreckage of glass strewn across the marble. Blood streamed from his arm.

"Paislee, don't touch me," he growled, but she ignored him and dropped to her knees, grabbing a hand towel and pressing it against the wound.

"Let me call someone."

He shook his head. "I don't need help," he muttered, though even speaking seemed to drain him.

"You're bleeding and collapsed on the floor. You need something."

His gave a breathless laugh. "Another towel."

Her gaze flicked over him and heat flared in her cheeks. She averted her eyes and grabbed another towel, doing her best not to notice how, even like this—bloodied, broken—he still radiated that same raw, unearthly beauty.

But as she knelt beside him, that sense of untouchable power began to slip. Not because he was trying to hide the damage. But because he couldn't.

Bruises from the crash were blooming beneath his skin. He'd taken the hit from the car for her, a hit no human could've gotten up and walked away from. But now, he was only getting worse.

The image of him in that moment etched itself into her. For the first time since she'd met him, the beautiful and dangerous creature she'd feared looked heartbreakingly...human.

He wrapped a towel around his waist and she slowly helped him to his feet. As they reached the doorway, he buckled over. His weight overwhelmed her, and they both fell.

She held her breath when she saw his fangs.

He gave up and remained sitting on the floor.

"I guess I'm in worse shape than I thought." His humor came in a light, breathy laugh.

"Yeah, no shit."

He met her gaze, his own was stern and unrelenting. "Paislee, get my phone."

"Will they get here in time?"

"Not if you keep asking questions," he said sharply.

His lips had curled back, and the sight of his fangs made her skin prickle. She brushed the dripping-wet, inky hair from his eyes and noted that the brilliance she'd witnessed before in their depths wasn't there. The sparkling embers of his gaze were now a dull glow. "Blood. That's what's wrong with you."

He braced his good arm on his knee and repeated, "Paislee, get my phone."

A new determination lit within her. She didn't think. She couldn't. Logic had been shouting at her since the moment she met him. Leave. Protect yourself. Don't get pulled in. And yet, there she was. "Let me help you."

Michael's eyes darkened. "I'll get my phone," he said, his voice again strained.

He started to stand up, but Paislee stopped him. She couldn't believe she was trying to steady him. Michael terrified her in ways she couldn't name. She told herself she owed him nothing. That whatever he'd done for her, whatever hold he had over her, it didn't mean she had to give him this. But now...seeing him this way, she couldn't separate the fear from ache. Something inside her recognized that moment—not as a mistake, but as a turning point.

"You wanted to contract me anyway," she said softly. "Let me help you."

"You don't understand," he said. "It would be your first time. It takes precision and control—neither of which I possess right now."

"You look like you're dying," she said, her voice trembling with urgency.

He waved her off weakly. "I will recover quickly," he said as he attempted to stand again.

Paislee cradled his face and brushed her lips against his, hesitant but deliberate. The contact sent a jolt through her chest, but she didn't pull away. She shivered as his sharp teeth grazed her tongue.

Michael stiffened, his instincts battling his restraint.

Somewhere deep, beyond reason, she knew she was part of this. That whatever had tied them together hadn't started the first night she had kissed him. That maybe nothing had ever been a choice at all. She deepened the kiss, boldly driving her tongue past his parted lips, savoring the unearthly sweetness that seeped into her senses.

At first, Michael didn't move. Then something shifted. Slowly, his lips moved against hers. Not urgently, but reverently. His hand slid up her arm, tracing the curve of her shoulder, sending more shivers down her spine. Michael had surrendered, fully and achingly, and the world around them faded into irrelevance. He deepened their kiss, a groan slipping from him, low and guttural. His hand trembled as he cupped the back of her head, pulling her closer. His fingers curled in hair, tilting her head back, exposing her neck.

She gasped as his lips brushed the edge of her skin, trailing the line of her jaw.

Michael grabbed the doorway, closing her between him and the vanity, his other hand still gripping her hair. His lips trailed down her throat, sending heat and a promise coursing through. His breath was a whispered warning in her ear before he pierced her skin.

His bite stole her breath, a searing pressure that struck like lightening and lingered like a kiss. Followed, was an ache so deep it made her entire body weaken. She cried out—a sound that landed somewhere between pain and release. Her body arched toward him instinctively. The sensation was unlike anything she'd ever experienced, a mixture of fire and elation—of being claimed. She felt her energy ebbing as Michael's strength had visibly returned. His breath was heavy in her ear, his grip tightened in her hair, holding her still as something ancient and primal passed between them. Michael's hold on the doorway tightened with such force, she heard the wood splinter.

Paislee's mind reeled. She should've been terrified by his growing intensity, by the way his savagery overtook his earlier gentleness. But she wasn't. It was strange how she wanted to give him what he needed, even at her own expense. Her body leaned into his, and their connection deepened as he drank from her.

When he finally withdrew, his breathing was labored. He nuzzled her neck, pressing his lips in featherlike kisses against her skin. "Thank you," he whispered, his voice raw.

She remained motionless for a long moment. Finally, she nodded...weakly, barely able to hold herself upright. He kissed her lips again, softly this time, brushing his lips against hers in a series of delicate, lingering caresses.

"Come on, ducizza," he murmured, scooping her into his arms as if she weighed nothing.

He cradled her against him, resting her head beneath his chin as he carried her into the master bedroom. He laid her down gently, keeping her close. Michael's arms wrapped around her protectively, and his warmth seeped into her.

Her eyelids grew heavy, and her body surrendered to him once more, sinking into the mattress as an indescribable exhaustion overtook her.

As sleep claimed her, she knew that nothing would ever be the same.

# Chapter Fifteen

T HE SUN SANK LOW over Michael's ocean view, casting streaks of amber and violet into the room as Paislee's eyes fluttered open. Her head felt heavy, and she hesitated before touching her neck. The wounds were faint but pulsed beneath her fingertips like a second heartbeat. Michael's bite wasn't just a memory. It was alive and lingering.

She rose unsteadily and made her way to the bathroom. Other than the doorway trim, no trace of the chaos that had unfolded there was visible. No broken glass, no blood. Her reflection in the mirror was a betrayal. She stared at the faint puncture wounds on her neck, raw and vivid. Her fingers trembled as they hovered over the marks; the skin around them was tender. It wasn't pain that unsettled her.

It was the awareness. This was more than a mark. It was a bond. A tether.

Her chest tightened as her mind replayed the moment—Michael's presence like a storm, his spell weaving through her until she was utterly his. The sharp sting of his teeth, the pull of him drawing her closer, draining her, and leaving her. No, it wasn't just a bite. It was a claim. And it had changed her. The woman in the mirror was familiar but hollow, a version of her that had been reshaped, leaving her former self nothing more than a shadow.

Muffled voices downstairs broke through her thoughts.

"It was no easy task, Michael, but it is done," a man said, his tone clipped and tense.

Another voice, sharp and commanding, spoke out. "You're Michael Chamberlain! Did you think no one would recognize you? This has to stop! Your mother and I are done with this feud."

Paislee crept to the top of the stairs, her heart racing as she recognized the voice of Michael's father, Saverio.

Michael leaned against the kitchen counter, watching his father pace the room like a caged predator. Saverio's anger was a storm brewing, but Michael had weathered worse. Saverio's fury always felt like a test—a reminder of the roles they were supposed to play—but Michael had grown tired of playing.

"You caused a pile-up on the north road over an uncontracted human!" Saverio's voice cut through the room, sharp and precise, each word a lash. "Do you have any idea what it cost to clean up your mess? Teams were dispatched, networks erased, lives silenced—all because you couldn't control yourself. For what? For her?"

Michael tilted his head, feigning indifference. Saverio's accusations washed over him like distant thunder. "But here we are. Crisis averted."

His words were deliberate, a knife under Saverio's armor. Michael knew exactly what the problem was. It wasn't Paislee, or even the incident on the north road. It was him. It was always him.

Saverio's eyes narrowed, dark and unyielding. "You think this is a game? You have no idea how close you are to tipping the balance. Every move you make—every careless spectacle—it's destabilizing. The Order doesn't have the luxury of enduring your indulgences, Michele. You're fanning the flames of tensions already rising, and you're inviting a scrutiny we can't afford."

Scrutiny. Control. Balance. Saverio's favorite mantras. "Flames," Michael repeated with a lazy lilt in his tone. "You act as though I'm the one holding the torch. Maybe you should be asking yourself why it's so easy to light. Maybe the Order is just broken."

His father stepped forward, and the weight of his presence filled the room. "Don't you understand that your influence isn't just a privilege—it's power?" Saverio's voice lowered, and the edge in it turned into something dangerous. "The lower classes look to you. The humans adore you without even knowing what you are. And the elites—" He exhaled sharply, his fangs gleaming as his control slipped further. "You're one of us. Your defiance doesn't just undermine the Order. It's dangerous. Loyalty is fickle, Michele. If you push too far, it won't be just you who burns. You'll take us all with you."

Michael's smirk faltered, and his fangs emerged as instinct took over. "After what was done to Katya, maybe it's time for shit to burn." His voice dropped to a growl. "If the Order is so fragile, maybe it deserves to fall."

His father's jaw tightened, and a vein pulsed at his temple. The room fell silent as the weight of Michael's words pressed down like a stone. For a moment, Saverio didn't move. Then he moved faster than Michael could blink, and his hand struck out in anger. The blow landed with a crack, sending Michael staggering into the counter. His cheek burned, with the sharp sting of the strike accompanied by a low, furious hiss from his father.

Michael's own hiss answered, low and guttural, as he straightened. His fangs were fully bared now, and his hand instinctively curled into a fist, though he didn't raise it. His chest heaved as the primal part of him screamed for retaliation, but he stayed still.

"How dare you speak such treason," Saverio growled, his voice trembling with rage. His fingers flexed at his sides, and the air between them seemed to hum with the charge of their barely restrained instincts.

Michael met his father's eyes, his gaze cold and unflinching. "If the truth is treason, maybe you should be asking yourself why."

Saverio surged forward again, but this time, Michael didn't move. His fangs glinted as, in a low and steely voice, he said, "Enough! This is my home. If you can't control yourself, you can leave."

Saverio froze, his body taut with fury. For a moment, it seemed that he might strike again. Then, with a sharp exhale, he stepped back, his fists clenched, the veins in his neck standing out like cords.

"You're a fool, Michele," he hissed, his voice barely above a whisper. "And fools always pay the price."

Paislee remained frozen on the stairs as Saverio stormed toward the door, his movements still charged with predatory grace. His dark, piercing eyes locked on her, and she felt her heart stutter.

"I hope you are worth the fire you've ignited," he said in a low and venomous voice.

She straightened and lifted her chin. If he'd wanted to intimidate her, he'd failed.

He slammed the door as he left, leaving silence in his wake.

Another man, dressed sharply in a long coat and carrying a leather satchel, lingered behind. He approached Paislee with a warm, practiced smile. "Ms. Sullivan, I presume? My name is Alexander Bishop." He offered her his card. "I understand you may be under contract. If you have any questions, please don't hesitate to contact me. I'll have a litigator assigned to represent you."

"Is that necessary?"

"For your sake, yes," he replied. "I recommend that all humans entering agreements understand exactly what they're signing up for." Paislee thanked him and glanced down at the business card he'd given her. She recognized the law firm's logo from Michael's contract. "You witnessed Saverio's rage and stood by when he struck Michael," she said, her voice barely above a whisper. She met his gaze, and there was a flicker in his eyes of something unspoken. "Why?"

He gave her a faint, almost weary smile. "Intervening would have cost me far more than my silence. You'd do well to remember, Ms. Sullivan, that it's a dangerous game to forget where you stand."

With that, he offered her a cordial nod and departed.

Outside, Michael lounged on the porch in a wicker chair, his ankles crossed on the railing as he stared at the streaks of color fading into twilight. His handsome profile was illuminated by the dying light. He seemed deep in thought. And unreachable.

Paislee hesitated before stepping outside. Curling into the chair next to him, she allowed the quiet to stretch between them as they watched the light slip beneath the horizon. Finally, she stole a glance at him.

"You look better," she said, offering him a faint smile.

He met her gaze and held it for a beat too long. "I have you to thank for that," he said at last. "I know it wasn't your choice."

"You saved me from something worse," she replied softly. "I owed you that much." She wasn't lying. But it wasn't the whole truth either.

His gaze wavered, and another stretch of silence lingered.

There was something else, an undercurrent between them she didn't have the language for. It tugged at her in that quiet moment, and it was unsettling. It felt ancient. Personal. Dangerous. But she wasn't ready to say that aloud. Not to him.

"Are you truly in trouble with the Order for what happened?" she asked.

"Am I in trouble?" He laughed, low and quiet. "No, ducizza. My father has always chastised my unruliness, but I don't answer to him. Or anyone." His gaze returned to the horizon. "Your car is being repaired. It'll be delivered to your address in Pennsylvania. My jet will take you home in the morning."

Her fingers toyed with the loose threads on her pants as she found the courage to ask, "What if I don't leave the Hamptons?"

Michael turned to her, and her heart pounded in her chest as she held his gaze. The words hung between them like a lit fuse. She hadn't planned on asking. Not really. But once it was out, she felt the shift, the moment where the thought became a choice, and choice became consequence. It wasn't a hypothetical. It wasn't small.

"There's only one way you stay," he said, his voice low and deliberate. "If you sign my contract. Then, you are mine, Paislee. Entirely."

Her breath caught, and she felt the weight of his words settle over her like a shroud. She knew what staying meant. Signing that contract wasn't just paper and ink, it was surrender. It was stepping into his world and letting it shape her life. It was binding herself to something powerful and irreversible.

To him.

And she couldn't take it back.

She squared her shoulders, willing herself not to falter. "Three years?"

"Yes."

"I want to read it," she said.

# Chapter Sixteen

P AISLEE FOLLOWED MICHAEL TO his office, where he retrieved the red folder from a locked drawer in his desk. She returned to the porch and started reading the contract. Honestly, it was a dream offer with a complete health and dental package, even an opportunity for retirement and pension depending on the number of years she stayed with him. She had to live and travel with him, be available anytime he chose. She had to remain free of toxic substances. She couldn't use any sort of birth control, so she was required to go to the doctor every month to confirm ovulation times. That was, of course, *if the largitor sanguinis so chooses to engage in sexual acts.*

Reading between the lines, she also couldn't ask questions about the Dominium Cardinalium. She was sworn to silence, or else permanent termination would result. She was reminded of Michael's chilling warning. If she'd told anyone, both she and the person she told would be eliminated. Killed. Executed. That gave her chills, and it reminded her just how serious the situation was. What was the Dominium Cardinalium, or the Cardinal Order, as Michael had also called it? What kind of power did they have to surpass a country's sovereignty with their own laws and government bodies? Yet, they remained hidden in the shadows.

Paislee spent a long time sitting on the porch, staring at the contract, reading and rereading, until she finally set it down and walked to the beach. She searched for answers to her dilemma in the unsuspecting moon.

When she returned, the tension in Michael's house seemed lighter. The television was on, and he was on the couch, with a laptop and paperwork scattered around him. It all looked so...normal. He looked like any other working man. He met her gaze as he closed his laptop and handed her his phone.

"You might want to message Kendra and let her know you're fine. I ordered something simple. You were out there a while; you must be hungry."

She glanced at the pizza box on the counter.

"Thoughtful. Do you always handle everything?" she asked.

"I want to ensure that you're healthy and all of your other needs are met."

She blinked, a smile tugging at her lips despite herself. She gave him a look, half teasing, half bemused. "You know I'm not your pet, right, Michael?"

He paused, eyes meeting hers with quiet intent. "No. You're not. But you're my responsibility, Paislee."

In the kitchen, he handed her a plate of pizza but didn't take a slice.

"You're not eating?"

He looked at the box with mild disdain. "That's not pizza."

Her head snapped towards him, eyes wide. "What's wrong with it?"

"Everything," he said.

"Wow." She grinned. "You're such a snob. Why'd you order it, then?"

"It's popular," he said, deadpan. "You drink dessert and call it coffee. I assumed your questionable taste would be... consistent."

She stared at him for a beat, then laughed. Full and unguarded.

"Well, you assumed correctly," she said, breathless, and grinning. "I love it. I'd happily eat it cold."

He tilted his head slightly, like he was filing that reaction away. "You're surprisingly easy to please."

"And you're impossible," she shot back, but her tone was soft, almost fond.

He didn't argue that, just watched her with that quiet, unreadable gaze. The kind that made her forget to breathe.

The laughter lingered in the air for another beat, then faded.

She toyed with the edge of the pizza box, her fingers suddenly restless. "I have questions about the contract," she said.

His expression shifted, only slightly. "Go ahead."

"It says I can only give my blood to you."

He cocked his head at her. "Would that be a problem?"

"I donate at blood drives."

He nodded. "That's fine—just not to other cardinales."

"Cardinales? You mean vampires?"

"I've said it before that *vampire* is a human term, and one I despise." She recalled when Seth had said as much. "We're the prime species, superior to humans. Homo sapiens are humans. Cardo sapiens are cardinales."

She hesitated. "It's strange to find that humans aren't at the top of the food chain."

He shrugged. "Nothing's ever what it seems. Just let me know when you donate, and I'll adjust."

She nodded, though her mind spun. "And we can't talk about your kind?"

"That's correct. There are rules about what I can share. But I'll tell you what I can."

"It also says I must travel with you. How often do you travel?"

"Often."

"I hate airports."

"We don't use them, Paislee."

"You also said I have to be available anytime."

"Do you have a packed schedule?"

"I have school."

"Not anymore," he said, and she stared at him, stunned.

"If I sign your contract, I have to quit school? I've already lost my job at the club."

"Yes, and you're to stay away from the clubs, completely."

"I can't go dancing with my friends?"

"Not without me," he said, matter-of-factly. "It's not safe."

"I feel like I'm being locked up."

He met her gaze. "Do you know how many cardinales are out there?" he said, his tone sharp. "You're marked. That makes you a target."

He opened the contract folder, made a few edits, and initialed the changes. "Anything else?"

She hesitated. "There's one more thing."

# Chapter Seventeen

MICHAEL LEANED BACK, HIS arms crossed over his chest. "I suspect this is going to be a good one."

Paislee straightened her shoulders. "I'm not ready to commit to three years. How about a six-month trial?"

"A trial period? That's for me to invoke."

"You need my blood. I need to ensure that this doesn't ruin me."

"You'll know in six days, not six months."

Her voice wavered. "How often...will you need it?"

"At first, consistently. Once I'm healthier, much less."

His bluntness left her flustered. She swallowed hard. *You can sign a lease. You can renegotiate a salary. You could say no and walk away. But this...this was different.*

"Why me?" she asked quietly, barely audible.

Michael stilled.

The weight of it all pressed down on her. The loss of her job, school, the danger she hadn't asked for, the impossible choices. She blinked hard, trying to stop the burning behind her eyes. "You could've found someone willing to sign without negotiation."

"True," he said, "but I want your blood. And you need my protection."

Her lips parted, searching for a retort, but his words had the ring of truth. And somehow that made it worse. "Rather convenient," she muttered, barely aware she'd said it aloud.

Michael's gaze narrowed. "What do you mean?"

Her chest tightened as anger flickered beneath her fear. Paislee looked away, her pulse thudding in her throat. "I didn't ask for any of this," she said, voice strained. "Esben, the attack, losing my job, and school. Now, I'm being told the only safe option is to stay and allow you to feed on me."

Michael lowered his gaze slightly, his jaw tensed.

A sick thought stirred in her chest, one she didn't want to believe. "Was all of this meant to back me into a corner?"

Michael froze. The slight curl of his lip revealed the edges of his fangs. "Careful, Paislee."

She tried to shove it away, but the words came anyway, almost broken. "Did you use Esben? His rage? To force me into a contract?"

The shift in the room was immediate. The air tightened around them.

Michael didn't speak right away. He just looked at her, as if seeing her differently. And then, his eyes darkened to near black, and when he spoke, his voice was cold and deliberate. "If I wanted to control you, I'd already have done it."

Paislee flinched.

"Don't mistake my restraint for lack of power," he said, his voice dangerously quiet.

"The night I asked for your help, you provoked him," she said, her voice laced with accusation. "Everything has happened so fast and it all leads back to you. Esben takes by force—you use manipulation. It might seem more civilized, but you're still no different!"

Michael's fist slammed into the counter with a deafening crack. The marble split beneath his hand. She shrieked and stumbled back, her pulse hammering in her ears.

His veneer of civility shattered. His breathing was ragged, and his fangs fully visible. For a moment, she was certain he'd lost all control, and her body braced for an attack.

He turned away sharply, gripping the fractured counter as if anchoring himself. Slowly, he straightened, running his hand through his hair. When he faced her again, the storm in his eyes had quieted, but the danger lingered, palpable and undeniable.

"I don't play games, Paislee," he said, his voice low and menacing. "Not with Esben, and certainly not with you. Don't push me."

She lifted her chin, her body trembling as the last echoes of his outburst faded. Backing closer to the door, she stared at the damaged countertop, the cracked edges gleaming in the warning.

Michael closed the distance between them before she had time to register his movements. He forced her to face him, his eyes softened slightly, though the tension in his posture didn't fully dissipate.

She hated how small she felt in that moment, hated the helplessness that clawed at her chest, her mind a tangle of what-ifs.

"I'm not your enemy," Michael said, his voice softer now. "I've done nothing to harm you."

"I don't trust you," she admitted quietly.

Michael nodded as though he expected this. "Trust comes later. Survival first."

"You scare the hell out of me. And yet, you require my signature."

"Your safety needs more than good intentions, Paislee. It demands action. Decisions. Commitments."

The words stung with their simplicity, their finality. Her hand instinctively brushed faint marks on her neck.

"Six months," she said finally, her voice firmer now. Her mind raced as her fear battled with a stubborn streak of defiance. "That's all I'm willing to give."

Michael lifted his head, studying her. "Short-term contracts aren't a thing. Far too much paperwork and a drain on resources for only six months."

"Make it a thing," she shot back, surprising herself with her boldness. "It sounds like you've bent the rules before. What's one more exception?"

For a moment, he was silent, his expression unreadable. Then, to her surprise, he smirked. "You're stubborn, I'll give you that."

He motioned her to follow him to his office, where he crossed out several lines. "Fine. Six months. But understand this—if you change your mind, there's no starting over."

She nodded, gripping the pen tightly as she signed. Her hand shook; the commitment felt as heavy as the granite counter he'd broken. When she slid the contract back to him, Michael melted red wax and pressed his cardinal seal into place with precision.

"How medieval," she muttered.

"The Dominium Cardinalium values tradition," Michael replied, his tone returning to its usual calm. "Tomorrow, we'll have it notarized, and I'll have a copy for you. Then we'll set up your first payment."

"Do I need to file taxes?"

His grin softened the tension. "We'll handle it, though explaining your 'job' to H&R Block would be...entertaining."

Despite herself, she laughed weakly as he led her out of the office. "And the rules?" she asked, her voice quieter now.

Michael's lips quirked into a slight grin. "You'll follow them. Or you'll learn why they exist."

The hour had grown late, and the silence stretching between them had grown heavy. Paislee suppressed a yawn as she finished eating and flicked through the channels, not really watching anything. She was too aware of Michael seated nearby, just close enough to remind her that it was real. The contract was signed. Her future had been redrawn in ink and silence.

He hadn't pushed for conversation, and she was grateful for that. But it also left space for the weight of everything to creep in.

She caught his gaze from the corner of her eye. "So... now what?" she asked, trying for lightness, even as uncertainty prickled under her skin.

Michael set his laptop aside. "Now you rest. I'll show you to your room."

"I get my own room?" she asked, rising slowly.

He gave a small smile, as if the answer should've been obvious. "Of course you do."

Across the hall from Michael's bedroom was one nearly as large as his, with tall ceilings and huge windows. The room was elegant, with pastel furnishings and cottage décor. She crossed the soft carpet and glanced in the massive closet, another room entirely. Then she checked out her equally impressive bathroom.

"I can't believe this is mine," she said, taking a full spin. She quickly calculated that this one room had more square footage than her uncle's entire house. "It doesn't feel right to live here for nothing." She turned to Michael as he leaned against the doorway to the hall. "Are you sure I can't pay you something?" She winked. "I'm making pretty decent money now."

"Yes, you are." He chuckled and shook his head. "But no, your money is yours."

She tilted her head and smiled at the way he leaned in the doorway, filling the entry in his usual stance, his arms loosely crossed over his chest. "You're generous, Michael."

"Providing a place of sanctuary for my largitor is standard, Paislee. Besides, I like my privacy, as I'm sure you do."

"Oh."

Protocol. She was his responsibility. He wasn't being nice or generous because he liked her; her care reflected upon him. His *largitor sanguinis*. His generous bestower of blood, as he'd explained. It sounded elegant, ceremonial. But she was just a donor, bonded in blood. In status. And in silence.

If she wanted to survive the coming months without losing her sanity, she would have to adjust to that harsh reality. He wanted his privacy. He had a life of his own. She wondered if he was in a romantic relationship. How did that work? She had no idea. And it wasn't her business to know. She was his blood source, nothing more. He was kindly reminding her of that fact.

"Your belongings should be here tomorrow. I rerouted your car. It'll be returned to your uncle's house. I have vehicles you can use, so I figured you might want Kendra and Tessa to have it." He laid a tee shirt onto a plush chaise. "The bathroom is stocked with your basic needs. You can use one of my shirts if you'd like to take a shower." With that, he disappeared from the doorway.

# Chapter Eighteen

A SOFT BREEZE STIRRED the sheer curtains as morning crept into Paislee's room. Light filtered across the bedding, warm against her cheek.

She blinked, disoriented for a moment, before memory rushed back like a tide. Part of her wanted to burrow back beneath the covers and pretend the world could pause a little while. She sat up slowly instead, her hand drifting to her neck. Her fingertips brushed the marks on her neck, now barely there. How had they healed so quickly?

There was a light rap on the door as she pulled back the covers and sat at the edge of the bed. "Yeah?"

Michael opened the door and stood in the doorway. His hair was damp, casually tousled, and a faint stubble shadowed his jaw. He was dressed down, but only technically. A pale linen shirt, sleeves rolled loosely to his elbows, the top buttons undone just enough to be unfair. Darker trousers and no shoes, he looked impossibly effortless. Like a man that didn't have to try to be devastating.

And yet, he hesitated.

"I, uh..." He glanced down at his sunglasses loose in his hand. "There's a café a short walk from here. Thought you might want... you're kind of coffee."

Her brow lifted. "With all that foo-foo I put in it?"

A faint smile tugged at his mouth. "I haven't that stuff here."

She laughed, standing up. "Give me five minutes," she said, brushing her hair off her face.

His eyes lingered. Not too long, just enough. "Take your time."

When she came down the stairs, Michael was coming out from his office. He observed her appearance, not critically, just quietly aware. "Are you ready?" he asked, motioning her towards the back deck.

The morning air was cool and clean, tinged with salt and the faint scent of wild beach roses. Paislee walked beside Michael in silence, her hands tucked into her sleeves, her eyes still adjusting to the quiet elegance of the Hamptons.

She hadn't noticed his neighborhood before, with the weight of everything happening. But now, she saw it. The wealth there wasn't loud. It was understated. Perfectly manicured lawns, sleek cars, and houses with walls of glass that hid nothing and everything all at once.

Michael blended into this world effortlessly.

His shirt fluttered with the breeze, the linen catching the light. He hadn't said much. Just walked, relaxed. But people noticed him. Not with stares or whispers. With deference. Glances that lingered just a second longer than normal. A quiet awareness. Like he was power in motion.

A man walking his dog gave Michael a slight nod. The woman beside him offered him a gentle smile before her eyes shifted to Paislee, and stayed there a bit too long.

Paislee glanced down at her clothes. Not bad, but not polished. Certainly not Hamptons-polished. She tugged at her sleeve and refocused on the sand-dusted sidewalk.

"You look fine," he said, his voice low and easy.

"I didn't say I didn't," she replied.

"No. But you fidget when you don't feel like you belong."

She shot him a sideways glance. "Is that in your handbook of how to read people?"

"It's in the footnotes under 'humans who lie with their body language.'"

She huffed. "Charming."

The cafe came into view with it's whitewashed trim, small-paned windows, and brick steps. As they approached the chalkboard menu, the aroma of espresso wafted out the open door. Something about the simplicity of it made her shoulders ease.

She felt Michael's eyes on her. "More comfortable?" he asked lightly.

She nodded with smile, and for a brief moment, it almost felt normal.

The morning had been pleasant. The quiet café. The sunlight slipping through the windows. The careful way Michael sat across from her, almost like he didn't want to scare her off. He noticed when she fidgeted with her sleeves, or nervously tapped her cup. Like everything about her mattered.

After coffee, they slowly made their way back home. As she slipped off her shoes in the entryway, Michael had retrieved his keys.

"I have to head into the city," he said. "I'll be back around dark. If you need to make any calls, there's a landline in my office."

Michael's gaze lingered, like he wanted to say something else. But he didn't. He just opened the door, then paused.

He turned back to her. Calm. Certain. "You're safe now, Paislee."

There was no hesitation. No theatrics. Just confidence, quiet and unwavering. It loosened something in her chest. It shouldn't have meant so much, but it did. It settled deeper than she wanted to admit.

The rest of the day passed in a blur.

She wandered the house, but touched nothing. She spent a good part of her day sitting on the back deck, watching the tide pull out, then wandered back inside when the breeze picked up. There was food in the fridge, she picked at some fruit, sipped a bottle of water, and tried not to think too hard.

At some point, she found herself standing in the doorway of Michael's office. It was clean. Modern. Tastefully expensive. Everything in it's place. But it felt...impersonal. No photos. No notes scrawled on a desk pad. No clutter.

The books on the shelves were pristine, their spines barely creased. The pens in the holder matched. Even the framed art, something abstract and in grayscale, looked like it had been chosen by someone else. It didn't feel like a space someone worked in. It felt like a space someone kept.

She didn't linger. Just turned and walked away, the sound of her footsteps oddly loud on the polished floor.

By the time the sun dipped low and shadows began creeping into the corners of the house, she'd retreated to her room.

After a long, hot shower, Paislee sank onto the bed, legs crisscrossed in the center, and she thought she'd fall asleep right there. She glided her hands over the soft white duvet, her fingers tracing the small, embroidered flowers.

There was a brief knock on her door and, after hours of silence and solitude, she was startled.

Michael opened the door and leaned in, setting down her bags. Then, he held a phone out to her. He didn't cross the threshold, and his hesitation caught her attention.

"You can come in, Michael. It's your house."

"This is your sanctuary," he said softly. "I can't come in without your permission."

Her lips curved into a smile. "You have it."

He crossed the threshold, his movements unhurried and deliberate. When he handed her the phone, her fingers brushed his, and for a fleeting moment, the room felt warmer.

"Wow," she murmured, turning the sleek device over in her hands. "This year's model."

"It's next year's," he said with a slight tilt of his lips.

Her eyes widened. "Then how..." She shook her head. "Never mind."

"You needed an upgrade," he replied, his voice a shade softer. "But breaking your old one...well, I shouldn't have done that."

"No argument here," she teased, her grin widening. "It was a little dramatic, even for you."

His laughter was quiet, almost reluctant, and she liked the way it smoothed the sharpness of his features.

"Sit," she said, patting the bed beside her. "I thought of a few more questions."

Michael sighed but complied, settling at the edge of the bed. The mattress dipped under his weight. She tossed aside the towel from her hair, letting her damp waves fall over her shoulders. His gaze lingered, not intrusive but observant, and she felt the heat rise in her cheeks.

"Are all cardinales so successful and attractive?"

"We have a much longer time to build our fortunes, so most of us are successful. Our looks are designed to lure in humans."

Paislee's lips pressed into a thin line before parting again. "So, you have superhuman strength and speed. And just kissing me can make me abandon all reason."

He smirked. "Yes, it can. It's complicated, but everything has an explanation," he said, leaning back on his hands. "My venom, for instance, it's just a biochemical compound that influences your brain chemistry. I heighten pleasure, reduce your fear. Evolutionary design, if you will."

She let out a laugh and then leaned forward, resting her elbows on her knees. "Your species has really fine-tuned seduction, haven't they?"

His smirk returned, slow and self-assured. "It's effective."

"So, it's not magic? Just biology?"

He smiled. "Science, Paislee. No spells or potions."

"Disappointing," she quipped, her tone light. But the curiosity in her eyes betrayed her playful words.

She tilted her head, studying him with an almost childlike curiosity. "But you do drink blood, and you heal like...instantly. And that's also just science."

"Yes."

She shook her head with a grin. "And you just...live with this? All these gifts? These abilities?"

He raised a brow, clearly amused by her incredulity. "Wouldn't you?"

"Are you happy?"

His expression shifted, part startled, part puzzled. "Am I happy?"

"Your kind doesn't age. You're rich, powerful. You're stronger than anyone I've ever met. And still...I don't know if I'd want it."

"We age. We just live so long, it's an incredibly slow process." His eyes flickered just barely. "Why wouldn't you want it, Paislee? You can have everything."

Paislee studied him. Then glanced at the room, its pristine order, the stillness, the cold beauty of it all. She remembered his office. No personal touches. No signs of a shared life. "You're right. Everything here is perfect. Just like you and your life. But your kind walks quietly among us humans. We admire you, desire you, even fear you...but we can't see you. Not really." Her voice dropped, thoughtful. "The cost of being exceptional seems...lonely."

Michael didn't respond, but the silence felt heavier. She hesitated, then asked softly, "Do you enjoy being a vamp—a cardinalis?"

Something about the question seemed to knock the air out of the room. The silence stretched, almost awkward.

She was about to speak again, to pull the question back. Perhaps she'd crossed a line by voicing her thoughts.

But he moved suddenly. The shift was deliberate, light and teasing. He captured her ankle and pulled her toward him in one fluid motion. She let out a surprised laugh, and her heart pounded as he crawled over her. His face was so close that she could feel the heat of his breath.

"You ask a lot of questions," he murmured, his voice dropping to a velvety timbre.

"And you dodge a lot of them," she shot back, though her voice wavered slightly under his intense gaze.

A slow smile tugged at his lips. "Touché."

Paislee felt her body react to his closeness, a mix of nerves and excitement bubbling under her skin. When his head dipped closer. The moment he kissed her, that familiar sweetness washed over her, intoxicating and smooth.

His lips barely brushed hers, soft and deliberate, before he pulled back just enough to meet her gaze. "Nervous?" he asked, though the slight curve of his mouth suggested he already knew the answer.

She nodded faintly, her breath uneven. "A little."

"You don't need to be," he murmured, his voice low and steady. "In about two minutes, you won't care what I do to you. We've done this before."

The words sent a shiver through her, equal parts of anticipation and unease. "But that was to save your life. There wasn't time to think about it."

His fingers traced a slow, deliberate path along her jawline; his touch was light but grounding. "I understand."

Her eyes searched his, looking for reassurance. She wasn't afraid of him in that moment, she knew the bite itself wasn't painful. But this felt different, heavier. Her choice settled in her chest, along with an unspoken acknowledgement of the connection it might forge...at least for her.

His expression shifted, with something gentler flickering in his gaze. "Extend me some trust."

She exhaled sharply, trying to muster the courage to respond, but before she could, his lips found hers again. This time, his kiss was deeper, laced with more of that intoxicating sweetness she couldn't resist. It seeped into her senses, melting away the tension in her shoulders, softening the edges of her thoughts.

"Why does it feel like this?" she whispered against his mouth, her voice barely audible.

He pulled back slightly, resting his forehead against her. "I feel like we've been through this, ducizza." His lips brushed hers again as he added teasingly, "My venom alters your perception of reality."

"Can I see them?"

He tilted his head at her, and a flicker of uncertainty flashed across his face. "See what?"

"Your fangs," she replied.

His mouth parted just enough to show his surprise, but no words came out. His lips twitched, caught somewhere between a frown and a faint smile, before they curved into an almost imperceptible smirk.

She inspected his teeth. They were perfect, and his fangs were insanely sharp. That gave her pause, and she slid off the bed, smoothing her hair before she moved toward the door. "What are some other differences between our body structures?" she asked, her tone overly casual, as if she hadn't just fled the moment.

"You're stalling."

"Am I?" she countered, tossing a glance over her shoulder. "Maybe I'm just curious. You did say I could ask questions."

He took measured steps toward her, his movements unhurried, almost lazy, but there was a glint of mischief in his eyes. "Your curiosity seems particularly well timed."

She ignored him, gesturing vaguely toward the hall. "What else—"

"What else can I do?" he finished for her, his voice low and amused.

Her steps quickened as she headed toward the door.

But he appeared in front of her before she even registered him moving, and blocked her path to the hall. "I can hear your heartbeat. From far away, I can hear the blood pulsing through your body."

Her heart leaped, though she tried masking it with a scoff. "Interesting."

She took a step back, only for her shoulders to meet the wall.

"And," Michael leaned forward, his palms braced on either side of her, caging her in, "you can try to run, but I'll always catch you."

She swallowed hard, her gaze darting anywhere but his face. "I wasn't running. I'm allowed to walk around my sanctuary, right? You can't technically stalk me here."

"You invited me in," he reminded her, his tone rich with amusement.

*Shit.*

She opened her mouth but then closed it. A flicker of shock crossed her face as she scrambled for a clever response. "I...my neck... It's extremely sensitive. I just need another day to recover—"

He chuckled softly, and his breath brushed across her cheek. "Sensitive, huh? What other parts of you are sensitive, Paislee?"

Her cheeks flushed crimson, and she quickly ducked under his arm, darting out of her sanctuary. "To be clear, I'm not running away," she declared over her shoulder, though her words rang hollow. "I'll be right back. I just need some water—"

Michael straightened and turned to follow her with the deliberate pace of a predator. "You're a terrible liar, Ms. Sullivan."

Her heart race as he closed the distance between them; his presence was overwhelming and magnetic. "I-I just think we should talk about—"

He caught her wrist gently and spun her to face him. His eyes gleamed with quiet triumph as he guided her into his bedroom. "We'll talk," he promised. "Later."

# Chapter Nineteen

M ICHAEL SCOOPED PAISLEE INTO his arms with an ease that left her breathless.

"Stop overthinking," he said softly.

Her heart raced as he carried her into his room.

"I'm not overthinking," she countered weakly, her voice faltering as he set her down on the bed. His gaze locked onto hers.

"You are," he insisted, his lips brushing hers in a whisper of a kiss.

Michael's hands moved with a purpose that sent shivers down her spine, tracing the curve of her waist. Her pulse quickened and her body responded instinctively.

When his lips trailed down her neck, a soft gasp escaped her. The light graze of his teeth sent a thrill racing through her. She knew what was coming, but it wasn't fear she felt—it was anticipation, a strange, inexplicable trust.

"Michael," she said, her voice barely above a whisper.

He paused, his breath warm against her skin. "Yes?" His tone was steady but laced with something deeper, something fragile.

"I'm not going to run."

"Good," he murmured, his voice like silk. "Because I wouldn't have let you."

Her laugh, light and teasing, broke the tension. "You're relentless."

"And you," he said, his expression darkening with intensity, "are irresistible."

Before she could respond, he leaned in. Deliberate, calculated.

Her resolve crumbled.

His lips founds hers slowly, pressing with warmth that wasn't rushed. It wasn't hunger, not yet. His kiss didn't just take her breath, it softened her thoughts, blurred her reasoning.

Her hand rose instinctively to his chest, feeling the steady rhythm of his heart. It was a reminder, no matter how unnatural he seemed, he was very much alive.

His palm slid up her back, guiding her closer. She should've noticed the tension in his body, the strain barely held in check. But the taste of his venom was creeping in, dulling the alarms.

A haze settled over her thoughts as his mouth traced a path down her jaw, slow, careful.

Her pulse surged against his lips as they found the base of her neck.

She knew what was coming. She gripped his shoulders, bracing herself. When he finally opened his mouth, letting his fangs graze her skin, just enough to promise what would come next, her heart stuttered. Then, she surrendered.

The faintest prick of his fangs followed, sharp but fleeting, and then a wave of euphoria. Warmth spread through her, heightening every sense as her body surrendered to the connection.

Michael's grip tightened, and his breath came raggedly as he drank. The intimacy of it overwhelmed Paislee, but it didn't frighten her.

When he pulled back, his lips brushed over the mark in a tender kiss. "Are you all right?" he asked, his voice softer now, his gaze searching hers.

She nodded, though her body still buzzed with the aftereffects. "I think so," she whispered.

His lips curved into a faint smile, but tension lingered in his eyes, a quiet restraint that hinted at his internal struggle.

She watched him in the silence that followed. The dim lighting carved shadows across his face, but didn't hide the restraint in his eyes. Or the sorrow buried beneath it. He looked like someone at war with himself, straining something far older than this moment. And yet despite everything, he hadn't taken what he so clearly craved.

That should've scared her. Once, it would have.

But something about him haunted her. Not the sharpness of his fangs or the hunger in his eyes. But the way he held it back. The way he chose her safety over his satisfaction. Again and again.

No one had ever made her want to give in without question. But she wasn't afraid. She felt drawn.

She should've created space.

Instead, she reached up and brushed the trace of blood on his lips, fingertips ghosting over the curve of his lips. Her touch was curious, but reverent, like she was trying to understand something sacred. The gesture surprised them both, and the air between them thickened. He didn't flinch. He didn't breathe.

Her heart thudded against her ribs, not in panic, but clarity. Maybe it was madness. But before she could stop herself, she closed the distance and kissed him.

He stilled beneath her lips.

For one terrifying heartbeat, he didn't respond. She'd overstepped, she knew it. He was too strong, too tightly wound to ever—

Then he broke.

A sound escaped him, ragged and low, like something primal that had been caged too long. His hands caught her waist with bruising urgency as he pulled her closer, his mouth claiming hers with a heat that nearly tore the breath from her lungs. He kissed her like something inside had cracked open and flooded free. His restraint shattered and she felt the tremor in his breath. The way his body tightened, the way his hands gripped in her hair.

The world narrowed to just the two of them. For the first time in forever, Paislee stopped thinking and let herself feel.

As the kiss deepened, Michael groaned against her lips. He pulled her closer, and his hands roamed her curves. His hunger was palpable, and she matched him, letting herself get lost in him.

Her hands slid down his chest, tugging at his shirt, and he helped her. The fabric disappeared in a blur, and she ran her hands over the hard planes of his chest, marveling at the strength beneath her fingertips. When her hands moved lower, finding the button of his pants, he tensed but didn't stop her.

"Paislee," he said, his voice hoarse, but the warning was weak as his resolve faltered under her touch.

Her confidence grew, and she pushed him back onto the bed. Her lips trailed down his neck, and her tongue teased the line of his collarbone as her hands worked him free. The sound he made when she wrapped her hand around him was raw, primal, and it sent a thrill straight through her.

His head fell back against the pillows as her touch dismantled him, piece by piece.

She inched down, and her tongue trailed the center line of his abdomen, flicking over him, savoring the way he jerked beneath her. She took as much of him as she could into her mouth, and the sound that escaped him sent another delicious thrill through her.

His hands tangled in her hair, guiding her rhythm with unspoken urgency. Each thrust pushed deeper, brushing the back of her throat, as his ragged moans filled the room. Each motion more deliberate, sending a pulse of heat through her as his breaths grew harsher, more erratic. She felt his body tense and his control slip as she pushed him closer to the edge.

But just as he began to lose himself, Michael suddenly pulled away, his chest heaving. "Damn it," he said, his voice ragged but firm. "We can't do this."

She frowned as frustration flared in her chest. "Why not?" she demanded, reaching for him again.

He caught her wrist, and though gentle, his grip was unyielding. "You don't understand," he said as his eyes searched hers.

"I understand, Michael," she argued, her voice steady despite the heat in her cheeks. "I'm a virgin, not a saint."

"The venom is clouding your judgment," he said firmly. With a shake of his head, he swung his legs over the side of the bed, putting space between them. "This isn't real," he said quietly, his voice almost pained.

"Don't do this," she said. Her jaw tightened as anger and hurt warred within her.

"Good night, Paislee," he said, his tone cold and final.

The words hit her like a slap. She stood and, her dignity barely intact, walked out of the room. Once behind her own door, the tears she had fought so hard to hold back finally fell, and she muffled her sobs by pressing her hand to her mouth.

Back in his room, Michael stood alone with his fists clenched at his sides. Silence pressed against him, oppressive and unrelenting. Sex was a natural part of the relationship between a cardinalis and their largitor. In the past, he'd indulged freely with his donors; their connection often extended beyond mere blood transactions. But this—Paislee—was different. It was dangerous, tangled in layers of complications he couldn't afford to unpack.

His gaze lingered on the spot where she'd stood moments ago. His chest tightened as a dull ache spread through him—a feeling he refused to name. He had done what he'd thought was necessary: reminded her of her place, drawn a line to protect them both.

So, why did it feel like he'd shattered something irreparable?

He paced the length of the room as his thoughts churned. Her hurt expression burned into him, her quiet strength breaking under the steely edge of his rejection.

"Damn it, Paislee," he muttered, his voice low and rough with frustration. He clenched his fists as he struggled to regain control, but no matter how hard he tried, he couldn't push away the image of her—her lips on him, her touch bold and insistent, her eyes glistening with unspoken defiance.

She wasn't like the others. She unsettled him in way no one else had, ways that unraveled his carefully constructed walls. He'd told himself that he was protecting her, shielding her from the truth of what it meant to be tied to him. However, deep down, he couldn't ignore the selfishness of his actions. Pushing her away hadn't been for her—it had been for him because she made him feel, and feelings for a largitor were a dangerous luxury in his world.

The tension in his chest became unbearable. His resolve was paper thin, and his carefully measured control threatened to slip through his fingers. With a growl of frustration, he grabbed his discarded shirt and yanked it on with a roughness that mirrored his mood.

He snatched up his keys and stormed out of the room; the need for distance clawed at him. The confines of the house, the scent of her lingering in the air—it was too much. He needed space, a distraction, anything to drown out the chaos she'd left in her wake.

The drive to Allusion was a blur, and he gripped the steering wheel tightly. The bar had always been his haven, a place to drown himself in the predictable pandemonium of others, where he could escape parts of himself he didn't want to face. Yet, even as he sped down the streets, a knowing sense of emptiness settled in his chest. He didn't want distractions...

Michael's thoughts spiraled as he parked and stepped into the familiar dim haze of Allusion. The thrum of music and low hum of conversation should have grounded him, should've pulled him back into the version of himself that he knew best. But tonight, everything felt hollow.

No matter how much distance he put between himself and Paislee, she was still there. Paislee Sullivan wasn't just under his skin. She was in his blood. And for the first time in centuries, Michael felt like he was losing control.

Seth was behind the bar, cleaning glasses with his usual calm efficiency. His eyes tracked Michael's approach, and his brow furrowed slightly.

"The struggle looks real," he said, sliding a tumbler in Michael's direction. He didn't need to wait for Michael's order to pour; the amber liquid in the glass spoke to how well he knew him.

Michael grunted as he collapsed onto the stool and ran a hand through his hair. "It is," he muttered, his voice rough with exhaustion.

Seth studied Michael for a long moment and observed his troubled appearance. From the way he tapped his fingers against the glass, to the raw edge of his expression. "I take it back. The struggle seems more like a disaster," Seth observed dryly, leaning against the counter.

Michael shot him a glare but didn't argue. Instead, he downed the drink in one swallow. The burn did little to numb the ache in his chest. He pushed the glass back toward Seth with a wordless demand for more.

"Your brother's dickery is the norm and never affects you," Seth said, pouring another measure. He huffed a quiet laugh, shaking his head. "So, it must be Paislee. She's in your head."

Michael's jaw tightened, his silence answering more than words could. He stared into his drink as the truth of Seth's words gnawed at him. "She shouldn't be," he said finally, his voice low.

Seth didn't respond immediately, giving Michael a moment to stew. When he finally spoke, his tone was even. "You can't just turn it off, you know. Doesn't matter how much you tell yourself it's wrong."

Michael opened his mouth to respond, but his words died as he caught the familiar scent of vanilla and jasmine—soft and inviting. He turned, and his gaze landed on a striking figure moving through the crowd.

"Naevia," he said under his breath, with a mix of surprise and irritation coloring his tone.

She spotted him almost immediately, and her lips curved into a knowing smile. His dark eyes glittered with amusement as she approached, her movements fluid and deliberate. Naevia had been a beautiful and cunning distraction he couldn't fully resist, even when he wanted to.

"Michael," she purred, sliding into the stool beside him. "It's been too long."

He didn't answer right away. His gaze flicked to Seth, who raised an eyebrow but then wisely chose to busy himself at the other end of the bar.

# Chapter Twenty

T HE TALL IRON GATES slowly opened as Michael's car rolled onto the Chamberlain estates. He stepped out, red folder in hand, and was greeted by Joseph.

"Good morning, Mr. Chamberlain," Joseph said warmly. "You look well."

Michael offered a nod as they climbed the steps. "Thank you. Is everyone inside?"

"They're in the breakfast room."

"Esben?" Michael asked, his tone hardening.

Joseph's neutral expression faltered for a moment before replying, "Yes, sir."

"Good."

As they entered, the faint scent of fresh paint lingered. Michael glanced at the ceiling, now an ornate imitation of the Sistine Chapel. His brow lifted slightly. "Mother's latest project?"

Joseph's lips twitched. "For the cameras. Her foundation is receiving considerable donations from the Catholic Church."

"Of course it is."

As Michael strode toward the breakfast room, its atmosphere seemed far too relaxed for his mood. His father was absorbed in the paper at the head of the table. Michael's mother sat to his father's right, and Esben was to his left, scrolling through his phone.

"Michael!" Alaitz exclaimed, her warm smile unwavering. She rose to embrace him. "Sit down. Breakfast will be out in just a moment."

Michael returned the hug briefly, but his focus was already on Esben. "I'm not staying."

The room fell silent as he crossed the space, his eyes like daggers.

Without hesitation, he dropped the folder onto Esben's empty plate. "Paislee Sullivan is under my protection now. If you so much as look in her direction, you'll regret it."

Esben sat back in his chair, and his smirk faltered as he opened the folder. "Don't be upset, brother. I was just having some fun," he sneered as he flipped through the pages. "Your scent is all over her. Gross."

"Now that she's under contract with me," Michael said, snatching the folder back, "you have no reason to even speak to her. If you return to her uncle's house or speak to anyone close to

Paislee—for any reason—I'll take it as a personal attack on her, and I'll rip out your fucking throat."

Esben stood abruptly, his chair scraping loudly against the floor. Tension snapped taut between them as their father barked, "That's enough!"

"You think you're stronger than me, *Micheddru*?" Esben asked, his voice a dangerous murmur.

Michael's jaw clenched. "We're going to find out one day, Esben."

Neither brother moved as their gazes locked.

Esben leaned closer. "Looks like we're going to have another Katya situation. Should we prepare the tribunal now?"

Michael lunged, but Saverio stepped in, his presence a wall between them. "Michele, stand down. Esben, leave it."

"Just leave it?" Esben's laugh was sharp and bitter. "Michael can disappear for fucking years and still be your golden child. I'm gone two days, and you have the Order up my ass!"

Michael gave his brother one last loaded look. "Stay out of my affairs."

"If you took your own advice, Mikey, we wouldn't have been brought up on charges," Esben shot back.

"You shouldn't have allowed your affairs to fall onto my doorstep," Michael sneered. "This is your final warning. Keep me and Paislee out of your mess."

"Oh, little brother, you won't even see it coming." Esben's grin returned, wicked and full of promise. "Neither of you will escape the suffering I have in store."

Alaitz swept in with her perfect poise, placing a calming hand on Michael's arm. "Walk with me," she said, her tone light as if nothing had happened. She looped her arm through his and guided him out. Silence ticked by slowly.

As they strolled the hall, she finally spoke, asking, "Is the club ready for my fundraiser?"

"It'll exceed your expectations," Michael said, his tone softening.

"And this latest drama with Esben?" she prodded, her smile fixed but her eyes sharp.

"Handled," Michael assured her.

She paused, and her grip tightened. "Esben is reckless. Don't underestimate him."

"I don't," Michael said firmly.

Her gaze was misty. "Don't let his hatred be your downfall. If you're brought to trial again—"

"I won't be." His voice was steady, almost too calm.

Alaitz studied him, her expression a mix of love and fear. "Good. Because I can't lose my son, Michael."

As he leaned down to kiss her cheek, his resolve hardened. However, behind the façade, Michael knew the storm brewing within the family wasn't one he could easily contain.

# Chapter
# Twenty-One

K ENDRA SLID OFF HER shades and scanned the grand space as though she couldn't quite believe what she was seeing. "This is his house?" she asked, her tone thick with awe as she wandered to the oversized windows framing the glittering ocean view. She paused, crossing her arms tightly over her chest. "What is all this, Paislee?"

Paislee's hands brushed nervously over her jeans. "What do you mean?"

"Don't play dumb," Kendra snapped, turning to face her. "You just met this guy. You don't know anything about him, and now you're moving in? Leaving me? What the hell is going on?"

Paislee bit her lip. Kendra's words had hit harder than she'd expected. She'd spent the morning rehearsing what to say, pacing until her nerves threatened to undo her completely. She wasn't sure she'd even believe the story she was about to tell. "It's not like that," she began, her voice softer than she intended. "We've really fallen for each other, and he asked to stay so we could—"

"Get to know each other?" Kendra cut in, her expression sharp. "Please, you've known this man, what, a week or so? This is ridiculous."

"Kendra, stop," Paislee said firmly, though her tone wavered. She knew Kendra wasn't wrong, but she couldn't tell her the truth—not about the contract, the Cardinal Order, or Michael. "You're just the least romantic person alive. If he doesn't treat me right, I'm out and moving back in with you."

"Like you did with Xavier?" Kendra's words sliced through the room. "You were so blind, Pais. He cheated on you for months, and when you finally figured it out, he nearly got you killed."

Paislee's chest tightened. "Screw you, Kendra," she shot back, her voice rising. "How dare you bring that up? You were pushing me to get to know him."

"Getting to know him, not move in with him when you barely know him." Silence stretched between them, heavy and painful. Kendra exhaled sharply, looking away. "I'm sorry," she muttered. "I just don't want to see you get hurt again."

Paislee's shoulders sagged as she exhaled slowly. "I get it, okay? I know you're just trying to look out for me, but this is my decision. I need to do this." Her voice softened, though the tension in her chest lingered. "Please, just trust me."

Kendra studied her a moment, her frown softening. "I don't like it," she admitted. "But I can't stop you, can I?"

"No," Paislee said quietly, and her lips twitched with a faint smile. "You can't."

They stared at each other for a beat before Kendra's arms opened and she pulled Paislee in for a tight hug.

"Just be happy, all right?" Kendra whispered, squeezing Paislee before stepping back. "And if this guy screws you over, I'm coming for him."

Paislee chuckled, though the laugh didn't quite meet her eyes. "Deal."

Kendra hesitated and then glanced at the sweeping staircase. "I still think this is crazy, but I'll try to be happier for you. For now."

Paislee didn't press her any further, knowing it was the closest thing she'd get to an approval. They were interrupted by the front door opening. Both turned to see Michael walk in, his keys flipping in one hand, a bottle of water in the other. As he glanced from Paislee to Kendra, a faint smile itched the corners of his lips. "Am I facing the firing squad?"

Kendra's brow arched, and a sly grin tugged at her lips. "Not yet."

Michael chuckled, entirely unbothered. "Firing squad or no, this is Paislee's home, too, and you're welcome here anytime," he said, his tone pleasant but nonchalant as he disappeared up the stairs.

As soon as he was out of earshot, Kendra turned to Paislee. "That man is too hot for his own good. Guess I can't blame you, I'd have moved in just for the view." She slid her shades back on. "And I don't mean the ocean view."

Paislee laughed. "Goodbye, Kendra," Paislee said, pushing her friend toward the door.

"All right, all right!" Kendra laughed, grabbing her bag. She paused at the doorway, her expression softening. "Take care of yourself. I'll call you later."

"Okay," Paislee said, wrapping her arms around her one last time. "And I'm not abandoning you. I'm here for you."

Kendra smiled faintly as she stepped back. "I know," she said, her voice quiet, before leaving.

Paislee closed the door and leaned against it, exhaling a long breath. The house was suddenly quiet save for the faint crashing of the waves in the distance. The stillness was pressing, bringing forth questions in her mind that she wasn't comfortable exploring.

While Michael was upstairs, she slipped out the back door and wandered toward the beach.

The sun was beginning to lower in the sky, casting warm hues across the sand and water. Paislee sat near the shore, wrapping her arms around her knees as she stared out at the horizon. Her thoughts drifted to last night. She didn't sleep much. Even when she opened her bedroom windows to the lull of the ocean outside, sleep evaded her. Michael's voice, cold and final, echoed. *Good night, Paislee.*

The memory flared every time she closed her eyes. Not just the rejection, but the way he'd looked at her right before. Like he wanted her. Needed her. And still chose to push her away.

She touched her neck absentmindedly, wincing at the tenderness. Her fingers trailed down to the faint puncture wounds hidden beneath her high-collared shirt. The memory of Michael's touch sent a shiver through her.

A soft rustle behind her broke her thoughts. She glanced over her shoulder and saw him approaching with a thin sweater in his hand. Without a word, he settled beside her and laid the sweater across her shoulders.

"How did it go with your friend?" he asked, his voice almost soothing.

"Kendra will be fine," Paislee murmured, pulling the sweater tighter around her. "Eventually."

Michael nodded, his gaze fixed on the water. For a while, neither of them spoke. The quiet stretched between them, not entirely uncomfortable but filled with unspoken questions.

She glanced sideways at him, studying him and the perfect lines of his profile. He looked calm, almost serene, as though the weight of the world didn't touch him. But she knew better. There was something dangerous lurking beneath his composed exterior—something she couldn't yet define. Last night, he'd stopped things. But there was a moment when he'd surrendered. And she'd felt it. All of it.

And that was the part she couldn't forget.

"How are you feeling?" he asked, looking out toward the sea. Calm, collected, as if nothing had happened the night before. But she knew better. His composure was a carefully drawn line. One she was starting to see through.

She followed his gaze to the waves as they teased the shore. Where a toddler darted between two parents, giggling wildly. The child's laughter seemed to rise with the salty breeze, but her question cut through it.

"Does your...*kind* have children?"

"Yes." His answer was straightforward, but his tone was unusually soft. "I was born, not turned."

She glanced at him, her curiosity deepening. "Humans don't just...turn into vamp—cardinales?"

He shook his head. "We can turn humans, but it's not as simple as the stories make it seem. And we can't turn anyone we please."

Her brows furrowed, and she leaned her chin against her palm. "Why not?"

"There are rules," he said. "We're governed by laws, just like humans. One of the most important is that we can't turn anyone without the Order's approval."

"The mysterious Order we're not supposed to talk about," she said, lacing her words with sarcasm.

A faint smile tugged at the corner of his mouth. "The very same. They've existed for centuries."

"Controlling you," she muttered.

He shrugged. "If we want to survive, we follow the code: ten core rules plus a slew of lesser laws. Break them, and you'll answer to the Order."

She tilted her head, pressing her lips into a thoughtful line. "So, why can't you turn whoever you want?"

"Population control is necessary," he said plainly. "If we want to turn someone, we submit an application. If it's approved, we're allowed to—but we're responsible for them. If they break the rules, we face the consequences."

"Why would you turn someone?" Paislee's mouth quirked in a half-smile. "What kind of application process is it? Do they need references?"

He chuckled, low and brief. "The most common reason for turning a human is to take a mate."

She blinked. "A mate—a partner?"

"Yes."

"So, cardinales commit, or can...fall in love with humans?"

"More often than you'd think."

"And if it doesn't work out?" she pressed. "You're still stuck being responsible for them?"

"It rarely fails. When we mate, it's...different than human relationships. And if something does go wrong, the Order intervenes."

"And if you don't agree with their decision?"

His laugh was sharper this time. "Appealing isn't an option."

She studied him, her curiosity deepening. "So, you've got some who are born and others who are turned. Are they the same?"

"Not exactly," he admitted. "You're getting into bloodlines—how pure your blood is. It's complicated, but generally, those who are turned are weaker. Blood purity determines status."

Her grin widened. "So, you have commoners and royalty?"

His gaze found hers, unwavering. "You could say that. Blood purity is encouraged, but harmony is more important than lineage."

"How noble," she teased.

His brow lifted in a warning. "It's not about nobility. We're a passionate species. Corner us, and we lash out. Nothing is more dangerous than discontentment."

She hesitated before asking, "Am I at risk of being turned?"

"Only if my blood infects you. Otherwise, no."

She turned her attention back to the water, her thoughts wandering. Vampires could love—loyally, deeply, passionately. What would it be like living with Michael? Could he love her? How did he even fall in love? Humans loved through time, connection, shared moments, and attraction. But vampires? She didn't understand how it worked for them.

"Are you hungry?" he asked, interrupting her thoughts.

She shook away her questions and smiled. "Starving."

"Come on. I'll take you to dinner." He stood, hoisting her up with him.

Her lips curved in a mischievous smile as they started back to the house. "I want a doughboy."

He stopped mid-step, turning to her with an incredulous expression. "That's not dinner."

"It's delicious, though," she countered. "The fair's in town. It'll be fun."

He turned without a word, heading towards the house again.

She followed, a step behind.

"Is that a yes?"

"I thought it was clearly a no," he said over his shoulder. "You see how I rudely walked away?"

She darted around him, cutting him off before he could reach the door. Her smile was dazzling, her tone light. "You don't like the fair?"

"It's noisy and dirty," he said simply.

"Afraid of dirt?" she teased.

His jaw tightened. "Humans at fairs are...unruly. And their offspring...distressing."

Her laughter burst out before she could stop it. "Distressing? You're at a club full of humans every night."

"That's different. The people at Allusion are refined."

"They have money and look like models," she said, her voice tinged with mock understanding. "Oh. You *are* a snob."

His growl was low and immediate. In one swift motion, he scooped her up and tossed her over his shoulder.

"Are all cardinales this arrogant?" she asked, laughing upside down. "Or is it just you?"

He carried her through the porch and into the kitchen, where he deposited her on the counter. "I'll take you anywhere for dinner—the best restaurant in town. Why the fair?"

Her laughter hadn't entirely faded as she met his gaze. "I want to see you mingle with us peasants."

He sighed, rubbing his temples. "Seriously?"

"Well," she said, her tone thoughtful, "there's also the hamster."

"The hamster?"

"The biggest stuffed animal you've ever seen. I want to win it. "

He stared at her, unblinking, before his tone turned drier than the desert. "If ever there was a reason to mingle with peasants, that would be it."

She let out a victorious whoop and hopped off the counter. "Let me grab my sneakers."

# Chapter Twenty-Two

P AISLEE WATCHED MICHAEL'S PROFILE carefully as they entered the fair, noting how people couldn't stop staring at him. He looked otherworldly—his chiseled features, smooth gait, and calm detachment screamed unattainability, perfection. Her curiosity about her enigmatic "employer" had grown into something else entirely: a budding fascination.

"You're not as scary as you want people to think, you know," she said with a sly smile, looping her arm through his.

Michael raised an eyebrow but didn't pull away. "Am I supposed to be offended or flattered?"

"Both," she teased, taking a bite of her doughboy.

Despite his nonchalance, she could tell the crowds were making him uncomfortable. He walked as if he were dodging landmines, careful to avoid brushing against anyone. It was a stark contrast to the suave demeanor at the bar, where he thrived on attention.

"Do you fly or turn into any creatures?" she asked, and he laughed, shaking his head.

"Now I think you're trying to annoy me," he said. "No, I don't change. And if I want to fly, I get on a plane like everyone else."

"Would you like to fly right now?" she asked with a smile, spotting the rollercoaster. "Because we're riding that."

His gaze followed hers, landing on the coaster's towering loops and screaming riders. "Absolutely not."

"Oh, come on!" She tugged at his arm. "Where's your sense of adventure?"

"Firmly rooted in the ground, thank you."

Ignoring his protests, she dragged him toward the line. Moments later, the attendant was strapping them into the seats, and Paislee couldn't suppress her grin.

"Just don't puke on me," she teased with a wink as the ride began its slow climb.

The look he flashed her just before the ride plunged into chaos was priceless.

Paislee hollered. She grabbed Michael's hand mid-loop, forcing him to release his death grip on the bar. By the time the ride screeched to a halt, she was breathless from laughter.

"You looked like you were having fun," she said as they disembarked.

Michael smoothed his disheveled hair. "Define 'fun.'"

Paislee laughed, but her amusement was cut short when a man staggered off the ride behind them. The poor guy made it two steps before doubling over and vomiting on the pavement.

Paislee's eyes widened, her stomach twisting at the sight. "Quick, let's go. Or I'm going to be next."

Michael cringed, and then he grabbed her arm to steer her away. "Revolting."

She bolted toward the souvenir shop, with Michael in tow. Her eyes lit up. "They took pictures on the ride! Let's see ours."

Michael groaned but followed her to the screens. When their photo popped up, she burst into laughter. His expression communicated a mixture of terror and disbelief.

"I'm buying it," she declared.

"No, you're not," he said, but she was already handing over cash.

They wandered toward the game booth where Paislee spotted her nemesis: the giant hamster.

"This is the year," she said as determination gleamed in her eyes.

Michael crossed his arms over his chest, amused. "What's the obsession with the hamster?"

"It's not just a hamster. It's *the* hamster. I visit my uncle in the summers, and I've been trying to win it for years."

Michael inspected the game. "How many people actually win this thing?"

The attendant smirked. "None, really."

Michael leaned closer to Paislee and said, his voice low, "You know you could just buy it."

"That's cheating," she said, scandalized. "I'm winning it fair and square."

He observed the pitching setup and then picked up the softball, looking at her with raised brows. To her surprise, he rolled the ball into her palm and whispered, "Then let's make it happen."

His unexpected support bolstered her confidence. With precision and focus, she landed pitch after pitch, slowly trading up for bigger prizes. The crowd around them grew as she approached the final round.

Her hands trembled as she prepared for her last throw. "I'm going to miss," she muttered.

Michael stepped in front of her and lifted her chin with his finger. "Breathe."

Before she could respond, he leaned down and kissed her. It was brief but intoxicating, leaving her steadier than before.

"You've got this," he said, stepping back.

The ball flew and sank perfectly into the hole. The crowd erupted into cheers, and Paislee jumped up, victorious.

"Suck it!" she shouted at the game booth, earning laughter from onlookers.

She claimed her prize and proudly marched back to Michael, who shook his head in disbelief.

"That thing's almost bigger than you," he said, smirking.

"It's perfect," she declared, clutching the hamster like a trophy. "Dinner?"

"I see no need to stay any longer. I've conquered this fair," she said, haughtily tilting her head and waving her hand flippantly. "So long, peasants!"

"Smartass."

As they walked toward the exit, he slung his arm around her shoulders. "You're impossible."

She grinned. "And you love it."

# Chapter Twenty-Three

MICHAEL TOOK PAISLEE TO a restaurant far above her usual dining standards, perched right at the water's edge. She looked down at her street clothes and sneakers, then at the white tablecloths and candlelight.

It was the kind of place she wouldn't have dared step into on her own, let alone without reservations. Yet somehow, Michael effortlessly bypassed all that. The second they walked in, the staff greeted him warmly and whisked them to a private, glass-enclosed room overlooking the ocean.

Dinner was filled with stories and laughter, easing some of the tension that seemed to follow them. Michael listened intently as Paislee shared glimpses of her past, his curiosity genuine.

"So, you really are country," he teased after hearing about her childhood on her family's farm.

"To the bone," she said proudly, flexing a bicep in mock strength. "I grew up cleaning stalls, making cheese, and hauling farm equipment. My brothers never made it easy, though—they called me a sissy every chance they got."

Michael chuckled, shaking his head. "I can't picture it. You, hauling farm equipment."

"Believe me, it wasn't glamorous," she said, smiling despite herself. "But it was home. My parents kept me busy to keep me out of trouble. Working the farm, selling produce at the markets on weekends, horse shows, all that. They were protective, kept me pretty close—especially after my accident."

His glass paused in midair. "Accident?"

Her smile faltered for just a moment. She shifted in her chair, uncertain as to how much to say. "I...got hit by a car a couple of years ago. It's not a big deal anymore; all that's left is a scar running down my back."

The words hung in the air, but Michael didn't seem convinced. "How did that happen?" he pressed gently.

Paislee hesitated, feeling the weight of his gaze. "I was in a bad situation. Let's just say it was a mistake I won't make again." She let out a small, nervous laugh, trying to brush it off. "Anyway, when you shielded me from the cars on the highway, you saved me from a similar fate. I hope you realize how much I appreciate not having to go through that again."

His expression darkened at the reminder of Esben causing her to stumble into traffic. His jaw tightened but didn't speak. Something in his expression shifted. She looked away, reaching for her glass.

"To be honest," she added lightly, trying to shift the mood, "I didn't expect dinner to get so confessional."

Michael leaned back, eyes still on her. "We don't have to talk about any of it."

"No, it's fine," she gave a faint smile. "It's just weird how easily we fell into it. I feel like you already know too much."

He raised a brow. "Do I?"

"Maybe. Or maybe we just met before."

Michael blinked, looking caught off guard. "Before?"

"In another life," she said, eyes dancing. "Maybe I was your enemy. Or your annoying neighbor. Or someone you passed on the street and never noticed."

He shook his head, a smile ticking at the corners of his lips. "You believe in that kind of thing?"

"Not sure," she said swirling her wine. "But I like the idea. That souls circle back. That people who matter to one another will find each other again, no matter how much time passes. You?"

Micheal's smile turned faintly skeptical. "I believe in physics, not fate."

"Of course you do," she teased. "You've lived long enough to get jaded."

He tilted his head. "You think I'm jaded?"

"I think," she said, setting her glass down, "you've seen enough to convince yourself the world is predictable. Logical. Safe in its cold little rules. But maybe....maybe something still surprises you."

"Like what?"

She shrugged, feigning innocence. "I don't know. Maybe someone who still believes in a little magic."

They held each other's gaze for a breath too long.

Then Michael murmured, "And if you had a thousand lives?"

She smiled. "I'd probably mess up most of them. But I'd try everything. Learn every language. Make a fool of myself in all the best ways. Fall in love just to see what it turns me into."

"Not all love makes you better."

"No," she agreed, "but the good ones show up again."

A moment passed, gentle and unspoken.

Then softly, almost to herself, she added, "You'd still be here, wouldn't you? Long after all my life is over."

Michael's gaze didn't waver. "Yes."

It was just one word. But it held centuries. A truth too big to sit with for long. So she reached for her wine again, as if that simple gesture could soften it.

"Well," she said lightly, "guess I better make this one count then."

By the time they left the restaurant, it was late, and Paislee fell asleep in the car on the way home. She barely stirred as Michael parked and carried her inside after adjusting her stuffed animal in her arms.

"Paislee," he whispered softly in her ear as he nudged her awake.

"Hmm?" she mumbled, half-asleep.

He chuckled, low and warm. "*Arrusbigliati, bedda mia.*"

"I don't know what you said," she murmured as Michael carried her through the house. She tucked her face into his neck, inhaling the crisp, clean scent of his cologne. The feel of his arms around her, his presence, stirred something deep within her—something undeniable. She released her prized trophy and tightened her fingers in his hair, pulling him into a kiss.

His response was instant, his mouth claiming hers with an intensity that left her breathless. For a moment, everything else disappeared—it was just them.

Until a voice shattered the moment.

"Bad timing?"

Michael froze. And Paislee blinked, disoriented, as a petite woman stepped into view. She was stunning, and confidence radiated from her as she approached, her stilettos clicking on the floor.

"Naevia," Michael said, clearing his throat. As he set Paislee back on her feet, his demeanor shifted in an instant. "What are you doing here?"

Naevia held up a key, her smirk razor sharp. "I still had yours." She cast a brief, dismissive glance at Paislee before turning her attention back to Michael. "After catching up last night, I thought we could grab a drink. If you need to feed, I'll wait. Better yet, I'll watch. Like old times."

Paislee felt like the ground had been ripped out from under her. Picking up her stuffed animal and clutching it to her chest, she mumbled an excuse and hurried upstairs, her heart pounding. She barely made it to her room before Michael was behind her, catching her arm as she reached for the door.

"Paislee—"

She yanked her arm free. "If you don't need me anymore tonight, Michael, I'd like to go to bed." Her words were soft but crisp, and her cheeks burned with humiliation. She didn't need Naevia to hear any more of this.

"Naevia was just kidding," Michael said, his tone low but urgent.

"You don't need to explain anything to me," she snapped. "I'm just a donor, right? A human."

"Paislee—"

"This is my sanctuary, Michael." She lifted her chin, willing her voice not to crack. "Please, leave."

There was change in his expression—hurt, anger, frustration—but he stepped back, his hands dropping to his sides. "You're right," he said quietly. "I won't bother you again tonight."

She nodded, her throat tight. With that, she shut the door, leaning against it as tears welled in her eyes.

Downstairs, Michael grabbed the drink Naevia had poured him and finished it in one gulp. He could still feel the weight of Paislee's words, her disappointment.

"That one's going to be trouble," Naevia remarked, swirling her own glass. "Cute, though. You'll want to get a handle on her."

Michael didn't respond. His mind was still upstairs, behind a closed door, with someone who made him question everything.

"I'm not in the mood to talk about my largitor, Naevia," he muttered, placing his glass in the sink.

Naevia stood beside him and leaned against the counter. She set down her glass, and her lips curved slightly as she met his gaze. "What are you in the mood for?"

# Chapter
# Twenty-Four

IT WAS STILL AND dark, with dawn not even a whisper beneath the horizon. Paislee couldn't bear another moment of sleeplessness, and her chest ached under the weight of unspoken thoughts. She'd lain awake, listening to the silence, as the void it had left gnawed at her until she couldn't take it. It had been hours since she'd heard Michael leave with Naevia.

Her bare feet whispered against the floor as she made her way downstairs. The house, bathed in the soft glow of moonlight, seemed to be holding its breath. She found Michael's bar with trembling hands and poured a drink, gulping it down in a vain attempt to dull her senses. The liquor burned, but it wasn't enough to quiet the storm inside her.

She turned to put the glass in the sink, and that was when she saw someone standing in the shadows. Startled, she dropped the glass, and her heart leaped as the sound echoed through the room.

Michael stood in the doorway, his figure half-shadowed and silent, his presence as striking as ever. She hadn't heard him arrive. He dangled his keys loosely in his hand before tossing them on the counter with a casual flick. The soft clink grounded the charged air between them.

He said nothing, his eyes fixed on her. A flicker of something unreadable danced across his face as he moved forward, each step deliberate, unnervingly quiet.

Paislee broke from her stare and started picking up the mess she'd made. Michael kneeled to gather the shards of glass, brushing her hand away. "I've got it, Paislee," he said, his voice low.

"No," she said, harsher than she intended, as the tension in her chest spilled over. The faint scent of perfume and liquor clung to him, needling her thoughts. "I can manage."

"You're barefoot," he replied, his tone firm and steady. "Step back."

She hesitated, but the authority in his voice left no room for argument. She rose and retreated, watching as he cleared the broken glass with meticulous care and then shrugged off his jacket. His movements were slow, deliberate, as he laid his jacket over the back of a chair.

When she turned to leave, he was suddenly there, blocking her path, his arms braced on either side of the island's countertop.

Paislee held her breath as Michael lowered his brow to the curve of her shoulder, his closeness drawing every nerve to her attention. His breathing was uneven, and his body felt rigid. He didn't speak, didn't move beyond that, yet the weight of his silence was crushing.

Instinctively, her hand found its way through his hair, threading through the dark strands. "Michael," she whispered, her voice trembling. "What's wrong?"

He didn't answer. Instead, his lips brushed the sensitive skin of her neck, soft at first, a whisper of a touch. Her breath stilled, and her body became rigid as he lingered there, caressing the curve of her neck. She inhaled sharply and braced herself. He wanted her blood, and she could barely blink back her tears. She reminded herself that it was her job. What he'd been doing all night with Naevia wasn't her business. The reality of her situation was raw and harsh, but again, she'd been warned. She tilted her head, focusing her gaze on the moonlight spilling in from the windows as his kisses trailed upward with maddening precision. When he attempted to kiss her mouth, she turned her head slightly.

He persisted, and she avoided his mouth again.

He paused, and his grip was firm as his fingers tangled in her hair, angling her face toward his, forcing her to face him. "Why are you fighting me?" he asked with a low, rough edge to his voice.

Her eyes met his, and she saw a glint of something raw and barely restrained. "You reek of perfume and whisky," she said, her voice catching. "If you're going to feed, then do it. Don't...make it more than it is."

A dark, humorless smiled curled at the corner of his mouth. "Is that what you think you want?" His words were a quiet storm, low and reverberating, drawing her further into his pull.

"I know it won't be as...painless," she said, nearly choking on the word, "but it's what I prefer."

"Is kissing me suddenly so terrible?"

Her eyes locked with his, and she lifted her chin despite his grip on her hair. "It's what I want."

"Do you know what I want, Paislee?" he asked, his mouth hovering over hers. "I want the torment you stir in me to subside."

She swallowed hard, and her pulse thrummed beneath her skin. "How can I possibly torment you?"

"You do so without even trying," he said through slightly parted lips, his fangs barely visible. His head dipped again as he tried to capture her mouth, but she refused his kiss again. "Why do you want me to hurt you?"

Her resolve wavered under his gaze, but she forced herself to speak. "I don't want an attachment, Michael. At least the pain will remind me why I'm here."

He leaned closer, and his eyes bored into hers. "If this is about Naevia—"

"Do what you must so I can go back to bed."

Michael stared at her for a long moment and then released his hold on her. She mumbled goodnight and attempted to leave, but he stopped her.

As he snaked one arm around her waist, his lips found the hollow of her throat, the curve of her collarbone, the line of her jaw. Each kiss was a deliberate claim, a slow unraveling of her defenses. Her body betrayed her, arching into his touch, and she gripped the counter with both hands for balance. His hand slid to her breast, teasing the taut peak with his thumb. She gasped as her body reacted with waves of sensations shooting through her.

His kisses lingered over her shoulder and then fluttered like butterflies across the delicate line of her jaw before stopping at her mouth, waiting for her invitation. He didn't receive it. She wouldn't kiss him.

He sank to one knee, and his lips descended further down her stomach. He gripped her hips as his kisses went further down, and he inched up her t-shirt. His tongue teased her hot flesh through the thin fabric of her panties, making her gasp.

Michael paused, his gaze holding hers while he slid the laced garment down her thighs. Forcing her legs to part slightly, he discarded it. His eyes darkened into a pool of endless depths. He inhaled sharply. "I believe you will complicate my life in many ways, Paislee."

His gaze was captivating, causing a haze to seep into her thoughts. "Then I will make things simple," she said, her voice a little more breathless than she'd hoped. "Our transactions are just that. I don't need your merciful tactics."

"Is that right?" he asked. His eyes still held hers captive, and his tongue flicked between her thighs, causing an instant sensation to radiate through her.

Paislee held her breath, gripping the counter behind her as his tongue caressed her. He started massaging between the thighs, his tongue teasing her, flicking over her wet flesh. "Michael," she said, her voice pained, "I don't need any of this. I'm not Nae—"

He straightened so quickly that she flinched, her head spinning. The muscles in his jaw flexed. "Don't," he said, cutting her off. "Don't finish that thought." His fingers rolled into the hem of her shirt, and he peeled it off her. "Since the night you kissed me, I've wanted this," he murmured, his voice thick with hunger and anguish. "You say you don't need my mercy. Then, fine. You won't have it."

The tension in his words struck her as quickly as his measured movements, with each touch igniting sparks beneath her skin. He gripped the backs of her knees and swiftly lifted her, setting her onto the island's cool marble.

His mouth drifted to her breasts, teasing them one at a time, his teeth grazing their taut peaks. Suckling them, and not gently, he made her breath stutter, and she instinctively pressed harder against his mouth.

He laid her back onto the counter and sent kisses down the line of her abdomen, with each kiss pulling her deeper into a haze. He stopped at her navel before his head sank between her thighs and claimed her hot center, his tongue massaging her, igniting flames that surged through her.

Mercilessly, his mouth devoured her, sending her body shaking. She gripped his hair and gasped. His touch was unrelenting, coaxing every nerve to life until he drove her mindless. She trembled as shockwaves spilled through her with each savage sweep of his tongue. Her skin tingled as the peak of ecstasy closed in.

Her world narrowed to the press of his lips, the heat of his hands, the raw hunger of his touch. As Michael pinned her hip with one hand and gripped her leg with the other, he sank his teeth into the sensitive flesh inside her thigh. The sting was almost a relief—a grounding anchor in the whirlwind he'd created.

And still, he didn't stop. He pushed her higher, further, until she broke apart. Her cries were swallowed by the quiet night from both her climax and the punctures of Michael's teeth.

Silence etched the tension between them as they settled from their high. Their breaths heavy and labored, Michael gently kissed her inner thigh and then sent small kisses back to the center of her. Her body was so heightened, so sensitive to the touch, that she shook uncontrollably and jerked beneath his lips.

He slowly straightened and, without a word, lifted her off the counter and carried her upstairs, his movements gentle now, almost tender. He pulled back the covers, laid her in his bed, and gathered her in his arms.

As the first signs of dawn streaked across the sky, they fell asleep.

# Chapter
# Twenty-Five

E SBEN'S STRIDES CRUNCHED THE broken sticks and leaves scattered over the ground beneath his shoes. The early morning sun barely streamed through the trees overhead, and a slight fog hovered low, drifting eerily above the cemetery.

He stopped walking and turned on his heels as he found the stone with the name Katya Sokolov etched along the front. The stone was ancient and cracked, but her body had only lain there for four years, a common deception the Order used to keep their secrets buried.

As his gaze fixed on her name, his hatred for Michael slowly resurfaced

"Esben, why are we meeting in a cemetery?" a voice asked, coming up behind him.

He didn't turn around to greet Alexander Bishop; he knew what he'd see.

Elitist arrogance.

Esben didn't like him. Another relic from a world that had long since passed its expiration date. To Esben, he was just another elite who put himself above the rest of those from humbler origins. Even now, he could feel that look of disgust boring into his back as he stared at Katya's grave.

"This is rather morbid, wouldn't you say?" Alexander asked.

Esben finally turned to him. Alexander wasn't even courteous enough to remove his sunglasses. They weren't necessary, considering the early morning hour, but an indication that he didn't want to talk with Esben, or even look at him.

"Do you ever come here, Alex? Ever come to look at the Order's work?"

Alexander remained unmoved, his solemn expression as thin and cool as his black London Fog jacket.

"I have no reason to. I carry no blame," Alexander replied coolly. "However, if I were you, I'd come every day. You can remind yourself of your own part in her demise."

Alexander handed Esben a leather-bound folder with an embossed cardinal on it. "Go through the proper channels next time."

Esben took the folder and opened it, and then his eyes scanned the application inside. "How long does this take?" he asked.

"We're backed up, but it shouldn't be too long," Alexander replied. His tone was noncommittal, and Esben glared at him.

"You're the high adjudicator of the Cardinal Order and the archon of the Eastern Judiciary."

"And there's still a process I must abide by," Alexander said. "You can return the paperwork to me. I'm not meeting with you again. I don't need your dreary games, Esben."

Esben gave Alexander a quiet curl of his mouth.

Alexander turned around and marched out of the cemetery without giving the grave they had been standing at another glance. But Esben did after several moments of watching Alexander's back as he headed for his car.

Esben took one last look at Katya's stone and frowned. Then he spat on it. "Bitch," he muttered and then walked away from the grave.

As he sauntered through the old cemetery, he couldn't seem to shake that smirk from his face.

One thought kept replaying in his mind.

*Michael is finally going to pay.*

Paislee tied up her freshly washed hair in a loose bun, slipped on her shorts, and pulled a hoodie over her head before she descended the stairs. She could hear Michael on the phone in his office.

She went to the kitchen and found a macchiato waiting for her. Next to it was an appointment card for a clinic. It had her name on it, along with an address and time. She picked up the card and noted the cardinal in the clinic's logo.

Her steps were muffled by the thickly carpeted marble as she padded into Michael's office. She drank in the sleek, masculine décor, from his mahogany desk to the black leather chair positioned in the center of the gray and white-trimmed room. She inhaled the aroma of leather, lemon wax, and Michael's cologne.

He was dressed brilliantly in black suit pants, a crisp white shirt, and a silk tie. He looked up from whatever he'd been writing down and offered her the faintest smile. She tiptoed into the office and held up the card.

He nodded once, then he said something in Italian. The man on speaker replied, and Michael gave a short, amused response. He went back a forth with the guy on the phone another moment. She couldn't understand anything they were saying but it all seemed lighthearted, and Michael's hand movements were animated. She suppressed her smile, watching him talk with his hands.

She wondered why he didn't do that when he was speaking English.

Michael motioned her closer. When she got close enough, he pulled her in front of him, and she braced against the desk.

Michael had a mischievous yet hungry stare that was starting to feel familiar as he began sliding his hands up the length of her exposed legs.

He made so little space between his chair and the desk that she sat on the desktop, and he gave a satisfied grin.

"*Michele? Michele? Cosa stai dicendo?*" she heard the guy on the phone repeat.

Michael said simply, "*Arrivederci,*" and hung up.

The moment the call ended, the atmosphere grew still. Heavy.

He relaxed in his chair, and as he observed her sitting on his desk, several emotions crossed his face. The tension between them hadn't lessened since last night.

His eyes dropped to where his fingers had touched her thighs. Her skin flushed hot in response.

"I want to apologize for my behavior last night," he said, his voice lower now. "I should've shown more restraint."

She'd woken up naked in his bed, with vivid images of him going down on her on the kitchen counter flashing in her mind. Admittedly, she'd enjoyed every second of it, even, strangely, when he'd pierced her flesh. It was the most erotic moment she'd ever experienced—and almost seemed like a natural part of what they'd done.

"I didn't hate it," she said, softly. "And that scares me."

Michael stayed quiet.

She wondered what it would be like if Michael actually made love to her. Well, it wouldn't be love, though, would it? It would be just sex, Michael finally losing control and succumbing to his passion. But something told her that he wouldn't do that. And a part of her didn't want him to. She'd consent—there was no doubt—but with it, she'd surrender her heart. And the idea that Michael wouldn't accept it was devastating.

She cleared her throat and held out the card again, needing something to focus on. "I have an appointment this morning?"

Michael took it from her hand, brushing her fingers. "It shouldn't be too long. A car will be picking you up in about an hour."

She nodded and rose from the desk. But he stopped her with a hand at her hip. He stood up and lifted her chin with his finger. "Please don't avoid looking at me, ducizza."

He brushed her lips with his before grabbing his jacket, swinging it over his arm, and leaving the house.

Less than two hours later, Paislee was sitting on a medical table in her assigned clinic. Her doctor, Daniel M. Breton, was reserved but friendly. Quietly efficient. The kind of man who left no impression at all. He ordered a series of tests to be taken and about nine vials of blood.

There was a lot of paperwork, and the nurse walking Paislee through the screening process, Rosa, was pleasant enough. Her bubbly personality and shaking shoulders whenever she cracked a joke lessened the awkwardness and tension.

Paislee glanced at the lined up vials as Rosa prepared them. "Is that...a lot?"

Rosa paused, mid-label, then gave a sheepish laugh. "Oh—uh, usually it's six," she admitted, her smile tightening. "But Dr. Breton likes to be thorough."

There was a beat. Rosa's smile faltered slightly, and she looked toward the doctor. Dr. Breton didn't look up from his tablet.

"All routine," he said evenly, fingers still tapping his tablet. Then he swiftly stood up and left the room.

The air stilled for a second. Rosa cleared her throat and busied herself with the tray.

Something about the moment stayed with Paislee.

"Do you have any questions?"

"So many," Paislee said with a sigh. "None I think you're permitted to answer."

Rosa's pink cheeks rounded. "It's overwhelming, I know. But you'll get settled in soon enough, and life will feel more normal."

Paislee lifted a brow. "I don't think normal will ever be how I describe it."

Rosa chuckled. "As close to normal as it can be," she corrected. "I was where you are, once upon a time. Believe me, you'll adjust."

"You were a sanguinis..."

"Largitor sanguinis. Yes, I was, and I've processed many humans since then. You're strong, a fighter, which is what Michael Chamberlain needs."

Paislee shook her head. "I'm not sure about that."

Rosa placed a hand on hers and squeezed it gently. "Trust me. You've got what it takes, Ms. Sullivan."

Michael went into the city and was gone most of the day, so Paislee enjoyed the time to herself. It was quiet, but it gave her time to think. And think. Until she was tired of thinking.

When he returned, night had fallen.

He didn't say much, just went upstairs to get ready for the club as she lounged on the couch.

When he came back downstairs, he passed by her, dressed in black trousers, his white dress shirt rolled at the sleeves. His hair looked more casual, and he'd left the shadow along his jaw. She inhaled the scent of his cologne: sandalwood and musk with a faint citrus undernote.

"I'll lock up," he said, and then he grabbed his keys. "Don't wait up. I won't be back until dawn." He spun around and patted his pockets. Then he went back upstairs to look for his wallet.

As Paislee returned to watching the television, until someone rang. at the door. She rolled off the sectional and opened it.

She wished she hadn't.

Naevia breezed past her in a sparkling bodycon and strutted toward the kitchen in heels that, Paislee guessed, were about five inches. If Naevia hadn't been so short, she would've towered over Paislee.

Paislee tried to forget Naevia was there and headed back to the living room.

"Come here," Naevia called, snapping her fingers.

Paislee turned and placed a hand on her hip. "I'm not a lap dog."

Naevia's mouth tipped into a smirk. "Paislee, is it?" she asked, closing the distance between them. "You're a feisty human—"

"A feisty human who doesn't have to acknowledge your existence," Paislee said and turned toward the living room again.

Naevia snatched her arm and pulled her back with frightening speed and strength. "I think you're confused about something," she said. "I'm a cardinalis, and you'll show me the proper respect."

Paislee looked at Naevia's long fingers and perfectly manicured nails curling around her arm. "I'm not contracted to you, so I needn't show you a damn thing."

Naevia arched her brows and let out a soft laugh. "Michael always did like a challenge. I'm going to enjoy watching him break you."

Her words stabbed Paislee's chest, as she instantly imagined them as a couple, bending Paislee to their will. Would Michael really do that? Did their contract give her the freedom to deny Michael if that was what he'd wished to do? Suddenly, she regretted not taking the lawyer's advice for representation and a clarification of her rights and obligations.

Paislee looked at Naevia in all her sparkle and bit back the tears stinging her eyes. "I wish both of you luck in that venture," she said. She attempted to leave again, but Naevia's grip tightened.

Paislee lost her temper.

She spun around and swept Naevia's leg out from under her. With Naevia's high heels, it was easy to make her land on the floor with a thud. Whatever the backlash, it would be worth it just to see her hit the ground.

Paislee's victory was short-lived, though, as Naevia got up with remarkable speed. Hissing, her fangs flashing, she lunged at Paislee.

Somehow, Michael appeared between them and held Naevia back.

"The fuck is going on?" he demanded.

"Your human needs to be put on a leash, Michael," Naevia snarled.

"Fuck off!" Paislee shouted. "Vampire!"

Naevia's eyes widened to a psychotic degree, and she went for Paislee again.

Paislee prepared to be slaughtered, but Michael wrapped an arm around Naevia and lifted her off the ground.

"Let me go, Michael! I'm going to tear that bit—"

Michael growled and glared at Paislee as he held onto Naevia's flaring body. "Damn it, Paislee! Go upstairs!"

Paislee inhaled sharply. "Excuse me? I'm not a chil—"

"You're my largitor, and you will know your place! Go. Upstairs!"

Paislee's cheeks felt like they were on fire as she glanced from Naevia to Michael. Squaring her shoulders, she stormed up the stairs.

From her bedroom, she could hear Michael leave with Naevia.

Once she heard his car drive away, she buried her face in her pillows and cried.

# Chapter
# Twenty-Six

MICHAEL GRIPPED THE STEERING wheel tighter than was necessary as he drove with his jaw clenched and his eyes fixed on the road ahead. Naevia sat beside him with a smug expression plastered across her face. He could feel her gaze on him, waiting for him to speak, but he refused to give her the satisfaction. Not yet.

The evening air was cool, but inside, Michael burned with barely contained anger. The scene in the house replayed in his mind—Paislee's defiance, Naevia's arrogance, and his own harsh words. He itched with regret for the way he'd spoken to Paislee, whose face had been etched with hurt and humiliation before she stormed upstairs.

"Your resource is a problem," Naevia said finally, her voice dripping with disdain. "The pet thinks too highly of herself."

Michael's grip on the wheel tightened until his knuckles turned white. "They're not our pets, Naevia," he growled, and the words came out sharper than he'd intended.

Naevia smirked, clearly unfazed. "Call largitores whatever you want. Mine know their place. You should've let me handle her."

"Handle her?" Michael repeated, his tone dangerous. "You're out of line. She's under my protection. You had no right to even approach her."

Naevia leaned back, feigning indifference, but the glint in her eyes revealed her pleasure in riling him up. "Under your protection?" she echoed mockingly. "How noble you make it all sound. Wait. Don't tell me you're getting attached?"

Michael didn't respond. He couldn't. And his silence spoke louder than any denial he could have.

"Are you serious, Michael?" she asked, incredulous. "Falling for humans may be acceptable for the lower classes, but not a cardinalis of your status."

Michael shook his head. "Don't make more out of it than it is, Naevia."

"Oh, my." She released a bitter laugh. "Remember that emotions like love and affection are weaknesses in our world, vulnerabilities that are exploited."

Michael remained silent, wondering how Paislee had slipped past his defenses, worming her way into the cracks he hadn't even realized existed. Her fire, her stubbornness, the way she refused to back down—it infuriated him as much as it intrigued him. He'd convinced himself that his strong attachment to her was a result of his hatred for his brother.

It was a lie he could no longer tell himself.

Paislee cried until there was nothing left. Her tears dried and were replaced by a hollow ache in her chest. She stared blankly at the ceiling, trying to steady her breathing. Her phone broke the silence.

She glanced at the screen to see Kendra FaceTiming her. She wiped away her tears and answered, forcing a smile as Kendra and Tessa burst into an impromptu, off-key rendition of a song. It was loud, obnoxious, and exactly what Paislee needed.

"What are you doing, Pais?" Tessa asked, fluffing her curls as she adjusted the camera.

"Nothing," Paislee replied, swallowing back the lump in her throat.

"Were you crying?" Kendra asked. Then she demanded, "What's wrong?"

"Just bored," Paislee lied. Then she added truthfully, "I miss you guys. Miss home."

"Where's GQ?" Kendra asked.

"Working," Paislee muttered.

Tessa and Kendra let out exaggerated whoops. "Girl, we got you!" Kendra hollered. "Hang tight. We're on the way!"

Before Paislee could protest, they hung up. A genuine laugh escaped her lips as she dropped the phone onto the bed.

It wasn't long before the sound of pounding on the front door jolted Paislee from her quiet contemplation. Moments later, Kendra and Tessa stormed in, armed with a bottle of Jäger and Red Bull.

"It's on, Pais!" Kendra declared, holding up the liquor. "We brought the cure for all your woes."

"Wow, this place is insane!" Tessa twirled in the center of the living room, soaking in Michael's lavish beach house. Her strawberry curls bounced as she marveled at the decor. Kendra wasted no time syncing her phone to the stereo, and soon, the walls were vibrating with bass-heavy music.

Shots were poured, glasses clinked, and laughter filled the space. Kendra raised her glass. "To you, Pais! Even though you quit my dream job and ran off with Mr. Tall, Dark, and Broody, I'm not even mad anymore."

"I'd leave Kendra, too, if it meant living here," Tessa teased, leaning against the counter. "I can imagine what the wedding will look like!"

Kendra hooked her arm in Tessa's. "A honeymoon in Barbados!"

Paislee flushed. "God, we're not getting married."

"Yet," Kendra shot back, winking before downing her drink.

The shots multiplied. So did their energy. Soon, the living room became a makeshift dance floor, alcohol blurring the edges and loosening laughter. Tessa's voice rose above the music. "We should take this party out! Let's hit a club."

Paislee hesitated, remembering Michael's voice echoed in her mind. *No clubs. No excuses.* He'd made himself clear.

"I can't," she said, more to herself than to them.

"Why not?" Kendra asked, frowning.

Paislee's mind raced as she struggled for an excuse. The truth was too twisted. Too humiliating. The image of Michael scolding her earlier like a child still lingered. He'd defended Naevia. Punished her. And she swallowed it like she'd deserved it. Like she was beneath both of them. Heat climbed her neck.

"He wouldn't want me to," she muttered, barely audible.

"So?" Tessa pressed. "He doesn't own you."

*Yes, he does.* Paislee's grip tightened on her glass. The alcohol loosened her nerves, and defiance bubbled to the surface as she imagined him with Naevia. She forced a smile. "You're right."

But her stomach turned as the lie left her lips.

Minutes later, dressed to kill, the trio piled into an Uber. As they laughed and shouted over each other, the energy in the car was electric.

"Allusion," Tessa called out to the driver.

"No," Paislee interjected sharply. "The Zanzibar."

Her friends exchanged glances but didn't question her choice.

They entered the club of molten gold. Low lights flickered over pharaohs and Anubis statues that towered over the crowd, shadows dancing through the haze. The music was deafening, a pounding rhythm that matched Paislee's heartbeat as she followed her friends to the bar, where the bartender flirted shamelessly with Tessa.

They started with shots. One. Two. Three.

"To the Hamptons," Paislee called, and they hollered before they tipped back their glasses. Paislee nearly choked on the liquid as it burned its way down her throat. Her skin flushed. She was already buzzing from the Jäger at Michael's.

The alcohol coursing through Paislee's veins made her fearless. Soon, they were pulling each other onto the dance floor.

The crowd swallowed them. Music throbbed. Light cut across strangers' faces like strobes. They danced, spinning and laughing. Men approached, trying to edge into their circle.

Paislee turned, laughing at something Kendra said, and froze.

A man stood just outside their circle. His sharp features and hazel eyes gleamed under the lights. Watching. Unmoving. Something in his stillness made her breath catch.

As she spun away, trying to shrug the uneasy feeling that had crept up her spine, a hand clamped around her waist. She stumbled slightly, landing against a solid chest. She stiffened. The man's grip was strong, his voice smoother than silk. "Who do you belong to?"

She turned and was staring into the flashing hollows of hazel eyes. A cardinalis' eyes. She averted her gaze. "No one," Paislee replied, trying to step away. His grip tightened. He eased her away from Kendra and Tessa.

"Don't lie," he murmured. "You wear the scent of venom like a collar, but I don't see anyone protecting you."

Her blood ran cold. Her stomach dropped. "He's by the bar," she lied.

"I don't think he is. And if he wanted you safe, he'd be here." The man smirked. His teeth flashed as he leaned in. His breath brushed her neck. "So, I'm sure he won't mind if I borrow what's his."

Before she could pull away, his hand slid lower, gripping her bottom firmly. Panic bloomed. He'd dragged her another step toward the edge of the dance floor. And that was when she realized she couldn't see Kendra or Tessa anymore. They were lost in the sea of bodies.

Michael leaned against the bar at Allusion, surveying the bustling crowd. The club was alive tonight, filled with the scent of liquor and the pulse of music. Normally, this energy would have fueled him, but tonight, his thoughts were elsewhere. They drifted back to Paislee—her anger, the hurt in her eyes as he'd scolded her. An unfamiliar unease gnawed at him. He told himself she was safe at home, probably sulking on the couch.

A longtime friend of Naevia's, and a familiar face from Michael's wilder years, approached the bar. She leaned casually across the bar, her nails tapping the polished surface in rhythm with music. She wore nostalgia like perfume.

"What can I get you, Leslie?"

"You know what I like." Her smile curved with familiarity, as if nothing had changed.

Michael didn't look at her right away. Instead, he reached for the gin behind him. Top shelf, citrus-forward. He measured it precisely, added lemon juice and a touch of simple syrup. The shaker snapped shut in his hands, ice rattled.

He strained the mixture into a chilled coupe glass, topped it with champagne, and slid it across the bar without a word. No garnish. No flourish.

Leslie's smile deepened as she took it. "Still know me."

He finally met her eyes, flat, unreadable. "I know what used to work."

"Michael, you should come with us to the after-party," Leslie said, sliding onto the stool in front of him. As she toyed with the stem of her drink, her lips curled into a playful smile.

Naevia took the stool beside Leslie and leaned in next to her, clinking her glass lightly against Leslie's. Her presence was effortless, her smile already curling. "Seth can close tonight. Come have some fun with us, Michael. Relieve some of that tension."

His hand stilled on the shaker.

Just for a second.

The two of them. Dark-eyed, knowing, and beautiful. Perched together across the bar like specters of a life that used to thrill him. Used to consume him. Now, they just looked like ghosts in a place that no longer felt like his.

He shook his head as he reached for another bottle. "Not tonight."

Leslie tilted her head, mock-pouting. "Your loss, Michael."

Naevia swirled the cherry in her drink before slipping it between her lips, letting the stem fall back into the glass. "I don't know what's gotten into you, but it's strange seeing you so...distracted."

"I'm perfectly fine," he replied dryly, dismissing her with a glance. She laughed softly and they both sauntered to the dance floor. But her words lingered.

"Something on your mind?" Seth murmured as he slid a towel across the bar.

Michael shook his head, not wanting to discuss it. Instead, he grabbed a bottle of vodka and busied himself with pouring drinks. But then another familiar voice pulled him from his thoughts.

"Michael!" Jared greeted, slapping a hand on his shoulder. "Busy night, yeah?"

Michael gripped Jared's hand firmly in a friendly shake. "Always is. What can I get you?"

"A couple of beers," Jared replied, gesturing to the friend beside him.

Michael served their beers, but before he could move on, Jared leaned closer. "When did you get so lenient with your largitores, eh?"

Michael froze for a fraction of a second before he continued wiping the counter. "What are you talking about?"

Jared smirked, taking a long swig of his beer. "That sexy brunette. The one who used to work here. She's yours now, isn't she?"

Michael's jaw tightened. "Where are you going with this?"

"We just came from The Zanzibar," Jared said casually. "Saw her there, tearing up the dance floor with her friends."

"She's hard to miss," his friend David added with a grin. "She and her friends were causing a scene—looked like they were having the time of their lives."

The words barely registered over the sudden roar in Michael's ears. He reached for his phone and scrolled through his messages.

Nothing from Paislee.

His thumb hovered over her contact, but he didn't call.

Not yet.

"Think I'm getting soft?" Michael asked, his nonchalance carefully controlled.

"Just saying," Jared replied. "If I had someone like her, I'd keep her here where I could keep an eye on her."

Michael's grip on the bar tightened, the strain visible in the tension of his forearm.

David chuckled, oblivious to Michael's darkening mood. "Yeah, man, she was getting plenty of attention. I wouldn't let her out of my sight."

Seth, who had been silently observing, placed a hand on Michael's shoulder. "Go," he said quietly. "I'll cover for you."

Michael didn't need to be told twice.

With sharp and purposeful movements, he tossed the towel onto the counter and grabbed his keys.

# Chapter Twenty-Seven

MICHAEL'S MERCEDES SCREECHED TO a halt in front of The Zanzibar, and he stepped out. After swiftly slamming the car door, he marched toward the entrance. The bouncer manning the door saw him and immediately unhooked the chain reining in the long line. "Hey, Michael. What are you doing here?"

"I'm looking for someone," he said, his voice low and cutting, as he passed the line and entered the club.

The pounding bass of The Zanzibar hit Michael the moment he stepped inside. The club was packed, with bodies moving under flashing lights, but he cut through the crowd with ease. His sharp eyes scanned the sea of people, searching for her.

It didn't take long to find Kendra and Tessa, both laughing and dancing, surrounded by eager onlookers. But Paislee wasn't with them. His stomach tightened. Kendra saw him and let him past the guys encircling them.

"Michael," Kendra said, her face flushed from drink. "What are you doing here?"

Tessa's eyes widened. "Oh, my God, you're Michael?" she said, her words slurred.

"Where's Paislee?" he asked, barely able to keep his tone calm.

Kendra and Tessa glanced around. "She was just here—"

He stormed away and pushed further into the crowd, his senses on high alert as he searched the crowd.

And then he saw her.

She was off to the side, caught in the grip of another man.

Michael's eyes narrowed.

Adam.

A cardinalis with a reputation for pushing boundaries. His hand rested low on Paislee's waist, and his head was tilted close to hers. Her posture was subtly tense and she tried to pull away. Adam wouldn't let her.

Michael reached them just in time to hear Adam murmur, "Let me have a try."

Michael's voice cut through the chaos like a blade. "Adam."

Adam froze, his smirk faltering as he turned to face Michael. "Michael," he greeted. "Didn't realize she was yours."

"She is," Michael replied coldly. He stepped closer, his presence radiating menace. "Let go of her."

Adam raised his hands in mock surrender, but the smugness in his expression remained. "No disrespect, Chamberlain. Just a misunderstanding."

Ignoring the excuse, Michael briefly shifted his attention to Paislee. She leaned into his side, but he avoided her gaze.

"Wait," Adam called out as Michael began to lead her away. He reached out, saying, "Maybe we could—" but Michael's fist connected with his jaw before he could finish speaking.

Adam staggered back, and his hand flew to his face. "I meant no disrespect!" he protested as blood dripped from his split lip.

Michael didn't respond. He grabbed Paislee's hand and guided her firmly through the crowd. She didn't protest, though he could feel her trembling. When they reached the dance floor, Kendra and Tessa's laughter died as they spotted them.

"Let's go," he ordered, his tone leaving no room for argument.

The drive back to Paislee's uncle's house was silent. He dropped off her friends without a word before turning the car back toward the beach house. His knuckles were white on the steering wheel, and his jaw was locked as he struggled to contain the storm of emotions churning within him.

Paislee didn't speak, either, sitting with her arms crossed tightly as she stared out the window. By the time they arrived home, the silence felt heavier than anything they could have said.

He pulled into the beach house garage, and the engine cut off immediately. The tension in the car was suffocating, the silence more deafening than any argument. He continued gripping the steering wheel for a long moment, as if willing himself to calm down, before finally stepping out. He didn't wait for Paislee to follow.

Paislee slammed the car door behind her and followed Michael into the house, her anger simmering just beneath the surface. The crash of the door slamming shut behind him reverberated through the quiet space. His strides were quick and purposeful as he disappeared into the main room and poured a drink from his bar. After swallowing the contents of his tumbler in one gulp, he immediately poured another.

"You didn't have to drag me out of there like that," Paislee finally snapped, her voice trembling with a mix of anger and lingering embarrassment. "You humiliated me. Again!"

Michael slammed down his empty tumbler on the bar and spun around to face her. His expression was thunderous, and his dark eyes blazed with fury. "You embarrassed me—and humiliated *yourself*," he shot back, his voice low and dangerous. "Do you have any idea what you've done?"

"I went to the club with my friends," she said, crossing her arms. "I had fun. That's not a crime."

"You were forbidden to go to the clubs!"

"It may be your preference, but that's not in my contract. I guess you should've put that in there!"

"You want to talk technicalities, Paislee?" He laughed bitterly, the sound devoid of humor. "Was it worth putting yourself and your friends in danger? Worth letting someone like Adam get his hands on you?"

She flinched as the memory of Adam's grip on her waist flashed in her mind. But she pushed it aside, her defiance flaring. "I was startled, that's all. But I was handling it."

"Handling it," Michael growled, stepping closer. "He was about to drag you out of that club, and you were just going to let him."

"I wasn't—"

"Do you have any idea what he would've done to you? What could've happened if I hadn't shown up?"

Her anger boiled over, spilling out in a rush. "You don't get to act like I'm some damsel in distress! I didn't ask for your help, Michael. I didn't ask for *any* of this."

His nostrils flared, and his jaw tightened. "You think this is about you asking for my help? This is about your reckless stupidity putting yourself and everyone around you at risk!"

Paislee glared at him as anger flared in her chest. "Maybe if you didn't treat me like I'm beneath you, like some fragile thing you own, I wouldn't have to sneak out just to feel human!"

His laugh was cold, biting. "Feel human? Is that what this is about? Flaunting yourself in a club, letting men paw at you, makes you feel human?"

Her cheeks burned. "Feeling human is having a connection you clearly don't understand. And tonight was about having fun with my friends—because I'm a fucking adult and I can!"

Something snapped in him. "You can't!" Michael took another step toward her, his presence towering over her.

"I don't belong to you, Michael!"

"Wrong," he hissed, his voice low and venomous. "You're my largitor, Paislee. You *do* belong to me! That's the reality of this world."

His words struck like a blow, and for a long moment, she could only stare at him.

"You're right; you did warn me." Her voice was quieter when she spoke, but no less fierce. "But I can't belong to anyone."

She brushed past him, her movements stiff, her mind racing as she went for the front door. She needed to get away from him—his anger, his arrogance, his suffocating presence. But Michael was faster. His hand shot out, grabbing her and yanking her back. She stumbled, gasping as she turned to face him.

"You're not leaving," he growled, his grip unrelenting.

"Let me go," she said, her voice steady even as her pulse kicked into panic.

His eyes burned, hot and wild. And for the first time, she saw something had frayed in them. Not anger. Not control. Desperation.

"You're under a contract. You're not going anywhere, Paislee."

"Let the Order arrest me," she spat. "At least in a cell, I'll get away from you—and your brother!"

He flinched. Just barely. But then he took a step closer, like her defiance pulled something loose in him.

"You walk out that door," he said, voice low, "Esben *will* come after you."

She froze.

She knew he saw it. Hesitation, the edge of fear. And he seized it. "He knows you're mine and he will take you just to spite me."

Paislee's fist clenched. "I'm not a fucking bargaining chip between the two of you," she spat. "Let him come! I dare him."

Michael's jaw ticked. "Do you have any idea what you're inviting?" he asked, his voice rough.

"I guess I'll find out."

"Paislee—"

"I'm within my trial period. I can leave," she said, twisting her arm, trying to free herself from his iron grip. "You can't keep me."

His fingers trembled slightly against her skin before they tightened again. His chest rose and fell unevenly, and she saw something fracture behind his eyes.

She finally wrenched free his grasp, and stumbled back a step.

The pressure from his grip faded from her skin, but a chill followed, crawling into the space where his touch had been. She saw the tension lining his shoulders, saw it in the way his eyes tracked her as she backed away. Not like a lover, but like something being cornered.

Her chest ached, but she straightened, willing herself not to look back.

*Don't look back.*

Just walk. Just go. It's the right thing.

She turned toward the door.

"Paislee, don't leave me—"

"I'll have my stuff picked up later."

He moved before she reached the door knob. A gasp escaped her as his arm snaked around her waist, pulling her back. He turned her, not gently, and caught her hair in his fist, tipping her head before she could resist.

"Michael—" she started, but it was too late. Everything happened in a flash. She barely saw his fangs descending in the dim light before they sank into her neck. Her heart leaped in her throat as a pain shot through her, sharp and searing—then distant. His venom, fast and unrelenting, numbed her almost instantly.

She cried out, and her body went rigid as his grip on her tightened. She tried to push him away, but he was unyielding.

The room spun as the pull of his bite made her weak, and her legs threatened to give out beneath her.

Her thoughts blurred. Her body buckled, trembling against him. And then, just as abruptly as it had started, it stopped. He released her and stepped back as though he'd been burned.

Paislee stumbled, clutching her neck. Her fingers found the puncture wounds, and the sticky warmth of her own blood sent a shudder through her. She looked at him, her vision clouded by tears.

Michael stood frozen, his chest heaving. Blood stained his lips. His expression was a mixture of horror and shame.

He took a step toward her, reaching out, but she flinched away. "Paislee..." His voice was soft, almost pleading, but she cut him off.

"Don't touch me," she managed, her voice shaking.

The words hung in the air, heavy and final. For a moment, he didn't move, his hand falling limply to his side.

Paislee didn't wait to see anything else. She turned and ran up the stairs to her room.

When she reached the safety of her room, she locked the door and pressed her back against it, her chest heaving with sobs. Her fingers shook as they touched her neck again. As she slid to the floor, tears streamed down her cheeks.

Michael sat alone in the darkness, staring out at the ocean, his hands still shaking, the taste of Paislee's blood still on his tongue, a reminder of how far he'd fallen. He clenched his fists as a growl rumbled low in his throat.

*What have I done?*

The question echoed in his mind, over and over, but no answer came. Because there was no justification. No excuse. He'd done the one thing he'd sworn he'd never do. He'd hurt her. In a way he could never undo. The look in her eyes, the tears, the *hatred*—it would haunt him for the rest of his existence.

His instincts had taken over. That's what he told himself. That's what he wanted to believe. But deep down, he knew the truth. It wasn't instinct alone. It was anger.

It was fear.

It was the unbearable weight of everything he couldn't admit to himself.

She had pushed him, challenged him, threatened to leave. And instead of letting her go, instead of swallowing his pride, he had punished her. He ached just thinking about it, a sick reminder of the moment he'd crossed the line. He acted like the monster she now believed him to be.

The worst part was how right she was.

*Don't touch me.*

Her words cut deeper than any blade, deeper than anything he'd felt in decades. He'd taken something from her—her trust, her safety, her belief that he was anything more than the beast he'd accused Esben of being.

He leaned forward, burying his face in his hands. His chest felt tight, and his breaths were shallow and uneven. He didn't cry. He hadn't in lifetimes.

If that part of him hadn't been stripped away long ago, he thought he might now.

He'd destroyed everything. The thought hit him like a blow to the chest, stealing what little air he had left.

He couldn't even bring himself to go upstairs, to knock on her door, to try to explain.

What would he say?

What could he possibly say to undo what he'd done?

Nothing.

He clenched his jaw, his mind racing but landing nowhere. There were no answers tonight. Just silence. Just regret. Just the faint sound of her heartbeat, muffled by the walls but steady enough to remind him that she was still there. For now.

And for the first time in his long life, Michael was truly afraid. Not of losing control. Not of the monster within him. But of losing her—and knowing he had no one to blame but himself.

# Chapter Twenty-Eight

E SBEN TOSSED HIS KEYS to the valet and climbed the stone steps of the sprawling neoclassical mansion. As he rapped on the heavy double doors, his eyes were drawn to the weathered gargoyle leering from the archway above. The door creaked open, revealing an older man whose sour expression rivaled the stone guardian.

"Good morning," the man said flatly. "What brings you here?"

"I need a word with Lady Autry," Esben replied, his smile as sharp as his tone.

The man gestured him inside with a begrudging nod. "Wait here."

Esben wandered into the foyer, his steps echoing on the polished marble floor. His gaze flicked over the gilded frames holding somber portraits and pastoral landscapes, their artistry both beautiful and suffocating in their perfection. Time dragged as his reflection stared back at him from the glossy surface of a nearby console table.

"She'll see you now," the butler called, snapping Esben out of his thoughts.

Following the man down a long corridor, Esben soon entered a grand office. Mahogany furnishings gleamed beneath a plastered ceiling adorned with ornate trim, but his focus shifted to the far corner. Lady Autry, clad in sleek navy yoga pants, was on a treadmill, her steady pace exuding controlled elegance.

"Mr. Regnanti, my lady," the butler announced before stepping aside.

Esben lingered, watching her ease to a stop and grab a towel. She dabbed her brow, and he noted the graceful curve of her neck before she reached for a water bottle. The small act felt calculated in its casualness, as if she knew he was watching.

"Thank you, Hector. That will be all," she said, her voice dismissive.

Once the butler disappeared, Esben sauntered forward. "Lottie," he greeted; the familiarity in his tone was deliberate.

She turned, arching a brow as she moved to an overstuffed green and gold chair. "My friends call me Lottie, Esben," she said coldly, her voice cutting like glass. "You can address me as 'my lady.'"

Esben smirked, unbothered, as he slid into the chair opposite hers. "Still holding a grudge, are we?"

"I think everyone is, for one reason or another."

"Well, I refuse to address you so formally after already having you naked and on your knees," he replied.

Her eyes narrowed. "If you're here to dig up the past, I'll save you the trouble—it's buried. Now, state your business."

He leaned back, feigning nonchalance. "I have a small problem that you're uniquely positioned to solve."

Her laugh was dry, her eyes unyielding. "Whatever it is, I doubt it warrants my involvement."

"Then I'll cut to the chase," he said. "I've applied for an approval on a human transition. It's been delayed. Deliberately, I suspect."

"Hmm," she mused, taking a measured sip of water. "What makes you think I care?"

"You're on the board," he said plainly. "You could expedite things."

"And why would I do that?"

He hesitated just long enough to unsettle her. "Because it concerns Michael."

The sharp intake of her breath betrayed her otherwise composed exterior. She recovered quickly, narrowing her gaze. "Michael has nothing to do with you."

"Oh, but he does. This human I've requested? She's under his contract."

"Then you already know the answer, Esben. Her contract stands unless it times out or he terminates it."

Esben leaned forward, his grin wolfish. "What if I told you the contract is void? She was mine first, Lottie. I had initial claim and was already beginning the process before Michael swooped in."

Lottie shrugged and took another sip of water. "You failed to finalize the contract, Esben. That makes her fair game."

"No, it doesn't. The Order has rules for these situations, and I've filed a grievance. Once reviewed, you'll see this contract was invalid from the start."

"This is petty, even for you, Esben," she said, her tone laced with disgust.

"How important she must be for Michael to go such lengths," Esben said with a twisted grin. "You know what I'm insinuating."

Her eyes flickered with surprise before hardening. "This is a pathetic attempt to bait me. Michael's royalty. He wouldn't—"

"Wouldn't what? Take a human as his mate?" Esben chuckled darkly. "Tell me, Lottie, how many nights have you wasted convincing yourself he'd come back to you? You voted to end Katya because she threatened your delusion—"

"She was your largitor, Esben, and she couldn't handle being turned. The Order did what was best for everyone involved. Michael was trying to save Katya."

He clicked his tongue. "But Paislee is different. He won't let her go. He'd get himself killed first. That's more enthusiasm than he's ever shown for you—even when you were together."

Her fangs gleamed as she stood abruptly. "Get out."

Esben rose slowly, placing his palms on the desk between them. "You think I'm lying?" His voice dropped, coiling like a snake ready to strike. "Michael nearly killed me over her."

The room fell silent. Her posture stiffened, and her hands clenched at her sides. He could see the storm brewing in her mind, weighing every option against the flickering embers of jealousy.

"Approve the application," he said, his tone softening but no less venomous. "Let me take her off his hands. You'll be doing yourself a favor."

Her laugh was hollow. "And you think he'll just...let this go?"

"He'll have no choice," Esben countered. "But you? You might have his attention again."

She stared him down for several agonizing seconds. "You're despicable."

"And you're predictable," he replied, with satisfaction curling his lips. "I'll let myself out."

As he exited, his silence followed him, and a bitter triumph settled in his chest.

# Chapter
# Twenty-Nine

P AISLEE STOOD IN THE center of her sanctuary, though it no longer felt like one. The bed was made, and the closet was empty, with everything packed and lined up by the door. A sense of finality hung in the air, thick and suffocating. Her fingers ghosted over the marks on her neck, barely healed yet still tender, as if his presence lingered beneath her skin.

Days had passed since the fight—since he had lost control. Silence had settled between them like an unspoken truce, one that neither dared to break. She had barely left her room, and Michael...Michael had found ways to disappear. He buried himself in work, staying away as if distance could erase what he had done.

Her gaze drifted to the large stuffed animal she'd left slumped in the far corner chair. The sight of it sent a sharp ache through her chest. It seemed like a ridiculous thing now, and yet, it held a memory—one she wasn't ready to unpack.

A soft knock broke through the stillness, and her heart clenched. For a brief second, she hesitated. Then, inhaling deeply, she reached for the door.

Michael stood there, his hands shoved deep into his pockets, his shoulders slightly hunched, his gaze averted. He looked...small. Not in size, never in presence, but in a way that made him seem uncertain—hesitant in a way that was so unlike him.

"The car's here." His voice was low and rough around the edges.

Paislee searched his face, drawn to the flicker of something she couldn't name. Guilt? Resignation? For the first time since she had met him, Michael Chamberlain looked unmoored, as if he were grasping for something that kept slipping through his fingers.

"Thank you," she murmured, swallowing the tightness in her throat. "I'm ready."

His eyes lifted to hers then, and she forgot how to breathe. There was something raw in them, something stripped bare. His lips parted slightly as if he meant to say something—anything—but then, just as quickly, he straightened. Then he pulled his hands from his pockets, smoothed them over the front of his dark pants, and gestured toward her bags.

"I'll take those for you."

Paislee nodded, and she fell into step behind him as they made their way down the hallway. The distance between them felt greater than ever.

"I...uh, I'll contact Alex and terminate the contract immediately," Michael said, his voice measured as if clinging to professionalism. "In a few days, someone from the firm will reach out. There'll be a brief investigation. Then you'll be debriefed."

Her throat tightened. She nodded stiffly. "And that's it? It's over?"

Michael reached for the front door, but then he hesitated. His hand lingered on the handle before he turned back to her. "It'll be the end of your obligations to me." A shadow passed over his face. "What happens after that...remains to be seen."

Paislee lifted her chin, inhaling sharply. She knew what he meant. Esben. "Michael...thank you. For trying to protect me. But your brother's actions aren't your fault—"

"Yes, they are." The words were sharp, leaving no room for argument. His jaw tensed, and his gaze shifted past her to the window, where a sleek black car idled outside, the driver waiting. When he spoke again, his voice was quieter, almost bitter. "And it's my fault you're leaving."

Paislee's lips parted, but no words came. Too many emotions churned inside her—ones she wasn't sure she wanted to name. They stood in the hush of his grand foyer, trapped in a moment neither knew how to navigate.

Finally, she exhaled. "Goodbye, Michael."

Michael opened the door—and then shut it.

The veins in his forearm flexed as he gripped the handle, and tension coiled through his body as if he were physically restraining himself. His head was bowed slightly, his breath unsteady. Then, hoarsely: "Stay."

Slowly, he lifted his gaze, and she saw it—the storm raging behind his ethereal eyes. "Please, Paislee," he murmured. "Stay with me."

The plea cracked something inside her. It was like he had reached into her chest and taken hold. Tears burned the backs of her eyes, but she fought them, fought the urge to give in. Even now, even as her body longed to move toward him, a terrible memory surfaced—the flash of his fangs, the pain, the fear, the helplessness.

She shook her head. "I...I can't."

Michael exhaled sharply, and his throat bobbed. His expression hardened, but only barely. "I won't make excuses," he admitted. "Not for my temper. Not for what I did." His voice wavered, and he clenched his fists before forcing them open again. "But let me prove to you that I can be better. That I will be." As his eyes searched hers, desperation flashing beneath the surface. "Give me a chance to learn...how to treat you."

It would be so easy to fall into his arms, to pretend that the other night had never happened.

But it had.

And no matter how much she wanted to believe him, the memory of his loss of control—the terror—was still too fresh.

She blinked as tears slipped free. Then, barely above a whisper: "No."

Michael's gaze dropped. A beat of silence passed before he gave a small nod, his throat working as he cleared it. "I understand." His voice was distant now, like he was already pulling away.

This time, when he opened the door, he did not stop.

Paislee followed him outside, where the cool ocean air bit against her skin. Michael passed her bags to the driver and then opened the car door. She hesitated for a split second before sliding inside.

As she settled into the seat, she caught sight of a man approaching Michael. He was tall and dressed in a long coat and khakis, with sunglasses obscuring his eyes. They exchanged brief words and a handshake.

Paislee frowned.

Moments later, the man turned and removed his sunglasses. Then he slid into the seat beside her. Before she could question it, the driver climbed in, and the car pulled away from the house—away from Michael.

She dared one last glance back.

Michael stood on the drive, watching her go. His expression was unreadable yet somehow looming, like it would linger long after she was gone.

A voice pulled her back to the present. "Ms. Sullivan," the man beside her said, slipping his sunglasses into his coat pocket. He rapped lightly on the window, and the driver promptly closed the partition. "You can call me Lucas. I've been assigned to you."

Her brows knit. "Assigned?"

"To ensure your safety." His tone was polite yet firm. "I'll keep my distance, but you'll never be without protection. If you need anything—"

"Are you a bodyguard?"

A small, knowing smile. "Your security detail. I was informed of credible threats against you."

Paislee stiffened. "For how long?"

Lucas tilted his head slightly. "Until Mr. Chamberlain tells me otherwise."

She turned to the window, watching the coastline slip past. The ocean churned, relentless, its rhythm steady and inescapable. It reminded her of something she couldn't name—something constant, something inevitable.

Her fingers twitched in her lap.

The farther they drove, the more a creeping unease settled deep in her bones. Not in a loud, obvious way, but quiet, like she was stepping onto a path that wasn't meant to be taken, like a choice that scratched against something instinctive, something unspoken. She'd convinced herself that leaving was the right thing, the only thing. As each mile widened the space between them, she had expected relief. Instead, there was only this gnawing pull, an unanswered question stretching between them.

# Chapter Thirty

T HE OCEAN HAD ALWAYS been a source of clarity for Michael.

He didn't know how long he had been sitting outside, holding a tumbler of untouched whisky, watching the tide roll in and out as if it held an answer he couldn't grasp. The early evening wind pressed against him, cool and salt-laced, but he barely felt it.

She was gone.

And this time, there was no coming back.

The moment the car had disappeared from sight, something in him had cracked—silently, invisibly, like the slow fracture of glass under too much pressure. He had known deep down that this was how it would end. That everything he had done, everything he had been, had led them here.

Still, some foolish, desperate part of him had hoped.

Hoped that maybe, just maybe, she could have seen past his failures. Past the monster that had surfaced, past the fear he had etched into her bones. But there were some things you couldn't come back from, and he had no right to ask her to try.

His fingers curled more tightly around his glass.

He had meant what he said—he wouldn't make excuses. And yet, the weight of regret was unbearable. He had spent years mastering control, learning how to wear his power like armor, to ensure that nothing and no one could ever truly shake him.

Then Paislee had come along.

And in a single moment of weakness, he had ruined everything.

The world felt strangely muted without her presence. His home, already too empty, now felt like a hollowed-out shell. The silence pressed in, thick and suffocating.

He exhaled sharply and set down his glass, having no desire to drink.

"Michael?"

For a moment, he thought he was imagining Paislee's voice—that his desperate mind had conjured her out of nothing. But then he turned, and she was standing there.

She was real.

She had come back.

Michael stood but didn't dare move toward her. He couldn't.

If he did, if he so much as breathed the wrong way, he was terrified that she would vanish.

She had left. He had watched it happen. He had felt it happen.

And yet—here she was.

For the first time in his life, he didn't know what to say.

Michael's breath stalled. His pulse slammed against his ribs as he took a single step, then another.

She didn't move away, but she didn't move toward him, either.

He slowed.

Up close, he could see the tension in her frame, the wariness in her eyes. She had returned—but not to him. Not yet.

Michael knew that if he reached for her now, if he so much as lifted his hand, she would flinch.

And that thought nearly shattered him.

So, he didn't touch her. Didn't press, didn't demand.

He just stood there, close enough to feel the warmth of her presence, close enough to let her see—*I will not take what is not given.*

She was still hurting. She was still uncertain.

But she was here.

Giving him the chance to fix what he had broken.

And Michael—who had never begged for anything, who had never allowed himself to need—felt something raw and unspoken settle in his chest.

He would not waste it.

A long silence stretched between them, carrying the weight of everything unsaid. Then...

Paislee exhaled, and barely—just barely—her lips curved into something that wasn't quite a smile but wasn't far from it, either.

"I'm hungry," she murmured. "Isn't it your responsibility to make sure I don't starve?"

His head dipped forward slightly, and for the first time in days, something unknotted in his chest.

"It is." The corner of his mouth tipped up. "I did say I would take care of you."

"You did." Paislee lifted a brow. "And I'm holding you to that."

The hint of a smile lingered as he held out his hand. She hesitated only a moment before placing her hand in his, and his expression broke into something warmer—an easy grin. "Let me make you something."

And just like that, the weight, while it wasn't gone, became bearable. Because she was there.

And for now, that was enough.

Paislee perched on a high-backed stool, her elbows resting on the counter, as Michael moved through the kitchen with the confidence of someone who had done this a thousand times. There was an effortless grace to the way he worked, flipping a skillet with a flick of his wrist, his movements unhurried but precise.

She tilted her head, watching as he added what looked like bacon to the pan.

"Guanciale," he corrected smoothly, pouring her a glass of wine without missing a beat.

Her lips twitched. "That's just fancy bacon."

Michael shot her a pointed look, but there was a hint of amusement behind it. Instead of arguing, he busied himself with filling a blender—walnuts, ricotta, basil, garlic, sun-dried tomatoes, and olive oil—while water boiled for the pasta. The kitchen smelled incredible, warm and rich, and she hadn't even taken a bite yet.

Michael caught her staring and arched a brow. "You're laughing at me, ducizza?"

The soft lilt of his accent caught her off guard.

"No," she defended quickly. "Why would you think that?"

"You're smiling."

She hadn't even realized. "I'm thinking your mind is in Italy, right now."

His lips curved as he tasted the blended sauce. Muttering something in Italian, he turned and held out a spoonful for her to try.

The moment it hit her tongue, warmth bloomed in her chest.

"That's amazing."

Michael winked and then effortlessly tossed the pasta in the sauce, adding the crispy—not bacon—guanciale. Fresh basil and a dusting of grated cheese completed the dish, and he divided it onto two plates before sliding one in front of her.

She glanced at the clock. "You made that in less than thirty minutes."

"*Pesto ricotta e noci*," he said with a sweeping gesture of his hand. "*Mancia, mancia.*"

She took a bite and nearly melted into the stool. "I can't believe you cook, too."

Michael chuckled as he grabbed both plates, nodding for her to take the wineglasses and follow him outside. "I own restaurants in Bologna and Naples. I've spent a lot of time with my chefs."

The sky was painted in soft hues of pink and gold as they stepped onto the patio. A fire pit flickered to life with the flip of a switch, casting a warm glow over the outdoor lounge. Overhead, delicate strings of lights illuminated the space, making it feel intimate, almost surreal.

Paislee curled into the corner of the sectional, tucking her legs beneath her as she balanced her plate and wineglass. As Michael settled across from her, the golden light cast shadows along the sharp angles of his face.

They ate in comfortable ease, the conversation light, their laughter blending with the rhythmic crash of the waves. Michael was animated as he told stories from his travels, his voice shifting between English and Italian when he got carried away. She could listen to him talk forever.

And that was the sobering part.

Because no matter how long she lived, he would always look just like this.

By the time they finished the bottle of wine, a slow drowsiness had settled over her. Michael stood and stacked her plate on his before she could protest.

"I can get that," she said, moving to stand.

He gave her a look. "No, ducizza, I have it. Finish your wine."

"You cooked," she argued. "Where I come from, the one who doesn't cook cleans up."

Michael smirked. "Where I come from, you drink your wine."

"That was weak." She tipped her glass toward him, not quite hiding the smile.

"Hm." He leaned down and brushed a knuckle beneath her chin before straightening. "I'll be back."

When he returned, he had the rest of the bottle in one hand and a blanket in the other. He draped it over her shoulders before refilling their glasses, and that's when she noticed something on the inside of his wrist.

A mark.

Not a scar. But...what looked like a brand.

She reached for his hand and traced her fingers over the raised image burned into his skin. A cardinal. How had she never noticed it until now? She lifted her gaze to his, her expression filled with questions.

Michael took a slow sip of wine, seemingly unbothered by her discovery. "It is what it looks like. And it's required by the Order."

"I don't understand," she murmured. "Why?"

"We need to be marked and can't be tattooed," he said simply. "Our skin won't hold ink."

"Why?"

"It's thick—layered like armor. We heal too quickly. The ink gets pushed out before it can settle."

She frowned. "What is it for?" She ran her fingers over the mark again.

Michael turned his hand over, palm up. "If there's ever an emergency, this tells responders who we are so they can proceed accordingly."

Her stomach tightened. "Are there...a lot of emergency workers who know what this means?"

His expression didn't shift. "More than you realize. It sets a protocol in motion." He flexed his forearm, pointing to the smallest bump beneath his skin. "Microchip. Holds my medical history and contact information."

A chill ran through her.

A mark of control—proof that the Order left nothing to chance. Even someone like Michael, powerful in his own right, was bound to their rules.

Michael didn't seem fazed. But then again, maybe he had been under their thumb for so long that he no longer noticed the weight.

Paislee tucked herself deeper beneath the blanket and sipped her wine, stealing a glance at the firelight dancing in his eyes. Silence settled between them—not uncomfortable, just there. For the first time in days, she felt at peace.

The wineglass in her hand grew heavier, and she barely stifled a yawn.

Michael chuckled. "Ready to go inside?"

She shook her head. She didn't want to move, didn't want to break the moment.

Before she realized it, she had leaned into him, resting her temple against his shoulder. Michael stilled, but only for a breath. Then, he draped an arm around her and pulled her in, positioning her head against his chest.

His heartbeat was steady beneath her ear. Strong.

She should've been more afraid. Her body remembered what he'd done. Her neck still bore the phantom throb of his bite. And yet, there she was. Letting herself fold into him.

The ocean breeze picked up, rustling the strands of her hair.

"Are you cold?" she murmured. "I can share the blanket."

Michael huffed a soft laugh. "I don't really get cold. Nor do I get that hot," he admitted.

Paislee smiled sleepily. "One of those Cardo sapien things," she muttered.

"You could say that." His voice was quieter now, almost thoughtful.

She thought of every story she had ever heard about vampires—bloodthirsty, soulless creatures lurking in the shadows. Predators. Monsters.

But Michael wasn't cruel.

He wasn't just the bite.

He was also this.

The warmth. The stillness. The safety.

And maybe that's what frightened her most. That she could feel safe there, in the arms of the man who had once taken all her choices away.

She wasn't healed.

She wasn't naïve.

But she was still his.

Michael's breaths were slow and steady, and the rise and fall of his chest lulled her into warmth, into security.

And as sleep pulled her under, the last thing she felt was the weight of his arm, holding her as if he never wanted to let go.

# Chapter
# Thirty-One

Paislee's eyes fluttered open as a cold drop of water splashed against her cheek. She blinked, wiped the sleep from her eyes, and lifted her gaze to the sky. The moon glowed above, casting silver light over the terrace where she and Michael lay. Another drop fell. Raindrops. She inhaled the crisp ocean air as the wind picked up, stirring the scent of salt and night jasmine.

She glanced down at Michael. Still lost in sleep, his arms were wrapped protectively around her. A small smile touched her lips. For a fleeting moment, she simply watched him. Something felt different—not in him but in the way she saw him. His face was the same, flawless in its sharp perfection, but her perception had changed. She was falling. Whether it was right or wrong, whether it would be her downfall or salvation, it was undeniable.

He stirred beneath her, shifting slightly on the outdoor sectional, his hold tightening around her. She leaned in, and her lips brushed his in the lightest of kisses. His eyes, heavy-lidded with sleep, opened to meet hers. His fingers trailed up her arm and curled behind her neck, drawing her closer. He deepened the kiss, slow and unhurried, his mouth warm and demanding. She melted into him, and her body pressed against his as his hands found the curve of her hip. His touch sent a jolt through her.

"It's going to rain," she murmured against his lips.

"Let it," he said, pulling her back into the kiss.

His venom tingled on her tongue, heightening her senses, making every touch electric.

Then the sky opened. Rain poured down in sheets, drenching them instantly. Paislee gasped and then shrieked as the icy drops cascaded over them.

"*Minchia*," Michael said with a sigh. Swiftly and fluidly, he lifted her into his arms and carried her inside. The downpour pounded against the massive windows as the storm rumbled overhead.

Paislee wiped the wet strands of hair from her face, still laughing. "I told you it was going to rain."

Michael ruffled his soaked hair, shaking out the droplets. Then, in one smooth motion, he peeled off his drenched shirt.

Their eyes met. The storm outside faded into insignificance as he stepped closer. His hands found her waist, and his fingers splayed across the damp fabric clinging to her skin. She reached up, her palms skimming the planes of his chest, her fingers trailing to the back of his neck as she pulled him in.

Michael lifted her again, and his kiss was ravenous, consuming. His venom sent her spinning, leaving her senses spiraling in a heady rush. The things he could do to her no longer frightened her. She understood them now. Accepted them. Welcomed them.

A soft sound escaped her, and in an instant, he released her. His breath was ragged, and his eyes glowed in the dim light. She saw the fear in them.

He backed away like he'd just stepped too close to the edge, like her gasp had confirmed his worst nightmare. That she wasn't ready, that he'd taken too much.

"Are you all right?" he asked, his voice strained and tight.

She swallowed, still breathless. "Yes."

He let out a low, frustrated growl. "I don't want to hurt you."

"You're not," she assured him.

He was already pulling back. "But I did," he said, barely above a breath. "And I can... You have no idea of the things I want to do to you, Paislee."

There was conflict in his expression, shadows of restraint warring with something darker. She reached up and cupped his jaw, her thumb brushing over the sharp line of his cheek. "I'm here."

He straightened, and his hands were gentle as he cradled her face. He pressed a soft kiss to her lips before stepping back.

"Don't pull away from me. I don't understand."

He raked a hand through his wet hair, and his gaze shifted to the window.

His jaw tightened as he exhaled slowly. "This was never a problem before."

Paislee hesitated. "What do you mean?"

His fingers flexed at his sides. "I've had donors. I've had lovers. And it was never...complicated." His voice was rough, haunted. "I took what I needed. Gave them what they wanted. A simple transaction."

"But with me..." she said gently, her voice threading through the storm beating against the windows.

"It's different." He inhaled sharply through his nose, as if bracing himself. "It has to be."

She frowned. "Why?"

His jaw clenched. "My venom, Paislee." His voice was quiet, but there was an edge of frustration there, like he wanted to leave it at that, like he hoped that would be enough. "You already know what it does to you. What it makes you feel." He swallowed hard. "If I let myself have you, if I let this happen, I need to know you're with me—completely."

She stepped closer. "Then be careful. Don't kiss me."

"You think it's that simple?"

"Isn't it?"

A bitter laugh escaped him, low and humorless. He shook his head and raked a hand through his damp hair. "I don't know," he admitted. "This should be simple. It always has been. But now..."

He exhaled sharply, his frustration bleeding into the silence. "I've never had to stop before. I've never wanted anything like this."

Paislee stilled. "This isn't just about what your venom does to me, is it?"

He looked up then, eyes darker than she'd ever seen them. Not with anger, but with terror. The kind that came from knowing what you're capable of.

Paislee reached for his hand, and she threaded her fingers through his, grounding him. "What are you really afraid of?"

His grip tightened, just for a second, before he slowly pulled away

"I didn't snap because I was angry," he said. "I snapped because I was going to lose you. To Esben. To the Order. To your own will. And in that moment—" He shook his head, voice ragged. "In that moment, I wasn't thinking like *me*. I was thinking like something else. Something I don't recognize."

His chest rose sharply. "I've lived a long time mastering control. Refining it. Polishing it into charm and diplomacy and restraint. But that part of me—the part that...lost control—it doesn't care about contracts or apologies. It only cares that you're mine."

"I'm not trying to scare you," he added quietly. "But you need to understand what it means to remain here. What I fight every time I look at you. Every instinct I've ever buried comes clawing to the surface when you pull away. If I stop fighting this, I don't know what I'll become. And I don't even know what this is. Other than that it's something primal. You make me want in a way I can't control."

Paislee swallowed. "You're still you, Michael."

His jaw tensed, and he turned away. "Am I?"

The weight of his confession settled between them. She felt the truth of it. Every word.

He hadn't just lost control.

Even now, she could still feel the ghost of his bite, the echo of pain trialing her pulse. And yet, her heart didn't race from fear.

It ached.

"Why didn't you stop sooner?" she asked quietly. "Before..."

His gaze dropped to the floor. "Because stopping meant letting go. And I didn't know if I could live with that."

For a long moment, she just looked at him. He seemed stripped bare in a way she hadn't seen before. Not the polished predator or the charming heir. But something more and less human.

She exhaled slowly, reaching for the edge the counter. "You say you don't know what you'll become if you let yourself have this...have me. But what happens if you keep denying it? How long before that part of you you're so afraid of takes over anyway?"

He had no answer.

She stepped closer, not to forgive, but to confront it with him.

"You hurt me," she said, eyes burning. "You didn't give me a choice. You took control because it was easier than baring the truth to me, than asking me to stay."

"I know," he rasped.

"I'm not saying I understand. Or that I've forgotten it." She touched her neck, like she could press the memory into stillness. "But I'm still here."

His throat bobbed. "For now."

She nodded. "That's all either of us has."

Then, after a long pause, she reached for his hand.

Michael didn't pull his hand away when she touched him. He looked down at their fingers, his thumb brushing hers.

"I thought I lost you," he said softly.

The words lingered in the air, unsoftened, as the rain lashed against the windows behind them. Thunder growled low in the distance. A jagged bolt of lightening lit up the room in a brief, pale flash.

"I don't want your forgiveness," he said after a beat. "Not yet. I haven't earned it."

Paislee swallowed hard.

The silence stretched between them, but it wasn't empty. It throbbed with things unspoken. Pain, regret, the echo of fear still lodged in both their chests.

A louder crack of thunder made them both turn toward the sound.

Michael led her to the couch and reached for the blanket draped over the back rest. He handed it to her as they relaxed by the line of windows.

"I know you don't get cold," she said, handing him half the blanket. "But humor me."

He let the fabric settle over his lap.

She watched him carefully, still uncertain of what to do with the tenderness that flickered in her chest. A part of her wanted to rest against him again, to fall asleep to the rhythm of his heart. Another part felt like running.

He didn't push.

They let the silence carry them a little further into the night as they watched the glow of the storm.

"You said not all love makes us better," she said. "Why?"

He glanced at her, then back at the window. "It just...shows us what's already broken."

Her throat tightened.

She didn't respond.

They watched in silence as the sky broke itself apart and pieced itself back together in pulses of electricity and sound.

Paislee pulled her knees up and wrapped her arms around them. Eventually, her head dipped. No toward him, but closer.

He didn't move.

When she finally gave in and rested her head on the back of the couch beside his shoulder, he quietly shifted, angling himself so she wouldn't slide away.

No apologies. No more explanations.

Just the storm. And the two them, sitting quietly in the middle of it.

# Chapter Thirty-Two

T IME HAD SETTLED INTO something slower, easier. Time had passed differently after the night of the storm. And with it, some of what stood between Michael and Paislee. What had fractured was slowly mending. Not through declarations, but through quiet routines. Paislee no longer returned to her own room at night. He didn't ask, and she didn't offer. It was as if some unspoken agreement had settled between them.

Their days were filled with the rhythm of shared of space. Work, conversations, glances that lingered longer than necessary. Whatever they'd been before, it felt different now. Real. Unrushed.

The clock downstairs chimed twice, marking the early hours of the morning, when Michael returned upstairs. With their phones and a drink, he slid back into bed and pulled her close. She rested her cheek on his chest, listening to the steady rise and fall of his breathing. His phone buzzed. He responded to the message before wrapping his arm back around her.

"There's no contract between us," he murmured.

She lifted her gaze and rested her chin on his chest. "What do you mean?"

"It's just a guise to keep my brother away from you. I want you here on your own accord."

She frowned. "He's relentless."

"He hates me," he said simply, taking her hand and absentmindedly tracing her fingertips.

She tilted her head. "Why? I mean, I've fought with my brothers my whole life, but we still love each other. We don't want to destroy one another."

He let out a quiet laugh, but there was no humor in it. "Yeah, he's always hated me. Jealousy? Resentment."

"What would he be resentful of?"

"Our father marrying my mother, maybe."

Her brows furrowed. "Where's his mother?"

"Dead. She was...unstable. My mother told me that she caused a lot of problems for my father, and since he was on the Order's board, it created controversy. But she was his wife, so his loyalty to her demanded tolerance. Eventually, she lost herself completely and took her own life. He married my mother not long after."

"But that's not your fault."

"No, but my mother wasn't turned like his. Both my parents come from a long line of nobles, making me a pureblood and my father's heir. I also have the right to take a seat on the Order's board if I choose. Esben will never have that option."

She exhaled as realization dawned. "So, he lashes out however he can."

Michael held her gaze for several moments before nodding. "He's spent years trying to ruin anything he could."

"Like what?"

"He's sabotaged my relationships, tried to have my businesses shut down, even worked to turn my father against me. And in that..." His voice darkened. "I think he's succeeding."

"He sounds unhinged."

"Which is why I take his threats seriously. For a while, I thought we might move past the hatred, but then there was Katya."

She stilled. "Who is that?"

"Was," he corrected, his gaze flickering with something jagged and painful. "She was his largitor."

Paislee stiffened.

"She showed up at my door one day, barely conscious, beaten, and drained nearly to death. In their struggle, she'd been exposed to Esben's blood. She was turning."

A chill swept through Paislee. "Oh, my God."

Michael's jaw clenched at the memory. "I put her under my protection immediately. The Order came for her that same day, and I fought them. Literally." He exhaled. "You can imagine the scandal."

She stared at him. "You risked a lot for her."

"I didn't even know her," he admitted. "It was the principle. The Order believes they control all human life, that they alone decide who is worthy of transitioning. I knew what they were going to do to her, and it wasn't right."

"What happened then?"

"I took responsibility for turning her to protect her and Esben. If they had believed he was responsible, he could have been executed."

Her stomach tightened. "And you wouldn't have been?"

"My bloodline is royal. The likelihood of execution was slim. But I needed the case to be public. With the world watching, the Order had to tread carefully. A high-profile trial ensured my survival. And I hoped that by exposing their hypocrisy, I could save Katya."

"Did it work?"

His expression hardened. "For me, yes. For Katya?" He hesitated. "Almost."

Paislee leaned in, drawn by the gravity in his voice. "What do you mean?"

"The cardinalis population devoured the story. They romanticized it—spun some tragic love triangle. In their version, Esben discovered our 'secret affair' and beat her nearly to death in a fit of rage."

"And you didn't correct them."

He shook his head. "It would've been foolish. Suddenly, I was the hero, fighting to protect the woman I wanted as my mate. It was something the people wanted—needed. It sparked protests, fueled outrage, and forced the Order into the spotlight."

"Michael, you—" She sat up as realization dawned. "You turned their own system against them."

"The discontent had been brewing for years. Katya's case was just the match to the powder keg. The laws about seeking approval—about who we're allowed to choose as mates—had always been a point of contention. This made it personal because the public connected with me and Katya." He sighed. "But that was over four years ago. After the trial, I was reprimanded. Put on probation. Ordered to lie low or face...worse consequences. Esben was publicly shamed for his abuse, another humiliation."

Paislee shook her head. "You took the blame for him. He should have been grateful."

Michael's expression darkened. "No. The opposite. I ruined his reputation. Exposed him. My father had to denounce his actions publicly. And the world believed that his largitor had fallen for his brother."

The air in the room shifted.

Paislee swallowed. "Where is Katya now?"

Michael didn't answer at first. He toyed with a lock of Paislee's hair before tucking it behind her ear.

Her heart pounded. "Michael?"

He finally met her gaze. "She was never approved to transition. In the end, a vote was cast on her fate."

A breath caught in her throat. "What happened to her?"

He winced at the dread in her voice. "She was contracted, under Cardinalis rule. Bound to the Code. She was executed shortly after the trial. They kept it from the public."

Paislee sat upright as cold crept through her chest, and horror flooded her veins. "Executed?" The word felt sharp in her mouth. Her stomach turned. "That's monstrous."

Michael didn't argue. He didn't soften it, either. "The Order is absolute, Paislee. I tried to expose them. I tried to save her. But you don't fight them and win. Not really. When I turned against them, I put everyone around me in danger. My family. My friends. My entire class."

She stared at him trying to understand. "But you were doing the right thing."

He let out a quiet laugh, joyless and small. "Doesn't matter. She's still dead. And Esben's hatred for me has only festered." He reached for her hand and pulled her back down, his touch gentle despite the unrest in his eyes.

"So, now he targets all your largitores?" she asked, barely above a whisper.

Michael brushed a strand of hair from her face. "No," he murmured. "Just you. And now that he's finally discovered the one thing that can hurt me, he won't stop."

Silence hung.

Michael's phone buzzed again on the nightstand.

He sighed and leaned back.

Paislee blinked, the moment cracking slightly. "Your phone has been blowing up this whole time."

He eased her onto her back and brushed his lips across hers, then buried his face against her shoulder. "Seth. He's finalizing the Liberty Benefit details."

She exhaled, reached for the phone, and handed it to him. "Then maybe answer it."

Michael took one look at the screen, and hit decline.

She smirked. "You know they can tell when you press the 'fuck you' button, right?"

He studied her for a moment, then looked over her slowly, eyes lingering on her bare legs, the oversized t-shirt slipping off one shoulder. "You need a dress."

Paislee was caught off guard. "What's wrong with my pajamas?"

Michael's lips twitched. "They're not appropriate for my mother's fundraiser."

A surprised laugh broke out of her. "There's no way you want me to go to the Liberty Benefit."

"Yes, I do."

"Are all largitores invited to such a lavish event?" she asked, half a challenge, half disbelief.

"That doesn't matter," he said, lowering his mouth to her collarbone.

But it did matter.

A cold realization settled over her. The weight of what he was saying pressed against her chest. This wasn't about a dress or a party. It was a statement. To his family. To his class. To the Order.

The way they would see it...she was just a largitor. Like Katya.

And Katya was dead.

"Michael," She sat up, searching his face. "You just told me what happened to Katya. She was a human they believed didn't belong, wasn't their equal."

His expression darkened. "And?"

"And she was executed," Paislee whispered, as if saying it too loud would make it happen again. To her.

A muscle in his jaw flexed. "This isn't the same, Paislee."

Her voice was quieter now, urgent. "You're putting me in front of all of them. They'll see me as your human, Michael. Not as some date. As someone contracted to you."

He reached for her hand and brushed his thumb over her knuckles. "I won't hide you."

She swallowed hard. "Maybe you should."

The words stung even as she said them.

Michael's expression didn't change, but there was something in his eyes—something deeper, something dangerous. "No."

Her heart pounded. Would attending this event paint a target on her back? Would Michael really be able to protect her if that was the case?

"Michael—"

He dipped his head and pressed a kiss to her neck. "I want you there, ducizza."

He almost smiled, then added more quietly, "You'll get to say goodbye to my father before he dies from a brain tumor."

She froze. "What?"

# Chapter
# Thirty-Three

MICHAEL CHECKED THE TIME on his phone again, his fingers tapping idly against the polished face of his watch. She should've been down by now. Had he miscalculated? Had he gone too far?

When he'd returned from the city that evening with what he'd thought was a considerate gesture, he'd expected gratitude, maybe a smile. Instead, he'd been met with a stunned, wide-eyed stare before she'd all but fled upstairs.

He was halfway to her door when the knock at the front entrance pulled him back. He opened it to find Paislee's friends, Kendra and Tessa, grinning like they'd already had a bottle.

Tessa swept inside first, her eyes scanning him from head to toe. "Damn, Michael. You clean up nice."

"Wow," Kendra agreed, taking a dramatic step back to admire his Italian fitted suit. "Like, rich-villain nice."

Michael sighed, already feeling the oncoming headache. "Why are you here?" He tried to keep his voice polite. "Paislee and I are leaving soon."

"We don't know," Kendra admitted, glancing around. "She just texted urgently for us to come over."

"Like, now," Tessa added. "So, here we are."

Michael exhaled sharply. "I think I might've...screwed up."

Kendra raised a brow. "What did you do?"

"I bought her a dress," he said flatly.

Silence.

Then Tessa blinked. "The horror."

Kendra shook her head. "The audacity."

"Just go check on her," he muttered, waving them off.

They exchanged knowing looks before charging upstairs.

Paislee sat cross-legged on her bed, chewing anxiously on her thumbnail. The gown lay beside her, a deep red river of silk, shimmering under the glow of her bedroom light.

When the knock came, her friends barely waited before pushing inside.

"What happened?" they demanded in unison.

She pointed at the dress like it had personally insulted her. "That."

Kendra squinted. "He...bought you a dress?"

"Yes."

Tessa frowned. "And...the problem is?"

Paislee let out a strangled groan as she dragged her hands down her face. "I had a dress! I prepared myself! And then he walks in with that—like it's no big deal! Like—"

Kendra picked up the gown, whistling low. "Paislee, this isn't just a dress. This was made for you."

Tessa turned it in her hands, admiring the elegant drape of fabric that would cross behind her neck, the daring cutout at the hip, the slit that ran high along the thigh.

"Oh my god—the shoes," Kendra sighed. "He's been planning this."

"Exactly! He's downstairs, looking like he belongs on the runway, and he expects me to walk in wearing a dress that probably costs more than my car!" She threw up her hands. "His parents will be there!"

Kendra and Tessa froze.

"Oh," they said together.

"That's what this is about," Kendra said.

Paislee groaned and collapsed onto the floor. "I'm going to ruin this."

Silence.

Then Kendra took a deep breath, grabbed Paislee's wrists, and pulled her up. "No, you're not. You're going to look incredible. We've got this."

Tessa nodded, already rummaging through Paislee's makeup drawer. "We've so got this."

Michael knocked at the door. "Paislee, we need to go. Now."

Tessa cracked it open just enough to poke her head out. "Hi, handsome."

Michael frowned. "Can I have my date?"

"Uh, no," she said cheerfully.

His frown deepened. "Why not?"

Kendra's head popped into view beside Tessa's. "She needs a minute."

"Maybe two," Tessa added, politely.

Michael pinched the bridge of his nose. "You do realize I can't be late? I'm hosting this thing."

"She'll meet you there," Kendra assured him, and before he could argue, the door shut.

Back inside, Paislee stood barefoot in front of the mirror, fidgeting.

Kendra stepped up behind her. "Alright. Deep breath."

She obeyed. In. Out. It helped. A little.

Paislee slid into the gown, with the silk slipping like cool liquid over her skin. She admired the high neckline that hugged just below her jaw, sleek and elegant. Most importantly, covering the marks on her neck.

When she turned to face her friends, they both let out dramatic, appreciative sighs.

Tessa worked on her makeup with a careful hand, blending soft, smoky tones around her eyes. "You have the kind of cheekbones that make makeup artists weep," she murmured.

"And the jealous ones quit," Kendra grinned, sectioning Paislee's hair. "We're going elegant. Up, but not severe."

She brushed and teased, then gathered Paislee's hair into a chignon at the nape of her neck, letting a few tendrils fall naturally.

"Okay, you're ready, Pais," Tessa clapped.

"Go look," Kendra said, with a proud lift of her chin.

The room fell silent as Paislee returned to the mirror and studied her reflection. The woman looking back at her didn't seem fragile or small. She looked...timeless. She was tall, polished, and arresting. Her eyes seemed older, somehow. Sharper, knowing. The makeup was subtle but deliberate. Her hair swept up into a soft, elegant twist that whispered old money. And the dress—God, the dress—it made her look like she'd never known anything but champagne and French perfume.

That small-town girl with worn sneakers and dirt under her nails? She was still there, but fading. Somewhere behind the eyes. Tonight, she didn't look like someone who'd been pulled into Michael's world.

She looked like she belonged in it.

"Holy shit," Kendra whispered, almost reverent.

Even Tessa blinked. "Yeah. His parents won't know what hit them."

Paislee's breath caught. Her throat tightened.

Kendra didn't miss the doubt in Paislee's face. Her own expression hardened—not unkind, just sure. Sure of Paislee's worth. Kendra's smile curled as she stepped beside Paislee, and met her gaze in the mirror. "Let them all look. Let them whisper. You hold your head high. Don't give them a single reason to think you don't belong there."

Tessa snorted, crossing her arms. "And if they do? Fuck 'em. Because Michael is going to forget the whole world when he lays eyes on you."

"Now," Kendra smiled, and handed Paislee the matching heels. "Take a deep breath, Cinderella."

Tessa grabbed the whisky bottle. "And a sip for courage."

Paislee took a long drink and winced. "It burns."

"Good. Means it's working."

Kendra grabbed her wrist and dragged her toward the door. "Let's go before you change your mind."

The city shimmered as they arrived at the event. The entrance was swarming with dazzlingly dressed guests as camera flashes bounced off the walls. A red carpet stretched toward the doors of Allusion, and the bass of the music thrummed beneath their feet.

Paislee stared at the overwhelming scene. "I can't do this."

Kendra shoved the bottle into her hand. "One more sip."

She downed it and coughed, her eyes watering.

"Better?" Tessa asked.

"Ask me again in five minutes."

"Good. Now, get out."

Paislee hesitated. Then, taking a deep breath, she stepped onto the pavement before smoothing her hands over the silk. The night air felt cool against her skin. She turned—only to find Kendra and Tessa already driving away.

Her heart pounded.

Maybe Michael wouldn't notice if she didn't show up. Maybe—

"Paislee."

She spun around.

Seth stood a few feet away, dressed in an immaculate tux, a knowing smirk on his lips. "Planning your escape?"

She let out a weak laugh. "Um...no?"

Seth chuckled and offered his arm. "Michael sent me to make sure you don't bolt."

"He expected me to panic?"

"Oh, definitely." Seth guided her toward the entrance. "But he also knows you're stronger than you think," he added in a low voice and with another playful smirk.

Her fingers curled tighter on Seth's arm, and he led her inside.

Allusion was almost unrecognizable.

The usual low, pulsing lights and moody shadows had been replaced by something grand, something almost ethereal. Soft, golden illumination bathed the space, casting long reflections over the polished black marble floors. The walls, once cool and dark, had been adorned with climbing vines of delicate white flowers with tiny lights woven between them, creating the illusion of a twilight garden.

The bar, always a sleek, modern centerpiece, had been transformed into something almost celestial—a cascade of glass and crystal, with bottles stacked like constellations, each reflecting the warm glow of the chandeliers above.

And the chandeliers—God, the chandeliers.

They hung like dripping stars, shimmering with every movement in the room, casting delicate patterns across the crowd. The music wasn't the usual heavy bass but something richer, smoother.

Paislee had expected luxury. She hadn't expected...this.

It was intoxicating, overwhelming—a world so carefully curated, so effortlessly refined, that it barely seemed real.

But what unsettled her most wasn't the grandeur.

It was the way she felt as if she had just stepped into a dream—one she wasn't sure she was meant to be a part of.

As if sensing her hesitation. Seth whispered, "Chin up, Country."

The music cut as they stepped further inside, and she saw Michael standing on a raised platform. His voice was steady, and his words were confident as he welcomed everyone, thanked donors, and introduced a guest speaker to the elite crowd before him. Clearly, he'd done this countless times—high-profile gatherings, all eyes on him as he played the role of host with effortless charm.

She watched him proudly, and when his gaze lifted mid-speech, they rested on her. She smiled.

The words died on his lips. It seemed as if every carefully rehearsed word, every line he was supposed to deliver, disintegrated.

The energy in the room changed, an electric current buzzing in the air.

Paislee swallowed. Her breathing was unsteady as Michael's gaze slowly traced the length of her, his expression unreadable—except for the molten spark in his eyes.

The pause stretched, and the crowd shifted in confusion at his sudden silence.

His lips parted, and a flicker of something passed over his face—something raw, something almost vulnerable. The air between them stretched, thrummed, shimmered with something silent yet loud.

Eyes subtly turned toward the entrance and rested on her.

The corner of Michael's mouth lifted, slow, deliberate.

Recognition.

Amusement.

Surrender.

The moment fractured as someone in the crowd cleared their throat. A few curious glances were exchanged, as Seth guided Paislee forward.

She playfully arched a brow at Michael.

Michael chuckled and shook his head—then cleared his throat to recover.

The room collectively exhaled, charmed by his momentary distraction.

Michael continued his speech, but his focus wavered. His eyes kept drifting back to her.

"He's been a part of the Long Island team for the past twelve years. He's a member of the American Society of Hematology and the American Society of Oncology. He's also been a mentor to the residents of Southampton. Everyone, please give a warm welcome to Dr. Andrew Acierno."

A polite wave of applause followed as the doctor emerged. He shook Michael's hand before taking the podium.

More speeches followed. Cycles of dignitaries and influential figures offered their thanks and remarks. Paislee listened, but her focus sharpened when Michael's mother stepped forward.

Petite, stunning, commanding.

There was no mistaking where Michael had inherited his presence. His mother exuded the kind of confidence that was effortless; her every word was spoken with a quiet authority. Then there was his father—unmistakable, even from a distance. Paislee would never forget the first words he had ever said to her, delivered coldly on the night he'd struck Michael in the kitchen.

*I hope you're worth the fire you just ignited.*

The memory sent a chill down her spine.

Michael returned to the podium after his mother, and his voice slipped back into that smooth, controlled tone. "Before we turn the music back up, I have a quick announcement. Tonight, we're encouraging everyone to 'drink for a good cause.' There's plenty of champagne making its way around, but from now until closing, all proceeds from drinks purchased at the bar will be donated to the foundation."

The crowd murmured with interest, but Michael wasn't finished.

"And I'm calling out Chamberlain Corporation to match whatever Allusion donates."

A spotlight shifted across the room before landing on Saverio. Seated casually with a glass of champagne in hand, Michael's father merely raised a brow. There was something in his gaze, something unreadable. He drained the rest of his glass before answering.

"I'll match you," Saverio said, his lips curling. "And I'll up you."

The room erupted.

Michael grinned, satisfied, but before he could speak, another voice rang out.

"I'll match whatever you donate, Saverio."

Walter Hemming, a key sponsor and Southampton's prominent boating magnate, stood from his table. The man squared his shoulders as the crowd turned to him, waiting.

"Then I'll double it."

The energy in the room spiked. Cheers, claps, and laughter echoed as the playful challenge took off. Other companies began chiming in, with executives and sponsors upping the stakes with competitive pride. The entire exchange carried an air of banter, but Paislee was beginning to understand—this was more than just a game.

Michael had expected this reaction.

He'd known exactly what he was doing when he'd singled out his father.

By the time the back-and-forth settled and the music returned, the mood had heightened. The room was buzzing with excitement.

Michael wasted no time in slipping away from the crowd, dodging eager socialites and business figures angling for his attention. His strides were purposeful and smooth, cutting through the crowd with a single goal in mind.

Paislee barely had a second to react before he was in front of her, taking her hand, his touch firm but careful. He leaned in and pressed a warm kiss to her cheek, his breath a whisper against her skin.

"*A tò bedda mi leva u fiatu.*"

She exhaled shakily. "I have no idea what you just said, but I really hope it was a compliment."

Michael's lips twitched. "You're breathtaking." His eyes swept over her again.

Paislee let out a nervous laugh. "Well, my friends worked really hard on me."

Michael plucked two champagne flutes from a passing server's tray. He handed her one and watched her down it in one go.

He raised a brow but said nothing, instead offered her his own.

She took it without hesitation. Another long sip. Another empty glass.

Michael gently pried the flute from her fingers and handed it off to another server. "Are you all right?"

She nodded, though she wasn't entirely sure she believed it herself.

His touch was soft as he cradled her face, and his lips found hers in a kiss that was warm, intoxicating, and soothing. His venom curled through her, settling her nerves, and the tension in her shoulders melted.

She deepened the kiss, tasting more of him, letting it settle her further.

Michael smiled against her mouth. "Did you have whisky?"

"Doesn't work nearly as well as your mouth."

His grip tightened at her waist. "Is that right?" he murmured. "Well, let me accommodate you further."

His lips brushed hers again, slower this time.

"Are you going to let me introduce you?"

The warmth drained from her limbs instantly.

Michael chuckled, already prepared for her reaction, and took her hand, resting it lightly on his arm. "You'll be fine," he assured her.

Paislee wasn't convinced. The walk through the crowd felt like an eternity. Every few steps, someone stopped him—polite hellos, introductions, questions. Michael handled each one effortlessly, his presence never faltering, his tone never rushed.

For Paislee, however, the entire experience was suffocating. *What am I even doing here?*

She wasn't meant for this world. The wealth, the power, the politics woven into every exchange. She was just a girl from the countryside, one who didn't belong in this gilded room full of elite figures—let alone standing beside Michael.

And yet...

His grip around her remained steady, reassuring.

As if, despite everything, despite the overwhelming odds and expectations, he wanted her there.

And maybe...just maybe...she wanted to believe that was enough.

"Why the hell would you bring her here?"

# Chapter Thirty-Four

P AISLEE TURNED, STARTLED BY the weight of an unimpressed gaze. Saverio, stood before her, his expression a careful mask of scrutiny.

"Surely, your hunger isn't so great that you need to bring your bestower?"

Michael's frown mirrored his father's. "She's not here as my largitor but as my date. And I expect her to be treated as such."

A woman's voice cut through the tension, smooth and lilting. "And she is lovely."

The sea of guests parted, as if by instinct, making way for Alaitz Chamberlain. Her smile reached her eyes, and to Paislee's relief, there was warmth in them.

Michael's features softened instantly. He watched his mother the way a man watches the sun break through the clouds—unexpectedly, reverently. She met him with the same warmth, her gaze filled with quiet pride.

"*Ciau, Mà*. This is Paislee Sullivan," Michael said. "Paislee, you already know my father. This is Alaitz Chamberlain."

Paislee's blood turned to ice. Alaitz Chamberlain. Even her name held a kind of unshakable power.

Alaitz tilted her head, and her voice was gentle. "Paislee, it's wonderful to meet you."

Paislee forced herself to breathe. "It's an honor, Mrs. Chamberlain."

"Ms. Sullivan." Saverio took her hand and kissed it politely, though his eyes remained unreadable. "Michele tells us you're not from New York."

"Pennsylvania," she managed.

"And what brought you to the Hamptons?" Alaitz asked.

"School. That was the plan, anyway."

Saverio hummed. "I suppose a contract with Michele derailed that."

Paislee stiffened as heat rose to her cheeks. Before she could respond, Alaitz's cool fingers wrapped around hers. "Paislee, darling, come with me for a drink."

Michael flashed her a reassuring wink, but she only managed a weak smile before Alaitz swept her away. The crowd melted before them as they moved, as if Alaitz carried the presence of a queen walking to her throne.

"Forgive my husband," Alaitz said smoothly. "He shouldn't discuss you and Michael's arrangement so openly."

"I just hope no one overheard."

Alaitz laughed, a sound like dark honey. As she tucked a dark curl behind her ear, diamonds flashed on her hand. "Eighty percent of the guests here already know exactly what you are, Paislee. Michael has, yet again, caused a stir."

Paislee glanced uneasily at the crowd. "I don't understand."

Alaitz motioned to Seth behind the bar. "Of course you don't," she said lightly. "You're a small-town girl. Your innocence is written all over your face. No wonder my son is fascinated by you."

Paislee's fingers trembled slightly as she accepted the champagne flute. "I-I don't know what to say, Mrs. Chamberlain."

"Call me Alaitz. And you don't have to say anything. I know my son very well. I also know humans very well—whereas Michael does not. He keeps his distance, merely using them as sustenance. Yet you..." She studied Paislee, her gaze sharp despite the warmth in her tone. "You're here. Meeting me."

Paislee's mouth felt dry. "I don't—"

"You love him."

The words landed like a stone in Paislee's chest.

Alaitz gave her a knowing smile, watching her closely. "And yet, you're human. A woman like you is content with a simple life—watching television, living in a modest home, growing old. That is what you want, isn't it?"

Paislee's spine stiffened. "And is there something wrong with that?"

"Not at all, darling," Alaitz said, setting her glass down. "But can Michael accept it?"

Paislee's stomach twisted. "Michael—"

"Michael has found his mate, Paislee. He just doesn't know it yet."

Paislee's breath caught in her throat. "I think you're mistaken."

"Perhaps," Alaitz mused. "But if I'm not, you will have a choice to make. Are you prepared for that?"

Paislee gaped at her, her pulse hammering. The sharp glint in Alaitz's eyes hinted at something deeper—a warning wrapped in silk.

"I'm an understanding woman," Alaitz said, her smile turning razor sharp. "But I'm a mother first. And seeing my son hurt..." Her voice dropped, and the warmth vanished. "Makes me protective."

Paislee swallowed hard, her fingers tightening around her glass.

Then, just as swiftly as she had turned cold, Alaitz softened, and she pressed a kiss to Paislee's cheek. "Good luck, Paislee, in whatever path you choose."

Paislee barely registered Alaitz sauntering away before Seth slid beside her, chuckling. He raised his glass. "Welcome to the Cardo sapiens' world, Country."

Suddenly, all the lights dimmed, and the club went silent. Like Allusion had taken a breath. Then, the music changed. The bass thrummed through the floor, intoxicating and electric. And neon beams pulsed in time with the music.

Seth called out, "Let's light this place up. Michael, cue the drama!"

Michael vaulted over the bar, stripping off his suit jacket. The crowd erupted in cheers. He and Seth lined up a row of shot glasses and then filled them with a shimmering liquid that caught the backlight like molten gemstones.

With a flick of his wrist, Michael ignited a stream of rum. The fire leaped to life, racing down the bar in a ribbon of blue flame, kissing each shot glass in a flawless cascade. The crowd gasped and then roared with delight.

Without missing a beat, he spun a bottle of vodka behind his back before pouring a cascade of liquid nitrogen into crystal tumblers. Fog rolled over the edges, thick and ghostly.

Paislee watched, transfixed. The Michael before her was completely in his element—reckless and magnetic.

He shot her a smile before tossing a flaming lime slice into the air and catching it between his teeth.

Paislee shook her head, grinning as the crowd roared.

The laughter behind her was familiar—too familiar. Paislee turned to see a group of women watching her, their diamond-studded wrists barely disguising their allegiance to the Order. They were regulars at Allusion, and she'd served them many times.

"Hi. Paislee, isn't it?" The tallest blonde, Leslie, smirked. "Country, they call you?"

Paislee's jaw tightened, remembering Alaitz's words earlier. Eighty percent of the guests already knew who—and what—she was. "Yeah, that's me."

Leslie feigned concern. And ignorance. "Did you get fired? We don't see you serving drinks here anymore."

Paislee forced a tight smile. "No."

Leslie adjusted the strap of her silk gown, her smirk deepening. "Did you come with Michael?"

Paislee's patience snapped. "Is it your business?"

Leslie leaned in, and her voice dripped with mock pity as she said, "You look a little pale, sweetheart. Maybe Michael's been drinking a little too much from you." Her smirk widened. "But don't worry. I'll tell him to go easier on you—later, in private."

Paislee went rigid.

The laughter from Leslie's friends felt like needles against Paislee's skin. Before she could move, Seth was there. "Ignore them," he said in a low voice. "You don't want to start something right now."

Leslie gave Seth a look, then dismissively turned away from Paislee.

Just as she thought it was over—

"Do you really think that Michael bringing you here means you have a future as anything more than his largitor?"

Paislee didn't need to turn to recognize Naevia's voice.

Paislee's lips curled, keeping her eyes on her drink. "He needed a date. I suppose his snack was better company than you."

Naevia's eyes blazed, but before she could speak, Michael appeared behind Paislee, and he curled his arm possessively around her waist.

"Naevia," he said with a nod.

Naevia sneered. "I understand that this is an event for the ill and unfortunate humans, Michael. But I didn't think you were bringing in the charity cases for display. It was hardly necessary."

Paislee's fingers twitched, and she started toward Naevia, but Michael guided her away. "Forget about her."

Paislee flashed her one more glare. "I'll show her how we do it in the country."

"I believe you." Michael chuckled as he led her onto the dance floor. "Dance with me."

The dance floor was alive—bodies swaying beneath the low lights, caught in the same low, sensual rhythm—but space seemed to open wherever Michael led her.

The beat dropped, something sultry that vibrated through the speakers. A low, sensual pulse filled the room as a breathy vocal wove its way through the rhythm. Michael's hand found Paislee's, and he pulled her closer. As they moved, it seemed like every eye in the room watched—not all with admiration. Whispers and sideways glances spread through the crowd.

Undeterred, Michael drew her in, pressing their bodies tightly together. He guided her with a confident touch. His hand rested possessively at her waist, his thigh pressing between hers. Paislee's pulse raced, both from the beat and from the awareness of the discontent swirling around them.

She met his gaze, and together, they began a slow, deliberate grind. Michael allowed her to lead for a moment—a subtle, teasing back-and-forth that sent more heat spiraling between them. Then he took control, turning her, pulling her back against his chest. He slowed their movements until every shift, every calculated dip, became a bold statement of intimacy and defiance.

Even as they swayed in perfect synchrony, the unspoken judgment of the onlookers loomed large. Each move on the dance floor carried the weight of centuries-old expectations—a defiance of the hierarchy that deemed her lesser. But in that charged moment, Paislee felt both vulnerable and powerful, caught in the thrill of rebellion.

Their bodies moved as one as the rhythm built toward a crescendo. Michael dipped her low, forcing her to hike up her gown. His lips hovered tantalizingly near her ear as the music swelled. In that suspended moment, every whisper, every disapproving glance seemed to melt away.

Then, as the chorus echoed, Michael spun her back, drawing her close so that their bodies pressed together in a defiant embrace. His voice, low and teasing, broke through the rhythm. "You, Ms. Sullivan, forgot your panties."

Paislee's cheeks flushed scarlet. Laughing into his neck, she said, "The dress you picked left no option."

He grinned, his eyes twinkling with mischief. "That's how I knew it was the right dress."

With a playful scolding and an intimate nudge, she said, "That's not what you were thinking."

"You don't think so? Well, no matter. I think we should go home and look for them."

The mischievous glint in his eyes told her that he wanted to leave, but the last thing he wanted to do was look for her panties.

"Wouldn't it be rude to leave your parents' fundraiser early?" she asked. "Aren't you hosting it?"

"I've done my part," he said, walking her backward, easing her off the dance floor and toward the exit. He took out his keys and ushered her out the back door. "Shouldn't you say goodbye—"

Her words died when he kissed her. All the while, as he was making her head spin, he was inching her toward his car.

# Chapter Thirty-Five

THE POUNDING ON THE door shattered the silence.

Michael jolted awake, and his eyes narrowed in the dark. Paislee stirred against his chest, murmuring sleepily as he reached for his phone. It was 4:30 a.m. His jaw clenched.

"Who the hell is banging on my door at this hour?" he muttered, sliding out of bed. He pulled on his pants and grabbed a shirt. "I'll be right back."

Paislee blinked sleepily as he stalked out. He was pissed.

Micheal pulled up the camera feed as he descended the stairs.

Alexander Bishop.

Michael's brow creased. This couldn't be good.

He wrenched the door open. "Alex." His voice was thick with sleep and irritation.

Alexander's smile was empty. "Can I come in?"

Michael stepped aside, his jaw tight. "Far be it from me to deny the Order anything."

As Alexander entered, Michael noted the folder in his hands, filled with paperwork.

He led Alexander into the kitchen.

"A top administrator at my door at four in the morning," Michael said. "Should I make coffee or pack my bags?"

"Coffee will be fine." Alexander slid onto a barstool and dropped the folder on the counter. His hand passed over the crack in the marble. "What happened?"

Michael started making coffee like he hadn't heard him. He kept his movements controlled, calm.

What the hell did the Order want now?

A soft shuffle on the stairs caught his attention. Paislee appeared, wearing his shirt over faded pajama bottoms, her hair tousled from sleep.

Michael's irritation flickered into something warmer.

Then she saw Alexander.

She stiffened and promptly turned to leave.

Alexander stopped her.

"Hello, Paislee." His voice was unusually gentle. "Do you remember me?"

Paislee hesitated. "I remember you, Mr. Bishop."

Alexander leaned forward. "Can you come here? I'd like to see your hands."

She glanced at Michael. He gave her a slight nod, though he watched Alexander like a hawk.

Paislee stepped closer and held out her hands as Alexander had requested. He took them and inspected her skin. Then he released them with a small, knowing smile.

"You're still human."

Michael stiffened. He moved to her side instinctively, sensing her unease. "Of course she is. Why wouldn't she be?"

Alexander didn't answer. "We need to talk. Privately."

Michael put a protective arm around her waist and opened his mouth to protest, but Paislee held up her hand. "I'll go upstairs. Goodnight, Mr. Bishop."

Alex responded kindly and waited for her to leave. Then he slid a document across the counter. "Michael, you have a problem."

Michael took the paper. His eyes skimmed the words—and his blood turned to ice.

His contract had been voided.

His grip on the paper tightened. "What the hell is this?"

"A grievance was filed. Your contract was put under investigation." Alexander exhaled. "It wasn't contested in time, so—"

Michael's temper ignited. "I never received anything to contest to."

Alexander rubbed his temples. "That's the problem. It was handled—strangely. I came as soon as I saw it."

There was only one person who could've pulled something like this.

Esben.

His brother's name burned through his veins like poison.

Michael's voice dropped, low and dangerous. "I'll contest it immediately."

Alexander shook his head. "You can't."

Michael's hands curled into fists. "What do you mean, I can't?"

"It's too late," Alexander said.

"Then I'll have her sign a new contract," Michael said with finality.

"You can't do that, either." Alexander pulled another document from the folder. "When her contract was terminated, another application was submitted."

Michael snatched the paper and scanned it.

His heart slammed against his ribs.

The name on the application was Esben's.

"This isn't a largitor contract."

"He doesn't want her as a largitor," Alexander said grimly. "He applied to make her his mate."

Silence.

Then—a chair scraped violently across the floor.

Alexander barely had time to react before Michael had him against the wall, with his feet dangling inches above the ground.

"Michael." Alexander's voice was calm despite the fingers pressing into his throat. "Put me down."

Michael's fangs were fully extended, and his body coiled with rage. Every instinct screamed to tear something apart.

"You knew my brother. And still, you let this happen?" Michael hissed.

"I didn't approve it," Alexander said, his voice tight from the pressure. "Now, let me go."

Michael inhaled sharply through his nose, as his body vibrated with restraint. It took everything in him not to break something. Slowly, he released Alexander.

He adjusted his collar with a sigh.

"Now," Alexander muttered, "about that coffee."

As Alexander calmly sipped his coffee, Michael paced the floor.

"Damn good coffee," Alex remarked. "What spice did you put in—"

Michael glared at him.

"Never mind," Alexander muttered.

"When Esben's approval crossed my desk, I had a feeling something was wrong. Anything to do with your brother puts me on alert."

"My brother isn't going anywhere near her, Alex," Michael said. "I can't imagine him being approved to turn anyone after what happened with Katya."

"He met with me not too long ago and asked for a transition application," Alexander said. "I gave it to him because I can't deny anyone the application. But when it was returned, I buried it, with no intention of approving it."

"Then how did this happen?" Michael asked. He couldn't imagine why the board would approve his brother after Katya. What strings had he pulled to have his application bypass Alexander? He stopped his pacing. "Fuck," he muttered as he came around the counter. He searched the papers. "Lottie," he growled. "She signed off on this."

Alexander looked stumped. "Why would Lady Autry do this?"

That was an excellent question. Michael recalled the last time he'd seen her. It had been at his townhouse in London. He'd walked into his own home, unsuspecting, only to find his brother buried inside the woman he'd trusted. His fiancée. The betrayal had struck deeper than any would. Lottie, in her infinite arrogance, had pleaded for his forgiveness.

Alexander set the cup down and sorted through papers. "I'll file a challenge. The termination of her contract was faulty. But Michael..." His gaze was sharp. "If Esben turns her before the paperwork goes through, it won't matter."

Michael's pulse pounded. "Can you delay his notification?"

"No. It's already been sent."

Michael cursed. His mind was already moving, calculating. If Esben didn't know Michael was aware yet, that was his advantage.

Alexander stood and gathered his papers. "Think carefully about this, Michael. She's just a largitor. Don't take the bait."

Michael's eyes flashed. "She is *my* largitor. If he goes anywhere near her, I will kill him, Alex."

Alexander studied him. "Interesting."

Michael's patience snapped. "If you don't stop him, I will."

Alexander sighed. "I'll do what I can." With that, he left.

Paislee found Michael standing by the windows, staring out at the ocean.

He was too still.

She hesitated, then stepped forward, slipping her arms around his waist. He flinched, just slightly, but enough to make her breath catch. After a long, silent pause, he let out a slow exhale and covered her hands with his.

Something was wrong.

Something was *very* wrong.

"What is it?" she whispered.

Michael didn't speak. His grip tightened around her fingers. His breathing was calm, too calm, like he was holding something in. But she could feel that something threatening to break loose. When he finally turned to face her, his expression was carved from stone—but his eyes burned.

"I should have seen this coming," he said, his voice low and furious. "I should have stopped it before it got this far."

Her stomach twisted. "Michael—"

"I want to take you away," he interrupted, his grip tightening around her fingers. "London. Dubai. Monaco. Anywhere. Just say the word. Where do you want to go?"

The way he said it—urgent, desperate—it sent a chill through her.

"Michael...that sounds like running." Paislee frowned as she studied his face. "Why?"

His jaw flexed. A muscle ticked in his temple. He looked out into the night, as if the dark horizon could give him courage. When he finally spoke, it was with effort.

"Michael," she asked, dread pooling in her chest. "Why was Alexander Bishop here?

Michael clenched his fists. "Esben." The name came out like poison. "He filed a grievance. Had out contract nullified. Then submitted a claim to the Order...to make you his mate. And it was approved."

It took a moment for his words to register. For a second, she didn't move. Didn't breathe.

"He has permission to change you."

A high-pitched ringing filled her ears. "That's not—" Her voice broke. "That can't be legal. I didn't agree to that. I should have a choice—"

"In our world," Michael said tightly, "a human doesn't refuse a mate. It's considered...an honor."

She backed away from him. Her voice trembled. "No. No, that's not an honor, that's a violation. It's my life. My body!"

Michael stepped toward her, but she pulled away. "Why would he do this?" she asked, her voice rising. "Is it just to hurt you? To prove something? That's a lifetime. That's forever. That's not just revenge—"

His silence was answer enough.

And it made her blood run cold. "He's abusing the system."

Michael looked sick. He didn't argue. He didn't have to.

"And when he gets tired of using me? When he's done proving his point?" Her voice broke again. "Michael...what happens to me?"

He remained silent.

She felt it hit like the floor dropped out from under her. Her legs buckled, and she would've collapsed if he hadn't caught her.

She gripped his arms with shaking hands. Her breaths came short as her panic rose.

Michael clenched his teeth.

She already knew the answer.

"I'll protect you," he said, his voice like steel. "He cannot have you."

She searched his face as her world tilted.

Unable to press down the nausea creeping up her throat, she imagined Esben touching her. Esben had been given the power to take her. Unless Michael stopped it, she would become something else. Bound to someone else.

"How does it happen?" she asked, barley audible.

"Paislee..." he said, and the pain in his voice was almost worse than his silence. "Don't ask me that?"

"I need to know," she said, her tone cutting. "What happens if..." She swallowed, her throat closing. "If you can't stop him?"

He looked as though her words sliced through him. "I will stop him," he said, fierce and absolute. A promise. A vow.

She wished she could believe it.

She didn't look away. "Tell me anyway."

He stared at her, and his lips parted slightly like he wanted to argue. Like he wanted to insist that it didn't matter, because it would never happen. But then he exhaled, slowly and measured. Controlled.

"It's slow," he said. "When you drink our blood, it starts to take over. You'll fall asleep. Your body shuts down while it...adjusts."

She latched onto that word. Adjusts.

"Is it painful?" she whispered.

"No," he said quickly, too quickly. "Not exactly. It's...strange. It feels like...dying. But you're not."

She felt cold all over.

"And then?" she asked, her voice quieter.

Michael's fingers tightened around hers as if to ground her. "Then you wake up, your senses are heightened. Your body is stronger. Venom glands form last."

She nodded faintly, barley absorbing the words. She was thinking about her blood. Her heartbeat. Her humanity. Everything that made her...*her*.

Michael was watching her. Waiting for her reaction. Bracing for it.

Paislee kept her gaze on their hands, tightening her fingers around his. Because the truth was, she was preparing herself. For the possibility that she might not survive this as herself. That she might not have a choice.

"Paislee." His voice was gentle now, almost broken. He touched her chin, tilting her face up. His eyes were wild. "This isn't going to happen."

She stared at him. She didn't know if he was trying to convince her or himself.

"Then why are you telling me?" she whispered.

Michael's lips parted, but he didn't speak. His silence screamed what he couldn't say.

*Because you asked.*

*Because you deserved to know.*

*Because we might not win.*

Instead, his brushed his thumb over her cheek, and spoke with a ragged edge. "I will never let Esben touch you. I will tear through the entire fucking Order before I let that happen."

She believed him. She did.

But she also knew that this wasn't just about Michael's will.

This was about the Order.

The law.

And the law didn't care about promises or vows, or the way Michael was looking at her now—like he'd burn down the world to keep her safe.

She nodded, swallowing hard. "I believe you."

Michael didn't let go.

But she knew he'd heard what she didn't say.

*I believe you. But I don't know if that will be enough.*

Michael drew her close. "Until I can sort this out, we need to leave, Paislee," he said. "Tell me where you want to go."

She looked past him, through the glass, out to where the ocean churned in the distance.

"I want to go home."

# Chapter Thirty-Six

T HE PAIN IN PAISLEE'S voice cut through Michael like a blade slipping between ribs, reaching a place he didn't know could ache.

"I can't take you home, Paislee," he said, his voice rough. "We'd endanger your family."

She hugged herself, though it didn't stop her trembling. "Then you pick. It doesn't matter."

Michael exhaled sharply. Then, without another word, he lifted her into his arms. She didn't fight him. He carried her to the couch and settled beside her, arms wrapped around her like a cage. Silence stretched between them, thick with unspoken words, while the rising sun bled over the horizon, staining the water gold. It should have been peaceful.

It wasn't.

Paislee dozed off against his chest, her breathing soft, unaware of the storm brewing inside him. His grip tightened unconsciously. The rage was growing, spreading like a sickness in his veins. He would end his brother for this. Esben had crossed the line—no, he'd obliterated it. And Lottie? He'd deal with her in time. The fact that she had aligned with Esben again, scheming behind his back, was infuriating enough. But this? This was different.

Paislee was his.

And Esben was going to pay for even thinking he could take her away.

Carefully, Michael shifted out from under her. After draping a blanket over her, he grabbed his phone.

Paislee woke to the sound of Michael's voice.

Groggy, she slowly sat up, and saw him pacing outside, talking on his phone. Tension rolled off him in waves. His posture was rigid, and his movements sharp. Everything was wrong.

Then his voice turned venomous.

She bolted to her feet just as, with a shout, he gripped the deck railing so hard the wood splintered beneath his fingers.

"Michael..." She rushed to him before he crushed the railing altogether. "Michael, stop."

His body was a coiled spring ready to snap.

"You're useless, Alex!" he roared. "I'll take care of this myself."

He hung up and turned with his keys in hand, already moving toward his car.

"Michael, wait!" Paislee grabbed his arm with both hands, but he barely seemed to notice her. "What's going on?"

Finally, he halted and slowly turned to face her.

"Mr. Bishop can't stop Esben, can he?" she asked, barely above a whisper.

Michael didn't answer. He didn't have to. She saw it in his eyes.

"So, what happens now?"

His white-knuckled grip on his keys, he slid on his sunglasses. "Seth is coming to keep an eye out while I'm gone. I need to handle a few things. Be ready when I get back."

Paislee's stomach twisted. "Michael—what are you going to do?"

His jaw clenched, and his muscles twitched under her touch as she gently reached up to brush her fingers against his face. He didn't pull away. She slid off his sunglasses and forced him to meet her gaze.

What she saw there crushed her.

Pain. Fury. A man cornered.

"Please," she whispered. "You don't need any more trouble with the Order. I'd rather endure the Order's bidding. Losing you would be more unbearable than anything Esben could do."

Michael exhaled, a slow, deliberate breath. "Nothing will happen to either of us, ducizza."

She wasn't convinced.

Then, suddenly, his lips were on hers—soft, slow, lingering.

"Road trip when I get back," he murmured with a grin.

His phone buzzed.

Esben's name flashed across the screen.

Michael's body went rigid.

She felt the change instantly—his grip tightening, his breathing deepening, his entire presence shifting from smoldering anger to something lethal.

He answered.

"What do you want?"

Esben's voice came through, light, almost cheerful.

"Mikey, I suppose you've heard the news."

Michael's fingers curled into a fist. "Come after me, Esben. Tell me where to meet you, and I'll be there."

Esben laughed. "Where's the fun in that? Sooo, where's the little morsel?"

Michael's entire body snapped tight. "You think I'd tell you?"

Another laugh. "If you're not going to release her, I'll be by—with agents. They'll take you into custody while I collect my mate."

Michael let out a sharp, humorless chuckle. "You want to have me arrested? Explain that one to Saverio."

Silence.

Then Esben's tone changed—no longer smug. Furious. "I guess you haven't heard. Our wonderful *poppa* has cut me off. This is your fault, little brother."

Michael's lips curled into a snarl. "Do you ever take responsibility for your own shit?"

"I have nothing to lose, Mikey." Esben's voice dripped with venom. "We're going to end this. The law is behind me. Hand her over."

Then, casually, as if discussing the weather, Esben said, "Tell me, does she taste as good as she looks? No, never mind. I want to find out for myself."

"Fuck you, Esben!" Michael roared, his voice so explosive Paislee stumbled back.

He hung up and charged toward his car.

"Michael!" she pleaded, reaching for him, but she might as well have been trying to stop a wildfire. His entire body trembled with rage.

Then headlights swept up the driveway.

Seth.

Michael didn't even hesitate. "Watch her," he ordered, already turning toward his car.

Paislee's heart clenched. "Michael, please—"

He spun, took her face in his hands, and kissed her—hard. It was desperate, claiming, as if this was the last time he'd ever get to.

When he pulled away, his eyes were still dark, still dangerous.

"I'll be back," he promised.

Then he was gone.

# Chapter
# Thirty-Seven

M ICHAEL'S CAR ROARED AS he peeled down the street. Tires screamed against the pavement as smoke curled into the air, leaving behind dark streaks of burnt rubber—a physical mark of his fury. Paislee stood frozen, her breath shallow as she watched his taillights disappear. The air still vibrated with tension, as if the house itself had absorbed his anger.

Seth exhaled. Removing his sunglasses, he turned to her. "I think you might want to fill me in."

Paislee tore away her gaze. "Did he tell you anything?"

Seth pushed open the front door and motioned for her to step inside. The lock clicked shut behind them. "Just that his brother's causing trouble again."

She drifted toward the couch, where she curled beneath the blanket, nausea twisting in her stomach.

Seth sat across from her, studying her carefully. The dim lighting caught the sharp angles of his face, and for a moment, she was struck again by just how inhumanly beautiful he was. All of them were. Michael, Esben, even Naevia and Leslie—they weren't just stronger than humans; they were something else entirely. Something dangerous.

Looking at Seth now, she saw beyond his easygoing nature, past his patience and charm. Beneath it all, he was just as deadly as Michael. Just as deadly as Esben.

"Why don't you claim your French heritage anymore?" she asked suddenly, needing the distraction.

Seth raised a brow. "I haven't lived in France in over two hundred years."

Her lips parted. "How old are you?"

He scoffed, waving a dismissive hand. "Don't ask such questions, Paislee. How rude."

She nearly laughed—Michael had given her the same evasive answer before. So, they were sensitive about their age. "Fine. Then why did you leave France?"

His expression darkened slightly. "I was a noble escaping persecution."

She frowned. "The revolution?"

"The cleansing period," he corrected. "When many nobles were sent to the guillotine."

A chill ran down her spine. "I thought that was about overturning the monarchy."

"It was."

She swallowed hard. "Were the nobles not...human?"

He shrugged. "Most weren't. And a lot of people knew. Some say the Order sabotaged us, scattering our stronghold in France to make us more compliant."

Paislee's jaw clenched. "The Order."

Seth gave her a knowing look before setting his shades on the table. "I traveled to New Orleans to escape execution. At the time, it was a small Spanish colony. I've stayed in America for the most part since then."

Paislee studied him, her mind racing with the weight of his words. How many lives had he seen rise and fall? How much history had he lived? "How did you meet Michael?"

Seth chuckled. "Oh, Michael's a young pup. I've been friends with his mother for many years. We were an item back in the day."

Paislee nearly choked. "Wait. You dated Michael's mother?"

He smirked. "Indeed. But then she met Saverio..." He trailed off, his gaze lingering on her as if searching for something. "The Regnanti family have a certain charm about them."

"You mean the Chamberlains?"

Seth grinned. "Ah, that's right. In your world, a woman surrenders her family name. In our world, bloodlines dictate who is dominate and who is property. Alaitz Chamberlain's bloodline is superior, so Saverio Regnanti had to publicly surrender his last name." He leaned back, amused. "But make no mistake—Saverio and his sons are very much Regnanti in blood."

Paislee shook her head in disbelief. "Michael's mother is badass."

Seth's expression softened. "She certainly is."

But then the thought of Esben crept in, and the warmth in Paislee's chest turned cold. "But I don't find much of the Regnanti family charming."

Seth sighed. "Time has worn on Saverio, hardened him. And Esben...has always been different. He carries his mother's burdens. She was ill. He watched her deteriorate—her violent outbursts, her paranoia. It shaped him."

Paislee shuddered. "That doesn't explain the lengths he's gone to."

"He's spent his life failing in Michael's shadow." Seth's voice was quiet. "Michael embodies everything a cardinalis would want in a child. Esben could never measure up. And every failure made him resent Michael more."

Paislee's throat tightened. "Michael trying to save Katya probably sent him over the edge."

"You know about Katya?" Seth's jaw flexed. "Yes. Michael was revered. Esben was disgraced. The Order took his properties, froze his accounts. He was forced to live under Alaitz and Saverio's roof again, like a youth."

Paislee frowned. "Better than death, I guess."

Seth nodded. "Michael saved his life. But imagine being rescued by the person you hate most. Imagine being at his mercy."

"What was Michael's punishment?" she asked quietly. "For Katya?"

Seth hesitated. "He is...more privileged than Esben. His punishment was minimal."

"Michael is treated like royalty everywhere we go. Everyone yields to him. It seems even the Order did."

Seth studied her for a long moment and then set his cup down. "Michael hasn't told you about his status?"

She shifted. "Not much."

Seth exhaled. "Then this is a conversation for him."

"I don't want him getting into any more trouble with the Order. Especially not because of me."

Seth's gaze darkened slightly. "Michael wants you to be ready when he gets back."

Paislee's heart pounded. Pack. Michael was taking her somewhere. Because Michael would keep fighting.

Swallowing hard, she stood abruptly. "I'm going upstairs to pack, then."

She stormed upstairs, where she yanked open drawers and shoved clothes into a bag. Her mind replayed everything from the day she'd met Michael and Esben—the danger, the secrets. Her gaze landed on the photos on her dresser—snapshots of another life, one untouched by this madness. Then she picked up the picture of her and Michael on the rollercoaster.

A sick feeling crawled up her spine as she traced the photo's edges. She set it down carefully. There had to be a way out.

He was ready to go to war for her.

And he couldn't afford to lose it.

She couldn't let someone take him from her. But she also couldn't be the reason he was taken.

Her decision settled like a stone in her chest.

# Chapter Thirty-Eight

M ICHAEL'S CAR HURTLED PAST the gates of Chamberlain Estates, barely slowing before he slammed the brakes, sending the vehicle into a sharp halt. The moment the tires stilled, he was out, and his steps thundered on the stone steps leading to the grand entrance.

Joseph barely had time to open his mouth before Michael shoved past him, his voice already ricocheting off the walls.

"Esben!"

Joseph flinched at the sheer force of Michael's voice. "Mr. Chamberlain—"

"Esben!" Michael bellowed again, his rage fueling every step as he stormed through the house.

The clicking of heels on marble cut through his fury. He turned just as his mother, Alaitz, descended the grand staircase, her dark eyes sharp with alarm.

"Michael, what's wrong?"

"Where is he?" His voice was raw and nearly shaking with the restraint he barely clung to.

"I don't know. What happened?" she pressed, concern deepening the lines between her brows.

"Where's Saverio?" Michael's words were clipped, with each syllable barely controlled as he continued moving.

"He's feeding," Alaitz said, falling into step behind him.

Michael gave her a humorless laugh. "Of course he is." He pushed through the double doors of the conservatory without hesitation.

Inside, Saverio was exactly where Michael had expected him to be—lounging on an oversized chaise. Jocelyne draped across his lap.

The second Michael entered, Saverio exhaled in irritation, and barely glanced up as he wiped Jocelyne's blood from his mouth.

"What the hell is this about now, Michele?"

Jocelyne, dazed, attempted to move, but her limbs were too weak. Joseph hurried forward, helped her to her feet, and guided her out of the room.

Michael didn't waste time. "Where's Esben?"

Saverio adjusted his collar, unbothered. "I wouldn't know. I told him to leave. I was finished with his games. I cut him off."

Michael let out a sharp breath. "Oh, well done. Finally disciplining your son—terrible fucking timing, though. You just made my problem worse."

Saverio leaned back in his seat and crossed one ankle over his knee, exuding the infuriating ease of someone who wasn't the least bit concerned. "I'm not inserting myself into another one of your childish feuds. You and Esben need to work out your own problems."

Michael clenched his fists so tightly that his nails threatened to break skin. "Childish feuds? Do you even know what he's done?"

Alaitz's gaze snapped to Saverio. Her voice cut through the tension.

"What is Michael talking about?"

"I assume you mean his legal action against your largitor?" Saverio scoffed. "Of course I know. And I cut him off because of it."

Alaitz's expression darkened. "Saverio, why didn't you think to tell me?"

Saverio waved a dismissive hand. "Because you already don't like my son."

"I don't trust Esben," Alaitz snapped. "And for damn good reason. Look at everything he's done to Michael!"

Saverio sighed. "Esben will drop the matter once he realizes he has no money."

Michael's laugh was sharp and bitter. "Oh, you think that's going to stop him?"

Saverio stood and walked to the windows. The glow of late morning cast his sharp features into shadow. "This is just another largitor, Michele. Let him have his fun. He'll regret it when he's bound to her for eternity." He turned, and his voice was cold, disinterested. "You're overreacting."

Michael's vision tunneled in red.

"She's not just another largitor." His voice was low, dangerous.

Saverio barely spared him a glance. "You're letting your anger toward Esben cloud your judgment—"

"If you don't stop this," Michael snarled, "I will. This is a courtesy, Father. If Esben touches her, I will fucking end him."

Saverio turned and closed the distance between them. "*My* son, Michele. *Your* brother." His voice was steel. "And you would kill him over some slip of a human?"

Michael's voice was unwavering. "She is mine! And if she's ever turned, it'll be by me, not by that miserable, pathetic son of a bitch who's as fucking insane as his mother."

Saverio moved fast, a blur, and his fist collided with Michael's jaw.

Pain detonated across Michael's face, rattling through his skull. His fangs snapped out as the taste of blood flooded his mouth. But he didn't hesitate.

He pivoted and swung. His fist connected with Saverio's jaw with enough force to send his father staggering back.

Blood splattered across the floor.

"Michael!" Alaitz screamed.

Joseph moved between them, shoving Saverio back, but it was too late. Michael and Saverio were both hissing, their fangs bared, the fight barely contained.

Alaitz stepped between them now, her eyes fierce. "Enough, both of you!"

Michael inhaled sharply, forcing himself to step back. As he wiped the blood from his mouth, his fingers trembled with barely suppressed rage.

Saverio's voice was deathly quiet. "If you kill Esben, Michele, I swear you will be shunned. You will no longer be my son."

Michael stilled. He met his father's gaze, his own anger burning just as fiercely. Then, slowly, he exhaled and shook his head.

"I don't think I ever really was," he said.

Then he turned and stormed out.

His mother called after him, but he didn't stop. He couldn't stop. His pulse thrummed with fury, with adrenaline.

As he reached his car, his phone rang.

"Seth?"

"Michael—"

His stomach clenched the moment he heard his friend's tone.

"She's gone."

Michael's breath stopped. His grip on the phone tightened and cracked the casing.

"What the hell are you talking about?" He started the car and peeled out of the driveway.

Seth's voice remained taut. "She was upstairs, packing. Then the shower turned on...but she was taking too long. I called up to her to check... She's gone. Jesus, Michael, you should've told me she was a flight risk."

A sick feeling curdled in Michael's stomach. His grip on the steering wheel tightened to the point where he thought he'd break it. "I didn't think she was." His throat was dry. "You don't think Esben—"

"No. If Esben took her, she wouldn't have had time to grab her things."

Michael's growl was sharp and violent. "She managed to leave with all her stuff? What the hell were you doing, Seth?"

"I didn't know she'd run. Where the hell is she going to go?"

"I'll find her," he muttered, tapping the tracking app on his screen. The signal flickered, buffering, taking too damn long.

His pulse pounded in his skull.

"Come on, Paislee. Where are you?"

Paislee sat in the back of the cab as the Hamptons disappeared behind her, the towering estates giving way to highways and city streets. The world outside blurred past—just streaks of color and concrete, faceless people going about their normal, safe, human lives. Lives untouched by the nightmare that had become hers.

She clutched her phone in her lap as Michael's name flashed over and over. Each missed call carved deeper into her chest. Seth. Michael. Seth. Michael. She ignored them all. Her heart hammered with each ring. Her thumb hovered over the answer button more than once, but she couldn't bring herself to do it.

If she heard Michael's voice, she'd break.

And if she broke, she'd run back to him.

That couldn't happen.

She checked into a hotel not far from Garden City. The concierge barely looked at her as he rattled off her room number, unaware that she was running for her life—or maybe from it.

Inside, the room was modern, soulless. A king-sized bed took up most of the space, dressed in crisp, untouched sheets. She tossed her bags onto it, moving on autopilot. The moment she locked the door behind her, her knees almost gave out.

She needed to think. To figure out her next move.

She stood at the window, pressing her forehead against the cool glass.

Four stories down, cars drifted down the street. People strolled in and out of coffee shops. A couple sat on a bench in the park across the road.

Paislee tried to remember what it felt like—to sit in the sun without fear. To plan for a future that wasn't already doomed.

Did she even have a future?

She tried to imagine it. What would she be in a hundred years? Two hundred? If Esben changed her, would she even make it that long? Or would he use her up, twisting her into something unrecognizable before finally getting rid of her?

A shudder wracked her body.

She closed her eyes, swallowing against the nausea clawing at her throat.

She just wanted to go home.

She wanted to sit on Kendra's bed and laugh about something stupid. She wanted to hear her dad shouting at the TV and her mom yelling at him to keep it down.

She wanted Michael—wanted the way his voice sent warmth curling through her, the way his touch made her feel safe, even when nothing else in her world was.

She wanted one night with him.

Just once. To know what it felt like to be completely his, even for a moment.

But she never would.

A sharp breath rattled through her and she straightened. She Bluetoothed her phone to the hotel's television and blindly selected a playlist. A '50s doo-wop song filtered through the speakers, and for a split second, she almost smiled.

She remembered making this playlist with Kendra. They'd danced around like idiots, talking about how they'd been born in the wrong era.

Right now, she missed her best friend so much it hurt. The weight pressing against her chest only grew heavier as she stared down at her phone.

Another voicemail from Michael.

She shouldn't listen.

But she did.

"Paislee, pick up the damn phone." His voice was tight, a little breathless. "You're scaring the hell out of me. Tell me where you are."

Her eyes stung. A lump burned in her throat.

She wanted to tell him.

But he'd come for her.

And Michael couldn't go to war against the Order.

Not because of her.

Her stomach churned violently. She gripped the window ledge, the drop below pulling at her like gravity knew her pain.

If she weren't here...Michael wouldn't have to fight.

Her fingers trembled as she stared at the ground below.

She was dead anyway, wasn't she?

What future was left?

There was no escape. Just this sick, spiraling free fall toward something worse than death.

Her pulse thrashed in her ears. Her breath came too fast, too loud.

She squeezed her eyes shut.

And then the panic cracked.

She spun from the window, pacing, her heart ricocheting inside. Her arms wrapped around her chest as if she could hold herself together. Her thoughts blurred into one frantic, wild heartbeat.

If she stayed there too long, he'd find her. If he found her, Michael would do something reckless. And it would get him killed.

A car honked somewhere outside, and she jumped so violently, her legs gave out beneath her. Her knees struck the floor, and she folded in on herself, gasping. Her body shook with sobs that had no sound.

She couldn't do this.

She couldn't stay.

She couldn't leave.

Tears streaked down her face as her mind grasped for something steady.

Michael.

That night. That kiss. That one moment when everything had changed.

She'd been desperate to get away from Esben.

And Michael?

He'd just been there. Some random guy at a bar, someone she'd chosen on a whim to throw Esben off, just to pretend she had someone else.

For five minutes.

That kiss—that single, impulsive kiss—had set fire to the entire course of her life. She could still taste it. Feel the way it shattered something inside her. Not fate. Not destiny.

It had been her choice.

And now, to protect him, she'd have to make another choice.

A broken breath shuddered through her. Her vision blurred, her gaze drifted back to the window.

Paislee's phone lit up again, and Michael's name blazed across the screen.

She squeezed her eyes shut, hitting Decline.

The tears came harder. She didn't try to stop them. Her heart and lungs ached from sobbing, and her body was wrecked with exhaustion. She buried her face in her knees, letting herself drown in it, letting herself break apart, letting herself feel the weight of the choice she was about to make.

She lost herself in it—so lost that when hands touched her shoulders, she screamed.

# Chapter
# Thirty-Nine

M ICHAEL DROPPED TO HIS knees beside Paislee, breathless and frantic. His hands trembled as they cupped her face, thumbs sweeping away the tears she couldn't stop.

"Paislee," he breathed. "What are you doing here?"

She laughed, but it cracked in the middle, tangled in a sob. "I could ask you the same thing."

He exhaled hard, a shaky thing that barely held him together. "Your phone," he said, his voice stretched thin. Then, his brows pulled together. "What the hell are you listening to?"

The soft croon of a 50s ballad drifted through the hotel room, slow and haunting. "The Platters." Through her tears, she huffed out a weak laugh. "It's a playlist Kendra and I made. She said if one of us ever died tragically, it should be to a soundtrack of dramatic oldies."

Michael shook his head. The worry in his eyes left no room for humor. "Morbid—and not funny."

She shrugged, murmuring, "It's a little funny. I can't believe you tracked my phone."

"I'll always find you, ducizza."

It wasn't a promise. It was a plea. A truth pulled from the deepest part of him.

The weight of everything pressed down at once, and no humor could lift it. Her chest collapsed inward.

"I can't stop crying," she whispered.

He gathered her against him, folding her into his chest, like he could shield her from the whole damn world. She clutched his shirt, shaking in his arms.

She pulled in a breath. "Did you find him?"

His arms tensed around her. "No. You come first."

"You'll be breaking the law if you stop him from taking me."

He pulled back just enough to tilt her face up. His hand cradled her jaw. "Then I'll break the law."

She wanted to believe that was an option. She wanted him to believe it. But that wasn't what scared her.

It was what breaking the law would look like. For him.

"Why did you run?" he asked gently, but his voice carried a quiet ache, like he was already bracing for the answer.

Tears pooled again. She blinked and they spilled freely. "Because I can't let Esben touch me. I won't." She swallowed hard. "I'd rather die."

He stilled. The words shattered something in him. His grip on her arms tightened, the air between them buzzing with panic.

"Don't—" His voice cracked, low and guttural. "Don't say that."

"You know what he's capable of." Her voice grew sharper, edged into despair. "You know he'll break me."

Michael stood suddenly, dragging her up with him. "Then let me turn you."

She stared at him, stunned.

"I'll do it now." His voice shook. "If you're mine—if I'm the one who changes you—he can't touch you."

For a moment—just one—hope stirred. She imagined it.

But then her heart dropped.

"I was approved for him, not you."

Michael's jaw flexed. "I don't care."

His hands found her face again, more urgent now. "We'll fight this."

But, there was no fighting the Order. He wasn't safe from them.

And if she let him do this...if she let him defy their laws again, he might not survive it.

"That's why I ran."

His expression faltered, confusion flickering.

"If I take myself out of the equation, Esben loses. The contract dies with me."

It took a full beat before her meaning landed. When it did, he recoiled.

"No."

"Michael—"

"No," he growled. "That's not the answer."

"We're both backed into corners," she said, voice shaking. "I've thought about it, really thought about it...but I'm scared it'll hurt."

He stepped back like she'd slapped him. His eyes flared wide, horror overtaking every other emotion.

"Don't say it."

She gripped his arm. "If you took too much—if it was you—would it hurt?"

A snarl tore from his throat.

"Stop," he bit out.

He turned, dragging her toward the door. "We're leaving."

She ripped free from his grasp. "I'm not letting you destroy yourself for me."

He turned slowly, his whole body shaking. His eyes were glassy, his voice a whisper of rage. "But you want me to kill you."

"It's better than what he'll do," she snapped. "You know that."

"No." His voice broke, shredded with fury. "He's not going to touch you."

She stepped closer, a breath away now. "You can't stop him—"

"And you can't ask this of me!"

Her voice dropped to a whisper, but it cut sharper than any scream. "I already have."

Silence crushed the space between them.

Then, softly...

"You don't get to choose how this ends for me, Michael."

Michael exhaled, but it sounded like he was breaking apart.

"I'm not asking for your permission," she said. "I'm only asking if...if you'll help make it painless."

He turned away, shoulders heaving. "Why are you giving up, Paislee?"

"Please," she whispered.

Michael turned back slowly. His voice broke on the words. "Why would you leave me now?"

She cupped his face, her thumbs brushing his cheeks, her own eyes burning. "Because if I stayed," she said, the words catching in her throat, "and something happened to you because of me, I wouldn't survive that."

Silence passed between them, filled with everything they couldn't say.

Her fingers slid to his jaw, memorizing every angle, every feature.

He drew a ragged breath and pressed his forehead to hers, like he could anchor them both with that one small connection.

"You're everything," he said, his voice nearly broken. "You have to know that."

"I do." A tear slid down her cheek.

His eyes searched hers, haunted. "I should've kept my distance," he choked. "You were never supposed to be part of this world. I pulled you into it. I did this. If I would've just walked away..."

"You wouldn't have," she said gently. "And neither would I."

Michael's throat worked around the lump he couldn't swallow.

"You asked me once what I'd do if I had a thousand lives."

His breath hitched.

She leaned in, forehead resting against his. "I'd choose you," she said, her voicing trembling. "In every one."

"Paislee..."

"I'd live them all," she whispered, "even knowing they'd end like this, I'd still pick you."

He closed his eyes, and a tear slipped free.

She kissed him. Soft. Final.

A kiss that said goodbye without ever saying the word.

Michael had never been afraid like this before.

Not when he'd stood in front of the Order's tribunal, facing their judgment.

Not when he'd felt Esben's schemes tightening around his throat.

Not when he'd taken the fall for Katya's transition, knowing it could cost him everything.

This? This was real fear.

Because Paislee was looking at him like she was already gone.

She wasn't sobbing anymore. Wasn't shaking.

Her voice was steady when she whispered, "I've already decided."

Michael felt himself unravel.

His stomach turned violently, and his fingers curled into fists at his sides. "You have no right—" His voice broke. He gritted his teeth. "You have no right to make this decision without me."

Paislee inhaled shakily, like she wanted to say something—but didn't.

This wasn't a decision he could change.

The air in the hotel room was suffocating, loud with meaning, too fragile. Behind them, the next song played. Another gentle and aching melody that wrapped around the room like a bittersweet memory too tender for the moment. It clung to the silence like a final thread, fraying at the edges. He wanted to smash the speakers.

Michael raked a violent hand through his hair as he gazed out the window.

His voice was low and strained. "Paislee...don't do this."

She exhaled as a small, tired smile curved her lips.

Like she was comforting him.

Like she wasn't the one who was about to sacrifice everything.

Michael's pulse thundered in his skull. He couldn't—he couldn't—

Before he could stop himself, his hands found her face and cupped it desperately, as if holding her there could make her stay.

"Tell me you don't love me," he whispered. "Say it, and I'll let you go."

Her lips trembled. Her beautiful, stupidly stubborn lips.

She said nothing.

Michael's breath shook. "You can't."

Paislee's eyes burned with too many things—but regret wasn't one of them.

"If you respect me, you won't try to stop me."

Something inside Michael snapped.

"No." His grip tightened, and he pressed his forehead against hers. As his hands tightened in her hair, his jaw clenching so hard it ached. "I swear I'll kill him."

She pulled back slightly, cupping his face. "And then what, Michael?"

Silence.

Michael squeezed his eyes shut, his breath coming fast.

She was calm. Too calm.

And he hated it.

He hated that he was losing.

That no matter how hard he fought—

She was still going to leave.

Her fingers found the hem of his shirt and lifted it slowly, deliberately. Then her hands skimmed up his stomach, his chest, his ribs.

Michael's breath caught. "Paislee—"

She kissed him.

A slow, aching kiss.

Her lips tasted like finality.

His hands dug into her waist, desperate, violent. He kissed her back harder, fiercer, like he could change her mind with nothing but his mouth.

She let him.

She let him hold her, let him kiss her like he was drowning and she was the only thing keeping him afloat.

But she didn't stop him from breaking.

Because this was goodbye.

And they knew it.

Michael's breath hitched as her fingers traced his jaw.

"Stay. Let me turn you." Michael's eyes burned. "Be mine for a thousand lifetimes."

She exhaled softly, a sound so tragically tender.

"No."

Michael's pulse thundered in his ears.

His hands shook as they skimmed down her back, his fingers desperate, unsteady.

She was slipping.

And he couldn't stop it.

The playlist switched songs, and the soft hum of another '50s ballad filled the silence. A sound low and eerie, almost like a dirge.

The song's opening crawled through the air like a ghost, too slow, too heavy. And then—

*"Forever, my darling..."*

The words drifted through the room like a vow neither of them could make.

Paislee smiled, something fragile and knowing, and reached for him again, swaying them both to the music like it was the only thing holding her upright.

Michael let her.

Because it was all he had left.

Her lips brushed his ear.

He clenched his jaw, trying to swallow the tremor in his throat.

He didn't want to.

He didn't want to give her this.

But he couldn't deny her.

Not now.

Her hands slid over his chest, her touch deliberate, certain.

And Michael knew.

Knew that in a few hours, in a few heartbeats, in a single breath—

She'd be gone.

And there wasn't a damn thing he could do about it.

# Chapter Forty

P AISLEE KISSED MICHAEL LIKE if she held him there long
enough—kissed him deep enough—the night wouldn't end.
That the universe would rewrite itself, and this wouldn't be their
first and last time together.

Michael's breath was uneven, his hands tightened at her waist.
Not gentle. Not careful. Like he was holding onto something
already slipping.

She leaned into him anyway.

Needed it.

Needed him.

Her hands slid down the length of his chest, fingers curling into
the hem of his shirt.

A request.

Or maybe a plea.

He hesitated.

Just a second—but she felt it.

Then he raised his arms, letting her strip him bare.

His eyes were dark, hooded with emotion, his jaw clenched like he was holding back something feral. But then she lifted her own arms, letting him undress her.

His restraint snapped—not just desire. Something sharper. Harder to contain.

Then his hands were on her, lifting, pulling, stripping away the barrier between them as his restraint gave way.

The moment her bare skin met his, Michael gripped her hips with a possessive, reverent desperation.

He kissed her like he was claiming every inch of her before something took her away. But when he reached her neck—he stopped.

Not pulling back. Not moving.

Just there. Breathing.

Her hands slid lower, urging, chasing the sensation that was undoing her.

He didn't kiss her mouth.

Instead, he held her like she was his last tether to this world—like if he just held her tight enough, he could keep her.

Her breath caught as his hands slid lower, teasing, tormenting, exploring.

She moaned softly, arching against him, needing his touch like air. Needing to forget everything but *this*.

Her fingers trailed the line of his waistband, then slipped beneath, wrapping around him.

His forehead dropping to hers, his body shuddering at her touch.

Then a sound tore through him—low guttural. Not quite human.

Michael dropped to his knees, his hands clutching her thighs, his breath hot against her skin.

He didn't move for a moment. Just breathed. Steadying something inside him.

Paislee's fingers slid through his hair, her chest aching at his hesitation.

It felt like control. Like it was the only way he could hold himself together.

When he finally looked up, his eyes were darker than she'd ever seen them.

Haunted.

A flicker of unease slipped through her.

A silent plea. A question.

*Can't this be forever?*

She could have lied. Could have told him yes.

Instead, she traced his jaw and whispered, "Michael..."

His hold on her tightened.

And then he kissed his way down her stomach, slowly.

She gasped as his mouth found her. His tongue warm and relentless, sent pleasure crashing through her.

Her fingers tightened in his hair, and her head fell back as his tongue sent waves of heat through her, her knees nearly giving out. But he held her steady, worshipping her, tasting her like a man desperate to memorize every part of her.

He turned her gently, his mouth following the line of her spine, slowing over her scar, until he stood behind her, chest to her back. His breath warm against her neck as his hands slid down her thighs, gently guiding her legs open.

She trembled.

One hand slid between her thighs, teasing her open, coaxing her higher. The other hand palmed her breast, commanding her body to surrender.

Paislee melted back into him, lost in the rhythm of his hands.

The sensation hit hard. Too sharp, too fast. Pulling a broken sound from her before she could stop it.

She turned in his arms, breathless, eyes wild.

His grip tightened—almost bruising. His eyes searched hers, begging. *Don't do this. Change your mind. Stay.*

But she held his face, her touch gentle. Her voice unyielding.

"No one will take this night from me."

Michael lifted her in one swift movement and carried her to the bed.

He laid her down like she was something holy.

She reached for him—but again, he wouldn't kiss her.

Instead, his lips traveled low, slow and thorough, until she was coming undone beneath his mouth.

He lapped her mercilessly, over and over, until her thighs and her cries shattered the silence. It tore through her—violent, sudden, all-consuming.

And still, he didn't stop.

Only when she lay trembling did he move over her—slow, controlled, like he was forcing himself to stay there and not lose it entirely.

She felt him press against her. Thick, hot, unrelenting. A flicker of fear cut through the haze—sharp enough to make her hesitate.

Michael stilled. Immediately.

His eyes locked onto hers, searching, holding.

Breath unsteady, and offered the smallest, surest nod. Her answer silent, but absolute. Giving herself to him completely.

Michael muttered something low in his own tongue. Then—

He pushed inside.

The pain hit first. Sharp. Splitting.

She cried out, her nails digging into his arms.

His body went rigid—suddenly, completely still.

She gasped, shaking.

Michael gripping her thigh to hold himself back.

And then he thrust again, deep and slow.

Her breath broke, rough and uneven as he filled her completely.

Again, he held still, shaking with restraint, whispering something in a language that sounded like a heartbeat.

Her body adjusted slowly. The pain dulled. The pleasure bled in.

And when it did, he moved.

His thrusts were slow—agonizingly slow—then deeper. Harder.

She gasped, cried his name, wrapped her legs around his hips and gave him everything.

Pleasure building like waves breaking over her.

She shattered.

Michael didn't stop.

He moved with hunger, like every thrust was a goodbye he didn't know how to give. His rhythm deepened, paced like he was holding onto her with every breath.

He didn't let up.

He took her, claimed her—his rhythm was fierce and unrelenting as he brought them both to the breaking point.

His fangs slipped into view and betrayed the control he was rapidly losing. Sharp and gleaming, like instinct taking over.

He growled something guttural, and then he thrust deep one final time and spilled into her.

Paislee's body trembled beneath his.

His chest heaved, his heartbeat racing, his breath warm against her skin.

Moments ticked by. Neither of them spoke.

Because there was nothing left to say.

Michael gathered her into his arms, her back against his chest, his hands splayed over her stomach, holding her like he couldn't bear to let her go.

Paislee listened to the steady rhythm of his heart, letting it lull her into sleep.

The last thing she felt was his lips pressing into her hair. His arms tightening.

And in that moment, she knew—

Michael wasn't going to do it.

He wasn't going to end her.

And that terrified her more than anything else.

Paislee woke to silence. Not just any silence.

A suffocating silence.

The kind that settled into your bones before you even opened your eyes.

The room was dark. The air thick with something she couldn't name. Grief, maybe. It clung to her skin, heavy as iron.

The sheets beside her were cold.

Her heart gave a slow, measured thud.

Then she saw him.

A silhouette against the window.

Michael stood perfectly still, shoulders drawn tight, hands braced on the frame. Not a single light was on.

Paislee sat up. The room felt unsteady. Hollowed out.

She licked her dry lips. "Michael?"

He didn't answer.

Just stared out the window.

But she saw his knuckles flex against the glass.

How long had he been standing there while she slept?

She exhaled softly, clutching the sheet around her as she shifted to the edge of the bed.

His shoulders flinched—just barely.

She closed her eyes for a moment. Then she stood, the cool floor grounding her as she stepped toward him like she was walking to her own execution.

She stopped just behind him. Close enough to feel his warmth. Close enough that if she reached out...

She didn't.

Not yet.

"Do you regret it?" she asked softly.

Michael exhaled sharply, his head bowing slightly.

His voice was low. Tense. "What?"

"Making love to me...might've made this harder. It has for me." Her own voice barely made a sound. "Do you regret it?"

Slowly, Michael turned.

So slowly it felt like the world itself had stopped just to watch him.

When his eyes met hers, her breath caught.

Because he looked broken.

Not angry. Not even grieving.

Just destroyed.

His chest rose too fast. His hands curled into fists at his sides. But his eyes...

They burned.

With sorrow. With the kind of pain that lives deep, quiet, and forever.

Michael took a step toward her. Then another.

Until he was so close, she could feel the trembling in his body.

Still, she didn't move.

Didn't flinch.

She had made this choice.

Michael reached for her—but not like her executioner.

Like someone about to say goodbye.

His fingers brushed along her jaw, his knuckles grazing her lips.

Paislee shivered.

He closed his eyes for half a breath, then exhaled. His hand slid to the back of her neck, and then he kissed her.

It wasn't rushed.

It wasn't desperate.

It was slow. Deep. Tortured.

Paislee whimpered against his mouth, holding onto him, wishing somehow she could stay inside that kiss forever.

But they both knew.

This was the last time.

The last time she'd feel him. Taste him.

The last time his hands would hold her.

A sob clawed its way up her throat, but she didn't let it out.

This was what she'd chosen.

Wasn't it?

Michael he pulled back just enough to whisper against her lips.

"Close your eyes."

She stared at him, searching. Begging for something, any sign he might change his mind.

But Michael was still.

Silent.

Already gone.

Her hand flattened against his chest, feeling the beat of his heart.

And then she closed her eyes.

Michael exhaled, rough and uneven.

One hand still held her face, thumb brushing a silent goodbye across her cheekbone, The other curved around the back of her neck, steadying her.

His breath ghosted across her skin, warm. Final.

And then the sharp sting of his fangs pierced her neck.

# Chapter Forty-One

A T FIRST, THERE WAS only warmth.

Michael's lips brushed against Paislee's temple, soft as a whisper.

Then came the bite.

The pain came fast and deep, a white-hot streak of lightening through her neck.

But just as quickly, it faded.

A breath caught in her throat. Her fingers tensed against his chest, but she didn't pull away.

She didn't fight it.

She let him take her.

Everything faded.

The venom worked fast—numbing her, flooding her, threading itself into her blood like silk and steel.

Her body relaxed without her permission.

Her limbs went heavy. Useless.

She tried to breathe, but her lungs felt thick.

Michael was taking her life.

And she—

She was letting him.

Her vision blurred at the edges. Not from tears, but from something else.

Something creeping and cold.

The room distorted, the darkness stretching, bending, tilting into strange angles.

Her ears rang. A soft, distant buzzing, like the world was pulling away from her.

Michael's arms tightened.

She focused on him. The shape of him, the trembling in his muscles, the way his grip refused to let her go too fast.

But even he was fading.

His warmth dulled.

His scent—that intoxicating mix of spice and something purely him—vanished.

Her heartbeat slowed. A heavy, weighted pause between each thud.

She tried to open her eyes, but couldn't.

Was he still holding her?

Was he still here?

She couldn't feel anything.

Not the floor beneath her feet.

Not her own body.

Not his arms.

She was suspended in nothingness.

Floating.

Weightless.

Drifting.

Distant.

Her ears were filled with the rush of the ocean. Pulling away, pressing forward again.

Something deep inside her ached.

She wasn't ready.

Not yet.

Her thoughts stretched apart, unraveled.

Memories bled into one another—Michael's smile. Kendra's laughter. The warmth of the sun on her face back home.

She reached for them.

Tried to hold on to something—anything.

But her hands didn't move.

Her fingers wouldn't curl.

Her body wasn't hers anymore.

Her breath caught—maybe.

She wasn't sure.

How long had she been standing here?

A few seconds?

A lifetime?

Something cold slithered through her chest.

No, wait—

But she was slipping too fast.

She couldn't speak.

Michael—

Her lips parted.

She tried to form the words.

Tried to whisper his name.

But all that came out was a soft, breathless exhale.

And then—

Nothing.

The world was slipping away.

Paislee's pulse was barely there, her breath fading—

And then—

A sound tore through the darkness.

Not a cry.

A roar.

It tore through the darkness, thunderous. It shook the walls, pierced through the haze of venom dulling her mind.

She flinched, her body jerked instinctively.

But Michael—

Michael was gone.

One moment, his mouth was at her throat, his arms wrapped around her.

The next—

He was ripped away.

The weight of him vanished—

And in its place, a wet, sickening gasp.

A snarl of pain.

A crack of bone on bone.

Then—

A crash. His body hitting the ground.

Paislee collapsed with him, her knees buckling beneath the weight of everything.

Her head spun.

The venom twisted the moment into something slow and dreamlike.

She heard breathing—shallow, ragged.

Not hers.

Michael's.

She forced her eyes open.

He was on top of her. Heavy. Too heavy.

Warmth bled through her the sheet she'd wrapped around her, thick and wet on her skin.

Blood.

Michael's blood.

Her vision swam.

Something cold and sharp pressed against her stomach—

And she saw it.

A blade. A long, wicked dagger dripping with blood.

Her mind reeled. Her lungs burned. But she couldn't move.

Then a voice, smooth and smug.

"Tsk, tsk."

Esben.

He gripped Michael's shoulder and yanked him back just slightly. Michael groaned, barely conscious.

She tried to scream, but no sound came.

She was trapped inside herself.

Esben crouched beside them, a silhouette carved from shadow. Triumphant.

"You should thank me, *bedda mia*." His voice was silk and razor wire. "I just saved your life."

Paislee's lips parted. Her head spun.

Michael's blood pooled beneath her.

"You didn't think it would be that easy, did you?"

Paislee tried to flinch. To move. But her body refused.

Michael wasn't moving.

Panic bloomed inside her, weak. But real.

She needed to—she had to—

Her fingers twitched.

There was something beneath them.

A phone.

Michael's phone.

The last of her strength pushed through the haze.

Paislee fumbled weakly, dragging trembling fingers across the screen. The first contact she saw, she pressed.

It connected.

"Hello?"

Alaitz.

Paislee's lips parted. She tried to speak, but her voice caught.

Alaitz's tone sharpened instantly. "Michael, what's wrong?"

Esben's voice reached her again. "All right, sweetheart. Time to come with me."

No. She had to move. Had tell Alaitz to help...

"Bitch." His face twisted. "Give me that phone."

Pain flared, hot and searing, but only for a second.

Then nothing again.

Her body was shutting down.

She couldn't feel Michael anymore.

Couldn't hold on.

Then—

A crash.

A voice.

"Esben!"

Seth.

It barely registered before her head dropped against Michael's chest.

Everything was too loud. Too blurry. Too far.

Shouting.

Fighting.

Michael's name.

Her name.

None of it mattered.

Michael remained so still.

Slowly, she found her voice. "Michael..."

Nothing.

She tried again. "Michael, please."

From the phone, a voice burst through, frantic.

"Michael! Are you there?"

Paislee forced her lips to move.

"Alaitz..."

Silence. Then—

A sharp inhale.

"Paislee? Where's Michael?"

Paislee swallowed, her throat tight and dry. "He's hurt," she rasped. "Please hurry."

Alaitz was yelling to someone else.

Paislee barely heard. Her body felt so cold now.

Michael wasn't breathing.

Alaitz was still talking, but Paislee couldn't understand the words anymore.

Her own voice was too quiet, too weak.

"Esben..." It was all she could say.

The phone slid from her fingers.

It hit the floor with a thud.

Her head followed.

Somewhere far away, Seth's voice called out.

Then sirens, and a rush of voices.

Footsteps. Hands.

They were shouting.

"Unresponsive."

"Massive blood loss."

"Get her on the stretcher—now."

She felt herself being lifted, pulled away from Michael.

No. No, she had to stay.

Someone touched her wrist.

"She's human."

Another voice cut in—lower, urgent.

"She's his largitor."

A pause.

"She's lost a lot of blood, but there's no wound."

Then—

"This blood isn't hers."

Confusion. A beat.

"She has a medical tag."

A sharp gasp.

"Right wrist."

Silence. Then:

"Jesus Christ. She's O-negative."

Everything stopped.

Then someone cursed loudly. "Fuck! Get that blood off her. Now!"

Hands grabbed her. Someone shouted for a saline wash. Another for a clean IV line.

They were stripping her down and scrubbing her skin.

Michael was being rushed out.

She tried to reach for him.

Tried to tell them to wait.

But the world was tilting, fading, falling away.

The last thing she felt was the sting of cold water against her skin—and then darkness.

Nothing.

# Chapter
# Forty-Two

A SLOW, CREEPING FIRE clawed up Michael's spine, spread through his ribs, and settled deep in his bones.

His eyelids felt heavy, his mind groggy—but the moment he inhaled, the scent of antiseptic and blood burned through him.

His eyes snapped open.

A ceiling. Machines. Beeping in his ears.

He turned his head. IVs. Wires. A heart monitor tracking his pulse.

A hospital.

Why?

His mind searched for answers, the last thing he could remember.

Then—it hit him like a freight train.

Paislee.

Michael ripped the wires off his chest, ignoring the flatline wail of the machine. The sharp sting of the IV in his arm was nothing compared to the sheer panic tearing through him.

Where was she?

A nurse rushed in, and her expression shifted to fear as she met his wild, enraged stare.

"Mr. Chamberlain, please, lie back down."

Michael growled, barely resisting the urge to shove her away. "Turn off that damned machine."

He pushed himself up—and his back ignited with pain.

He barely registered it.

He looked down at his jeans, stained with blood.

Memories slammed into him in flashes.

Esben. The knife.

Paislee collapsing.

A dark, guttural sound built in his throat. Had Esben taken her? Had he turned her?

The nurse pressed a hand to his chest, trying to ease him back down.

Michael's body tensed.

"Take out the IV," he commanded.

She hesitated. "Mr. Chamberlain, you're not stable—"

"Now."

His voice was low, deadly.

The fear in her eyes spiked, but she obeyed, and pulled the IV free. The puncture in his arm had already started to heal.

"Let me get Dr. Breton," she mumbled before scurrying from the room.

Michael was already on his feet.

The room spun. His body was still sluggish from sedatives, but he gritted his teeth and pushed forward.

And then he saw her.

Paislee. Unmoving. Hooked up to machines.

Relief flooded him. She was still here.

But as he drew closer, his relief twisted into something darker. She was so pale.

He could still see her chest rising and falling, but she looked lifeless in that bed, surrounded by wires and tubes.

The fear gripped tighter.

Michael braced himself on the bed rail and leaned in.

"Paislee," he whispered, his lips brushing her forehead.

No response.

A sharp, painful clench in his chest.

She should have stirred.

He kissed her again, murmuring her name against her lips.

Still nothing.

"Michael."

Michael's head snapped up. "Dr. Breton, is she alright?"

Dr. Breton hesitated, pushing his glasses up the bridge of his nose.

"She came into contact with your blood," Dr. Breton said as he shifted through the chart in his hands.

Michael gripped the rail tighter. "Is she changing?"

Dr. Breton rubbed his jaw.

"I can't say for sure, but I believe the EMTs cleaned her before it was too late." He gestured to the machines. "We put her under, just in case. We'll monitor her closely."

Michael's pulse thundered. His fingers clenched the rail so hard that the metal groaned beneath his grip.

Where was he? Where the fuck was Esben?

He turned to Dr. Breton. "What happened?"

The doctor flicked through his clipboard again, avoiding his eyes.

"Seth Bardin found you and kicked down the door. He struggled with Esben but managed to scare him off."

Michael stilled.

"Scared him off?"

Dr. Breton nodded.

"Is Seth all right?"

"Yes. Don't worry, Michael. Agents are looking for your brother now."

Michael's rage burned hotter.

Esben was still out there.

No more.

His fingers tightened around Paislee's hand.

His voice was a low growl. "I'll find him first."

Then—a memory. A voice at his ear, thick with amusement as a blade slid into his back.

*"It's time to finish this, little brother. If you want your girlfriend back, meet us at Allusion. I suspect it'll take you a while to recover. Don't worry. I'll take good care of her for you in the meantime."*

Michael's fangs ached. His vision burned red.

Pain medicine? Sedatives? It didn't matter anymore.

He grabbed the clothes left on a chair and tugged on a clean shirt.

Then his mother entered. "Michael, why are you out of bed?"

He didn't stop, didn't slow, and he was tying on his shoes when his mother placed a hand on his shoulder, her eyes wide.

Alaitz's voice wavered. "Please, stay here. Agents are looking for Esben."

Michael's eyes were cold, hard. "They won't find him before I do."

"Son," she whispered, "he doesn't fight fair."

Michael paused. Glanced at Paislee. His voice softened just slightly. "Watch over her for me?"

Alaitz covered her mouth as tears slid down her cheeks. She nodded.

Michael kissed her forehead. Then he was gone.

# Chapter Forty-Three

P AISLEE WAS TRAPPED. HER body wouldn't move. Her mouth wouldn't speak.

But she could hear everything.

Michael's voice—then silence. Was it a dream?

Then—she heard Alaitz.

"What do you expect, Saverio? After what you did?"

A pause.

A hand brushed her wrist.

"What's this?"

Someone tugged on her medical bracelet.

"She's O-negative." Alaitz's voice filled with horror. "How did no one catch this?"

There was a long moment of silence.

A longer silence.

Alaitz's voice sounded cold and unyielding. "She should never have been anyone's largitor—especially Michael's."

Saverio's voice was tight. "What do we do? Michael isn't going to let her go."

Paislee's heart slammed against her ribs. Something was very, very wrong.

More silence. The seconds stretched, each one a sigh too long.

She could feel Alaitz's fingers grip her hand and give it a small squeeze. "We're not going to do anything."

"Alaitz—"

"Nothing, Saverio," Alaitz said, and her tone carried a steely edge.

Paislee felt Alaitz remove the ID bracelet and heard her say, "Where is Dr. Breton? I think we need to have a chat. Obviously, he did a full exam on her when she became Michael's largitor. This should never have happened."

"How are we going to keep this quiet?" Saverio asked. "Reports are being filed. Four EMTs saw her bracelet. They had to wash her down just to keep her from changing."

"Hmm," Alaitz hummed. "We'll figure something out."

"What about Seth? He knows now, too, Alaitz."

"I'll talk to Seth."

Michael stormed toward Allusion; his body still ached, but his rage fueled him past the pain.

The club was locked—of course it was—but Esben had found a way in. Michael was sure of it.

Michael punched the security code. The bolt clicked, and he stepped inside, flipping on the lights.

The club's black walls swallowed the glow. Shadows stretched long in the recesses.

Then he saw him.

Esben stood on the balcony, his thigh resting on the railing, smirking.

"Mikey." His voice was mocking, indulgent. "You're here so soon. Paislee must be feeding you well to heal that fast."

Michael's fingers curled into fists.

Esben's smirk widened. "I bet she tastes *magnifica*. Bet she melts on the tongue."

Michael didn't rise to the bait. His eyes stayed locked on his brother, watching carefully as Esben pulled out a knife.

"Do you like this knife, little brother? Are you wondering if this is the one I plunged into your back?"

Michael's eyes narrowed.

Without warning, Esben tossed it to him.

Michael caught it out of reflex, his fingers curling around the hilt. It was cheap. Unbalanced. Unfamiliar in his grip.

A prop.

A taunt.

Then Esben drew another knife.

This one Michael recognized: a military-grade, seven-inch blade—Esben's personal weapon. He carried it everywhere.

"No," Esben said, twirling it between his fingers. "This is the one I put in your back."

He smiled like it was a private joke. "Don't look so offended. I wasn't trying to kill you. Just...leaving a message."

Michael's jaw flexed.

"I got your message." His voice was low, lethal. "You're fucking crazy."

"I'm not. Well...maybe a little." Esben laughed, still twirling. "I'm angry."

Michael's grip tightened. "At what?"

The smile vanished.

Esben stopped flipping the knife and pointed it at Michael. "You."

Michael didn't flinch.

"I've never done anything to you, Esben."

"No?" Esben exhaled hard. "Our father loved my mother. Not yours. He wanted me as his heir. Not you."

Michael stared him down. "Is that what Saverio told you?"

Esben's face twisted. "Yes. But your bitch of a mother wouldn't stop until she got what she wanted."

Michael's hands curled tighter.

Esben stepped down one stair, his knife catching the light.

"Do you know what it's like to be erased, Mikey? To know that you were first, then the moment you came along, none of it mattered?"

Michael said nothing.

Esben bared his teeth. "You took everything. And you didn't even have to try."

Michael exhaled slowly. "I never wanted it. I'm a Chamberlain. I want nothing to do with the Regnanti family—or their legacy."

Esben laughed. Bitter. Empty. "It doesn't fucking matter what you want." His eyes darkened. "Father was rewriting the bylaws. Making space for me on the board."

Michael scoffed. "No, he wasn't."

Esben's knife twitched in his grip. "You weren't there."

"I didn't have to be." Michael's voice was flat. "I seem to understand Saverio better than you."

A flicker of something raw passed over Esben's face. But it was gone in an instant.

He smirked again. "It doesn't matter."

Michael waited.

He tilted his head. "You know why?"

Michael said nothing.

Esben's smile stretched. "Because I've already joined the ones who are going to burn this world to the ground."

Michael's chest tightened. "The fuck are you talking about?"

"You don't even know what's coming, do you?" Esben grinned, flashing his fangs.

Michael's blade flew for his throat.

But Esben was ready. He dodged, slicing toward Michael's ribs.

Michael barely blocked it in time.

The fight erupted.

Steel clashed against steel. The club echoed with violence.

Michael's form was tight, controlled. Precision. Strength. Focus.

But Esben?

Esben was chaos. Wild. Fast. He fought like a storm—unhinged and unpredictable.

Michael forced him back.

But Esben spun, and grazed Michael's shoulder.

Michael hissed, stepping back. Blood bloomed and trailed down his arm.

Esben smirked.

"Does it make you sick?" Esben asked, breathless. "Knowing that no matter what you do, you'll lose her?"

"Shut up, Esben." Michael's voice grated. "Your tactics are obvious."

Esben's grin widened.

"*Dimmi, Micu,*" he said, circling like a vulture, "did you whisper something sweet before you sank your fangs into her? Before you started to suck the life out of her?"

Michael struck.

His fist cracked into Esben's jaw. Blood splattered across the floor.

But he laughed. "Ah. There it is."

Michael's breath was ragged, his vision burned red.

Esben spat blood and wiped his mouth with the back of his hand. Then, slipped in low, like a snake in the grass.

"Were you really going to kill her?"

Michael froze.

Esben's smile turned sly and knowing. "Because I don't think you were."

Michael gripped his knife tighter. "You don't know anything."

"Oh, but I do," Esben said, his voice dropped. "You've always been easy to read. You love her. And that love makes you...unreliable."

Michael barely saw the lunge—

Esben slammed him into the bar. Pain snapped through his spine. Then fire lit up his side.

Esben's blade buried itself into his ribs.

Michael gasped, his eyes wide. Breathing jagged.

Esben leaned close, twisting the blade like a lover's whisper. "You think I'm the villain. But she trusted you. And you hesitated. Long enough for me to stop it."

Michael snarled.

He yanked the blade from his side and drove it into Esben's.

Esben howled.

Michael shoved him into a table. Glass shattered, raining down like stars.

Michael advanced.

Esben laughed, spitting blood. "You couldn't do it. You froze."

Michael stiffened.

He remembered how Paislee had gone limp in his arms. How her pulse faltered. He felt her slipping—and still, he hadn't finished it.

Esben saw it. Smiled like a man winning a war.

"You were never going to finish her. Not really."

Michael's voice came low and bitter. "Not everyone discards human life like you."

"Ah, yes. Katya." Esben's tone changed. It was colder. "Here's a twist for you."

He leaned in, his voice a blade of its own.

"I didn't turn Katya."

A whisper. A grenade.

"Never touched her."

Michael stiffened. "You're lying."

"Am I?" Esben tilted his head. "Or were we both just pawns on someone else's board?"

Michael's expression darkened. "Whose?"

Esben's laugh was hollow. "Now, that is the question, isn't it?"

Michael lunged.

The fight turned brutal. Sloppy. Personal.

They crashed through chairs, slammed into walls, tore each other apart.

Michael got him on the ground, his blade to his Esben's throat.

"Go on, Mikey."

Michael didn't move.

Esben's breath was shallow, but the amusement never left his eyes.

"If you can't kill me," he whispered, "you never could've killed her."

Michael's hand shook.

"It doesn't even matter, does it?" Esben's voice turned cruel. "You were going to kill the woman you love...or you didn't have the balls to do it. Either way, she's already lost to you."

Michael's grip tightened.

Esben's eyes gleamed.

His voice turned mocking, singsong. "The Order will never let her be your mate."

Michael stilled. Cold washed over him.

Esben grinned through bloody teeth. "Think about it." He voiced danced. "Paislee should never have been your donor."

Michael's stomach dropped. "Why not?"

Esben smirk twisted wider.

Michael's vision blurred red.

His blade cut into Esben's throat.

Esben hissed as blood welled up at his neck.

"Why not, Esben?" Michael growled.

Then—

A voice cut through the shadows.

"Michael Chamberlain. Release him."

Michael stiffened.

More figures emerged from the dark.

The Order.

One agent stepped forward. "Michael. Put it down."

He looked at them, then back to Esben.

Esben was grinning again. "There it is. The moment you realize you were played, little brother."

"Michael." Another voice. Low. Stern. *"Thou shall not bring death upon thy kin."*

Michael's pulse thundered.

This was his chance.

He stared at Esben.

The brother who had stabbed him. Hunted Paislee. Threatened everything Michael held dear.

And now held answers.

He could end it here. To hell with the Order and their code.

His grip tightened.

But slowly, Michael let go.

He released Esben's collar and pulled back.

Esben coughed and rolled onto his side, wiping the blood from his neck.

The Order's agents moved in.

Michael stood there, his chest heaving, watching them drag Esben up and lock his arms behind his back.

Esben met Michael's gaze. "I won't be locked up forever."

Michael's jaw clenched. "You won't have to be."

Esben's grin faltered.

Michael leaned in, and his voice was low and lethal. "Because, next time, I won't stop."

Esben's laughter returned. But this time—it wasn't as confident.

The Order hauled him away.

Michael stood still, listening to their footsteps fade.

Then finally, he turned, and walked out.

# Chapter Forty-Four

MICHAEL WENT HOME TO clean up. He peeled off his bloodstained clothes and tossed them into the trash. The fight was over.

Or at least, that's what he told himself.

Under scalding water, he scrubbed hard. Rinsing away the blood, the sweat, the stench of battle. But it wasn't just blood that clung to him.

It was his Esben's words.

*"You were played, little brother."*

Michael's jaw clenched.

Esben was a liar. A manipulator. He twisted everything.

But not everything he said was a lie.

*"The Order will never let you keep her."*

Exhaling, Michael rested his hands against the shower wall.

He didn't have time for this.

Once dressed, he went to Paislee's room.

The wardrobe was nearly empty now, stripped bare of the few things she'd come with.

And yet, there in a bottom drawer, he found her ridiculous old pajama pants and bunny slippers.

Michael smiled.

How had she forgotten them?

His smile faded as something outside the window caught his eye. A black car.

It didn't move.

As if sensing his gaze, it rolled away.

Michael's eyes darkened. He grabbed Paislee's bag and headed out.

At the hospital, the same car was there. Parked across the street.

Watching.

He slammed his car door and strode into the building without looking back.

Paislee was still sleeping. His gaze landed on her the moment he walked in her room. Still, pale, but breathing.

Alive.

Dr. Breton looked up, pushing his wide glasses up the bridge of his nose.

"Michael, how are you feeling?"

Michael didn't answer. His eyes were locked on Paislee.

"Is she—?"

"She wasn't turned," Breton said with an easy smile. "She should be waking up soon. Would you like a minute?"

Michael nodded once. "Yes."

Dr. Breton hesitated a moment and Michael waited for him to say something else. But he didn't. Just turned away and left.

Michael waited for the latch to click, then walked to her bedside and turned off the monitor. Quiet returned.

Gently, he peeled the electrodes from her chest and hands.

Paislee stirred.

He leaned in, brushing his lips across hers. A whisper of a kiss. Not asking, just promising.

Her lashes fluttered.

"Michael..." she breathed.

A small smile touched his lips. "*Ciau, muri miu.*"

Her brow wrinkled. "What does that mean?"

"Sleeping beauty."

She laughed once, faintly. "You're such a liar."

Michael smiled again, fuller now. "You're awake. That's all that matters."

Paislee shifted, just slightly. And then he saw it.

The moment her memories returned.

Her breath hitched. Her hand shot up to his chest. Searching. Panicked.

"I thought you were dead."

Michael's jaw tightened. He caught her hand on his and pressed a kiss to her knuckles.

Tears filled her eyes before she could stop them.

He caught them with his thumbs and wiped them away.

"Esben, did you—?"

"Not quite," he murmured. Michael exhaled. "He's alive. The Order has him. It's over, Paislee."

A lie. But one she needed to carry right now.

She exhaled, shaky. Her eyes searched his face again. Needing to be sure.

Michael kissed her palm

"Don't ever try to leave me like that again, Paislee."

Her eyes softened. "I thought I lost you."

Michael's voice was low. "*Mi su' 'nnamuratu di tia profondamenti.*"

"I really need to learn Italian."

"Sicilian," he corrected, his voice warming. "I've fallen in love with you, Paislee Sullivan. Deeply."

Her lips curved, slow and sly. "Is that right, Mr. Chamberlain?"

Michael didn't flinch. Didn't joke.

"I mean it," he said. "You were willing to sacrifice yourself for me." His thumb traced circles on her skin. "That tells me everything."

He looked down at their joined hands and gave the barest hint of a smile. Then softly, he spoke again. "My intentions have changed."

She stilled. "How so?"

"I want a thousand years... a thousand lives with you." His voice stayed low, steady. "I would like you to consider being my partner."

The silence stretched between them, thick with meaning.

Heavy with everything unspoken.

Paislee's fingers tightened around his. Her eyes searched his—not rejecting, not retreating, just...taking him in.

"You have a way of making me believe in things I never thought I could have."

Michael's chest tightened.

Paislee smiled softly. "You're not the only one whose intentions have changed."

Michael's heart thudded in his chest.

She hesitated.

"I'd like to go home," she said quietly.

Michael's face fell. She had said those words before. She'd said those words before. And she'd meant Pennsylvania. She had meant goodbye. He lowered his head. He couldn't blame her. "All right."

But then she added, almost shyly, "You told me that your home was mine, too, right?"

He looked at her again. Really looked.

"I did."

"Then...can we go home now?" Her voice wavered. "To our home?"

The ache in his chest cracked open and filled with something warmer.

Michael leaned in, kissed her like a promise, and whispered against her lips.

"Let's go home, ducizza."

# Epilogue

T HE ELEVATOR DOOR OPENED, and Alaitz's heels clicked
sharply on the tile floor.

Dr. Breton's office was at the end of the hall. She didn't slow
down.

"Alaitz?"

She stopped and turned toward the voice.

Seth.

He was buttoning his shirt, stepping out of a hospital room.
Blood smeared his collar, but the wound beneath was already healed.

Alaitz scanned him, her sharp eyes softening just slightly.

"Did Esben hurt you badly?"

Seth glanced at his ruined shirt and then back at her. "Already healed."

She nodded once, but the tension in her shoulders didn't ease. "How's Michael?"

At her son's name, Alaitz's throat tightened.

"You saved his life." She hesitated and then added, "Thank you."

Seth tilted his chin up, offering her a small, reassuring smile. "I'm glad I was able to get there in time."

She brushed away a stubborn tear, but then her eyes darkened.

"You seem to care more about him than his own father does."

Seth's smile faded. His gaze dropped. Hands in pockets.

Alaitz didn't press him.

Instead, Seth asked, "Why are you going to Dr. Breton?"

Alaitz lifted her chin. "I have things to discuss."

Seth wasn't buying it. "Alaitz."

She sighed. She never could fool Seth.

"Paislee."

Seth's entire body went still.

"I know." His voice was low, unreadable. "And Michael wouldn't know; he's too young. The Order buried the truth about O-negative donors. Have you told him yet?"

Alaitz looked away.

Seth's hands gripped her shoulders. "You have to."

She pulled back. "Leave it alone, Seth."

His brows snapped together. "What if she's exposed to his blood again? Can you imagine how devastating it would be for him to watch her die in his arms?"

Alaitz's jaw clenched. "I'm not saying anything. And neither are you."

Seth shook his head, his lips forming a tight, bitter line. "You can't expect me to sit back and watch this play out. She's going to die—"

"No, she's not," Alaitz cut in, her voice dangerously quiet.

Seth's mouth snapped shut.

A long beat of silence. Then—he exhaled sharply. "What aren't you telling me?"

Alaitz's eyes filled with fresh tears. "Please, Seth, don't ask me any questions. Just trust me."

His voice was almost a whisper. "That's not how trust works, Alaitz."

She swallowed hard. "The only culprit in all this is Dr. Breton. He allowed this to happen, and I'm about to find out why."

Seth's jaw tightened. "And if I dig any deeper?"

Alaitz's gaze turned icy. "Then you'll be looking for trouble."

They stared at each other for a long moment.

Then Seth shook his head. Disappointed.

That hurt more than she expected.

Without another word, he turned away.

She watched the elevator doors close between them, and her heart sank.

*This is all Breton's fault.*

Her blood burned with fury. With renewed determination, she marched to his office.

Dr. Breton was standing by his filing cabinet, flipping through a manila folder. He didn't even flinch when Alaitz threw open the door.

"I expected Saverio," he said before snapping the file shut and locking it away. "Guess I should've known better."

Alaitz shut the door behind her. The air in the room shifted.

Breton felt it.

"You're going to wish it had been Saverio."

He cleared his throat and gestured to a chair. "Sit."

Alaitz didn't move. "How did this happen?"

Breton didn't pretend to misunderstand. He sighed. "Mrs. Chamberlain, I'm trying to find out."

"You want me to believe this was an accident?"

"I swear we followed protocol. We had her blood drawn. Everything was done according to procedure. We were just waiting on her records from Pennsylvania."

Alaitz's eyes flashed. "You didn't notice her medical ID?"

"No." A pause. "Paislee was a new patient. I'm not sure how her blood results got mixed up. But we will correct this."

Alaitz was silent for a long moment. Then, slowly, she sat down.

"You're going to leave everything the way it is."

Breton's brow rose. "Certainly, you're not implying that we pretend she's not O-negative."

Alaitz's voice was like a blade. "I'm implying that you keep your mouth shut."

Breton's jaw tightened.

Alaitz leaned in, her fangs slightly extending. "If you breathe a word to anyone—Michael and Paislee included—you'll be leveled into a bloody mass of destruction."

Breton's fangs flashed. "Do not threaten me, madame."

Alaitz's smile was ice. "I don't make threats, Dr. Breton. I make promises."

A long, tense silence.

Then Breton sighed, rubbing his temples. "Fine. For now."

Alaitz's demeanor shifted instantly. A dazzling smile. "Very good, doctor. Have a good evening."

She left, her heels clicking in perfect rhythm.

Breton exhaled as he stared at the empty doorway.

A moment later, his trusted nurse entered. She handed him a blue folder.

"Paislee didn't change," Rosa announced.

Breton tossed his glasses on the desk and flipped through the pages.

She hesitated. "Did you placate Alaitz?"

He closed the file. "I found her reaction…interesting."

Rosa's eyes gleamed. "What are you thinking?"

Breton's fingers tapped against the desk. "We've found Michael Chamberlain's weakness."

A slow, knowing smile.

"Paislee is the key."

Rosa's voice dropped. "What now?"

Breton leaned back, his smile widening.

"Call the brothers. Tell them to start recruiting."

Rosa hesitated. "But Esben—"

Breton's expression darkened. "Esben has become a liability."

He exhaled, almost amused. "But we'll be back on track. It's time."

A long pause. Then, softly—

"The revolution has begun."

# Acknowledgments

Thank you to my family for supporting this dream, and to those who encouraged me through every doubt, deadline, and rewrite. To the friends who listened, the readers who believed, and the quiet champions who reminded me to keep going—this story exists because of you.

Your support helped bring The Cardinal Code to life, and I'm grateful for every word of encouragement along the way.

Coming Soon

**The Order is watching.
And the truth they buried
is beginning to rise.**

Michael and Paislee
thought survival was the end of their story.
But it was only the beginning.

Every secret has its reckoning.
Every choice leaves a mark.

And the cost of their love
may echo through generations...

Because some love stories
are written in blood.

# The Cardinal Code
## Absolution

# AVERY STERLING

## About the Author

Avery Sterling fell in love with romance novels as a teenager, drawn to brooding heroes and slow-burn kisses. A dreamer, a traveler, and a hopeless romantic at heart, she believes love should be messy, steamy, and unforgettable. From the windswept coast of Maine to the sun-drenched Caribbean, she's chased stories across the map—always returning to the page to write about the kind of love that leaves a mark.

www.ingramcontent.com/pod-product-compliance
Lightning Source LLC
Chambersburg PA
CBHW030336120726
47901CB00007B/1809